A Heron Books Collection

CHRISTMAS HOLIDAY

W. SOMERSET MAUGHAM

CHRISTMAS HOLIDAY

with Original Illustrations by
Sydney Harpley

HERON BOOKS, LONDON

Published by arrangement with
William Heinemann Ltd., London

I

WITH a journey before him, Charley Mason's mother was anxious that he should make a good breakfast, but he was too excited to eat. It was Christmas Eve and he was going to Paris. They had got through the mass of work that quarter-day brought with it, and his father, having no need to go to the office, drove him to Victoria. When they were stopped for several minutes by a traffic block in Grosvenor Gardens Charley, afraid that he would miss the train, went white with anxiety. His father chuckled.

"You've got the best part of half an hour."

But it was a relief to arrive.

"Well, good-bye, old boy," his father said, "have a good time and don't get into more mischief than you can help."

The steamer backed into the harbour and the sight of the gray, tall, dingy houses of Calais filled him with elation. It was a raw day and the wind blew bitter. He strode along the platform as though he walked on air. The Golden Arrow, powerful, rich and impressive, which stood there waiting for him, was no ordinary train, but a symbol of romance. While the light lasted he looked out of the window and he laughed in his heart as he recognized the pictures he had seen in galleries; sand dunes, with patches of grass gray under the leaden sky, cramped villages of poor persons' houses with slate roofs, and then a broad, sad landscape of ploughed fields and sparse bare trees; but the day seemed in a

1

hurry to be gone from the cheerless scene and in a short while, when he looked out, he could see only his own reflection and behind it the polished mahogany of the Pullman. He wished he had come by air. That was what he'd wanted to do, but his mother had put her foot down; she'd persuaded his father that in the middle of winter it was a silly risk to take, and his father, usually so reasonable, had made it a condition of his going on the jaunt that he should take the train.

Of course Charley had been to Paris before, half a dozen times at least, but this was the first time that he had ever gone alone. It was a special treat that his father was giving him for a special reason: he had completed a year's work in his father's office and had passed the necessary examinations to enable him to follow usefully his chosen calling. For as long as Charley could remember, his father and mother, his sister Patsy and he had spent Christmas at Godalming with their cousins the Terry-Masons; and to explain why Leslie Mason, after talking over the matter with his wife, had one evening, a smile on his kindly face, asked his son whether instead of coming with them as usual he would like to spend a few days in Paris by himself, it is necessary to go back a little. It is necessary indeed to go back to the middle of the nineteenth century, when an industrious and intelligent man called Sibert Mason, who had been head gardener at a grand place in Sussex and had married the cook, bought with his savings and hers a few acres north of London and set up as a market gardener. Though he was then forty and his wife not far from it they had eight children. He prospered, and with the money he made, bought little bits of land in what was still open country. The city expanded and his market garden

2

acquired value as a building site; with money borrowed from the bank he put up a row of villas and in a short while let them all on lease. It would be tedious to go into the details of his progress, and it is enough to say that when he died, at the age of eighty-four, the few acres he had bought to grow vegetables for Covent Garden, and the properties he had continued to acquire whenever opportunity presented, were covered with bricks and mortar. Sibert Mason took care that his children should receive the education that had been denied him. They moved up in the social scale. He made the Mason Estate, as he had somewhat grandly named it, into a private company and at his death each child received a certain number of shares as an inheritance. The Mason Estate was well managed and though it could not compare in importance with the Westminster or the Portman Estate, for its situation was modest and it had long ceased to have any value as a residential quarter, shops, warehouses, factories, slums, long rows of dingy houses in two storeys, made it sufficiently profitable to enable its proprietors, through no merit and little exertion of their own, to live like the gentlemen and ladies they were now become. Indeed, the head of the family, the only surviving child of old Sibert's eldest son, a brother having been killed in the war and a sister by a fall in the hunting-field, was a very rich man. He was a member of parliament and at the time of King George the Fifth's Jubilee had been created a baronet. He had tacked his wife's name on to his own and was now known as Sir Wilfred Terry-Mason. The family had hopes that his staunch allegiance to the Tory party and the fact that he had a safe seat would result in his being raised to the peerage.

Leslie Mason, youngest of Sibert's many grand-children, had been sent to a public school and to Cambridge. His share in the Estate brought him in two thousand pounds a year, but to this was added another thousand which he received as secretary of the company. Once a year there was a meeting attended by such members of the family as were in England, for of the third generation some were serving their country in distant parts of the Empire, and some were gentlemen of leisure who were often abroad, and with Sir Wilfred in the chair, he presented the highly satisfactory statement which the chartered accountants had pre-pared.

Leslie Mason was a man of varied interests. At this time he was in the early fifties, tall, with a good figure, and with his blue eyes, fine gray hair worn rather long, and high colour, of an agreeable aspect. He looked more like a soldier or a colonial governor home on leave than a house agent and you would never have guessed that his grandfather was a gardener and his grandmother a cook. He was a good golfer, for which pastime he had ample leisure, and a good shot. But Leslie Mason was more than a sportsman; he was keenly interested in the arts. The rest of the family had no such foibles and they looked upon Leslie's pre-dilections with an amused tolerance, but when, for some reason or other, one of them wanted to buy a piece of furniture or a picture, his advice was sought and taken. It was natural enough that he should know what he was talking about, for he had married a painter's daughter. John Peron, his wife's father, was a member of the Royal Academy and for a long time, between the eighties and the end of the century, had made a good income by painting pictures of young women in eighteenth-century costume dallying with young men similarly dight. He painted them in gardens of old world flowers, in leafy bowers and in parlours furnished correctly with the chairs and tables of the period. But now when his pictures turned up at Christie's they were sold for thirty shillings or two pounds. Venetia Mason had inherited quite a number when her father died, but they had long stood in a box-room, covered with dust, their faces to the wall; for at this time of day even filial affection could not persuade her that they were anything but dreadful. The Leslie Masons were not in the least ashamed of the fact that his grandmother had been a cook, indeed with their friends they were apt to make a facetious point of it, but it embarrassed them to speak of John Peron. Some of the Mason relations still had on their walls examples of his work; they were a mortification to Venetia.

"I see you've still got father's picture there," she said. "Don't you think it dates rather? Why don't you put it in one of the spare rooms?"

"My father-in-law was a very charming old man," said Leslie, "with beautiful manners, but I'm afraid he wasn't a very good painter."

"Well, my governor gave a tidy sum for it. It would be absurd to put a picture that cost three hundred pounds in a spare bedroom, but if you feel like that about it, I'll tell you what I'll do, I'll sell it you for a hundred and fifty."

For though in the course of three generations they had become ladies and gentlemen, the Masons had not lost their business acumen.

The Leslie Masons had gone a long way in artistic appreciation since their marriage and on the walls of the handsome new house they now inhabited in Porchester Close were pictures by Wilson Steer and Augustus John, Duncan Grant and Vanessa Bell. There was an Utrillo and a Vuillard, both bought while these masters were of moderate price, and there was a Derain, a Marquet and a Chirico. You could not enter their house, somewhat sparsely furnished, without knowing at once that they were in the movement. They seldom missed a private view and when they went to Paris made a point of going to Rosenberg's and the dealers in the Rue de Seine to have a look at what there was to be seen; they really liked pictures and if they did not buy any before the cultured opinion of the day had agreed on their merits this was due partly to a modest lack of confidence in their own judgement and partly to a fear that they might be making a bad bargain. After all, John Peron's pictures had been praised by the best critics and he had sold them for several hundred pounds apiece, and now what they did they fetch? Two or three. It made you careful. But it was not only in painting that they were interested. They loved music; they went to Symphony Concerts throughout the winter; they had their favourite conductors and allowed no social engagements to prevent them from attending their performances. They went to hear the *Ring* once a year. To listen to music was a genuine delight to both of them. They had good taste and discrimination. They were regular first-nighters and they belonged to the societies that produce plays which are supposed to be above the comprehension of plain people. They read promptly the books that were talked about. They did this not only because they liked it, but because they felt it right to keep abreast of the times. They were honestly interested in art and it would be unjust even to hint a sneer because their taste lacked boldness and their appreciation originality. It may be that they were conventional in their judgements, but their conventionality was that of the highest culture of their day. They were incapable of making a discovery, but were quick to appreciate the discoveries of others. Though left to themselves they might never have seen anything very much to admire in Cézanne, no sooner was it borne in upon them that he was a great artist than in all sincerity they recognized the fact for themselves. They took no pride in their taste and there was no trace of snobbishness in their attitude.

"We're just very ordinary members of the public," said Venetia.

"Those objects of contempt to the artist, the people who know what they like," added Leslie.

It was a happy accident that they liked Debussy better than Arthur Sullivan and Virginia Woolf better than John Galsworthy.

This preoccupation with art left them little time for social life; they sought neither the great nor the distinguished, and their friends were very nice people who were well-to-do without being rich, and who took a judicious interest in the things of the mind. They did not much care for dinner parties and neither gave them often nor went to them more than civility required; but they were fond of entertaining their friends to supper on Sunday evenings when they could drop in dressed any way they liked and eat kedgeree and sausages and mash. There was good music and tolerable bridge. The conversation was intelligent. These parties were as pleasantly unpretentious as the Leslie Masons themselves, and though all the guests had their own cars and few of them less than five thousand a year, they flattered themselves that the atmosphere was quite bohemian.

But Leslie Mason was never happier than when, with no concert or first night to go to, he could spend the evening in the bosom of his family. He was fortunate in it. His wife had been pretty and now, a middle-aged woman, was still comely. She was nearly as tall as he, with blue eyes and soft brown hair only just streaked with gray. She was inclined to be stout, but her height enabled her to carry with dignity a corpulence which a strict attention to diet prevented from becoming uncomfortable. She had a broad brow, an open countenance and a diffident smile. Though she got her clothes in Paris, not from one of the fashionable dressmakers, but from a little woman 'round the corner,' she never succeeded in looking anything but thoroughly English. She naturalized whatever she wore, and though she occasionally went to the extravagance of getting a hat at Reboux she had no sooner put it on her head than it looked as if it had come from the Army and Navy Stores. She always looked exactly what she was, an honest woman of the middle class in easy circumstances. She had loved her husband when she married him and she loved him still. With the community of interests that existed between them it was no wonder that they should live in harmony. They had agreed at the beginning of their married life that she knew more about painting than he and that he knew more about music than she, so that in these matters each bowed to the superior judgement of the other. When it came to Picasso's later work, for instance, Leslie said:

"Well, I don't mind confessing it took me some time before I learnt to like it, but Venetia never had a

8

moment's doubt; with her flair she cottoned on to it like a flash of lightning."

And Mrs. Mason admitted that she'd had to listen to Sibelius' Second three or four times before she really understood what Leslie meant when he said that in its way it was as good as Beethoven.

"But of course he's got a real understanding of music. Compared with him I'm almost a low-brow."

Leslie and Venetia Mason were not only fortunate in one another, but also in their children. They had two, which they thought the perfect number, since an only child might be spoiled, and three or four meant a great expense, so that they couldn't have lived as comfortably as they liked to, nor provided for them in such a way as to assure their future. They had taken their parental duties seriously. Instead of putting silly, childish pictures on the nursery walls they had decorated them with reproductions of pictures by Van Gogh, Gauguin and Marie Laurencin, so that from their earliest years their children's taste should be formed, and they had chosen the records for the nursery gramophone with equal care, with the result that before either of them could ride a bicycle they were familiar with Mozart and Haydn, Beethoven and Wagner. As soon as they were old enough they began to learn to play the piano, with very good teachers, and Charley especially showed great aptitude. Both children were ardent concert-goers. They would scramble in to a Sunday concert, where they followed the music with a score, or wait for hours to get a seat in the gallery at Covent Garden; for their parents, thinking that it proved a real enthusiasm if they had to listen to music in some discomfort, considered it unnecessary to buy expensive seats for them. The Leslie Masons did not very much care for Old Masters and seldom went to the National Gallery except when a new purchase was making a stir in the papers, but it had seemed to them only right to make their children acquainted with the great paintings of the past, and as soon as they were old enough took them regularly to the National Gallery, but they soon realized that if they wanted to give them a treat they must take them to the Tate, and it was with gratification that they found that what really excited them was the most modern.

"It makes one think a bit," said Leslie to his wife, a smile of pride shining in his kindly eyes, "to see two young things like that taking to Matisse like a duck takes to water."

She gave him a look that was partly amused and partly rueful.

"They think I'm dreadfully old-fashioned because I still like Monet. They say it's pure chocolate-box."

"Well, we trained their taste. We mustn't grouse if they go ahead and leave us behind."

Venetia Mason gave a sweet and affectionate laugh.

"Bless their hearts, I don't grudge it them if they think me hopelessly out of date. I shall go on liking Monet and Manet and Degas whatever they say."

But it was not only to the artistic education of their offspring that the Leslie Masons had given thought. They were anxious that there should be nothing namby-pamby about them and they saw to it that they should acquire proficiency in games. They both rode well and Charley was not half a bad shot. Patsy, who was just eighteen, was studying at the Royal Academy of Music. She was to come out in May and they were giving a ball for her at Claridge's. Lady Terry-Mason was to present her at Court. Patsy was so pretty, with her blue eyes and fair hair, with her slim figure, her attractive smile and her gaiety, she would be snapped up all too soon. Leslie wanted her to marry a rising young barrister with political ambitions. For such a one, with the money she'd eventually inherit from the Mason Estate, with her culture, she'd make an admirable wife. But that would be the end of the united, cosy and happy family life which was so enjoyable. There would be no more of those pleasant, domestic evenings when they dined, the four of them, in the well-appointed dining-room with its Steer over the Chippendale sideboard, the table shining with Waterford glass and Georgian silver, waited on by well-trained maids in neat uniforms; simple English food perfectly cooked; and after dinner with its lively talk about art, literature and the drama, a glass of port, and then a little music in the drawing-room and a game of bridge. Venetia was afraid it was very selfish of her, but she couldn't help feeling glad that it would be some years at least before Charley could afford to marry too.

Charley was born during the war, he was twenty-three now, and when Leslie had been demobbed and gone down to Godalming to stay with the head of the family, already a member of parliament, but then only a knight, Sir Wilfred had suggested that he should be put down for Eton. Leslie would not hear of it. It was not the financial sacrifice he minded, but he had too much good sense to send his boy to a school where he would get extravagant tastes and acquire ideas unfitted to the station in life he would ultimately occupy.

"I went to Rugby myself and I don't believe I can do better than send him there too."

"I think you're making a mistake, Leslie. I've sent my boys to Eton. Thank God, I'm not a snob, but I'm not a fool either, and there's no denying it, it's a social asset."

"I daresay it is, but my position is very different from yours. You're a very rich man, Wilfred, and if things go well, you ought to end up in the House of Lords. I think it's quite right that you should give your sons the sort of start that'll enable them to take their proper place in society, but though officially I'm secretary of the Mason Estate and that sounds very respectable, when you come down to brass tacks I'm only a house agent, and I don't want to bring up my son to be a grand gentleman, I want him to be a house agent after me."

When Leslie spoke thus he was using an innocent diplomacy. By the terms of old Sibert's will and the accidents that have been already narrated, Sir Wilfred now possessed three-eighths of the Mason Estate, and it brought him in an income which was already large, and which, with leases falling in, the increasing value of the property, and good management, would certainly grow much larger. He was a clever, energetic man, and his position and his wealth gave him an influence with the rest of the family which none of its members questioned, but which it did not displease him to have acknowledged.

"You don't mean to say you'd be satisfied to let your boy take on your job?"

"It was good enough for me. Why shouldn't it be good enough for him? One doesn't know what the world's coming to and it may be that when he's grown up he'll be damned glad to step into a cushy billet at a thousand a year. But of course you're the boss."

Sir Wilfred made a gesture that seemed modestly to deprecate this description of himself.

"I'm a shareholder like the rest of you, but as far as I'm concerned, if you want it, he shall have it. Of course it's a long time ahead and I may be dead by then."

"We're a long-lived family and you'll live as long as old Sibert. Anyhow, there'll be no harm in letting the rest of them know that it's an understood thing that my boy should have my job when I'm through with it."

In order to enlarge their children's minds the Leslie Masons spent the holidays abroad, in winter at places where they ski and in summer at seaside resorts in the South of France; and once or twice with the same praiseworthy intention they made excursions to Italy and Holland. When Charley left school his father decided that before going to Cambridge he should spend six months at Tours to learn French. But the result of his sojourn in that agreeable town was unexpected and might very well have been disastrous, for when he came back he announced that he did not want to go to Cambridge, but to Paris, and that he wished to be a painter. His parents were dumbfounded. They loved art, they often said it was the most important thing in their lives; indeed Leslie, not averse at times from philosophical reflection, was inclined to think that it was art only that redeemed human existence from meaninglessness, and he had the greatest respect for the persons who produced it; but he had never envisaged the possibility that any member of his family, let alone his own son, should adopt a career that was uncertain, to some extent irregular, and in most cases far from lucrative. Nor could Venetia forget the fate that had befallen her father. It would be unjust to say that the Leslie Masons were put out because their son had taken their preoccupation with art more seriously than they intended; their preoccupation couldn't have been more serious, but it was from the patron's point of view; though no two people could have been more bohemian, they did have the Mason Estate behind them, and that, as anyone could see, must make a difference. Their reaction to Charley's declaration was quite definite, but they were aware that it would be difficult to put it in a way that wouldn't make their attitude look a trifle insincere.

"I can't think what put the idea into his head," said Leslie, talking it over with his wife.

"Heredity, I suppose. After all, my father was an artist."

"A painter, darling. He was a great gentleman and a wonderful raconteur, but no one in his senses could call him an artist."

Venetia flushed and Leslie saw that he had hurt her feelings. He hastened to make up for it.

"If he's inherited a feeling for art it's much more likely to be from my grandmother. I know old Sibert used to say you didn't know what tripe and onions were until you tasted hers. When she gave up being a cook to become a wife of a market gardener a great artist was lost to the world."

Venetia chuckled and forgave him.

They knew one another too well to have need to discuss their quandary. Their children loved them and looked up to them; they were agreed that it would be a thousand pities by a false step to shake Charley's belief in his parents' wisdom and integrity. The young are intolerant and when you talk common sense to them are only too apt to think you an old humbug.

"I don't think it would be wise to put one's foot down too decidedly," said Venetia. "Opposition might only make him obstinate."

"The situation's delicate. I don't deny that for a moment."

What made it more awkward was that Charley had brought back several canvases from Tours and when he had shown them they had expressed themselves in terms which it was difficult now to withdraw. They had praised as fond parents rather than as connoisseurs.

"You might take Charley up to the box-room one morning and let him have a look at your father's pictures. Don't make a point of it, you know, but let it seem accidental; and then when I get an opportunity I'll have a talk with him."

The opportunity came. Leslie was in the sitting-room they had arranged for the children so that they might have a place of their own. The reproductions of Gauguin and Van Gogh that had been in their nursery adorned the walls. Charley was painting a bunch of mixed flowers in a green vase.

"I think we'd better have those pictures you brought back from France framed and put up instead of these reproductions. Let's have another look at them."

There was one of three apples on a blue-and-white plate.

"I think it's damned good," said Leslie. "I've seen hundreds of pictures of three apples on a blue-and-white plate and it's well up to the average." He chuckled. "Poor old Cézanne, I wonder what he'd say if he knew how many thousands of times people had painted that picture of his."

There was another still life which represented a bottle of red wine, a packet of French tobacco in a blue wrapper, a pair of white gloves, a folded newspaper and a violin. These objects were resting on a table

15

covered with a cloth in green and white squares.

"Very good. Very promising."

"D'you really think so, daddy?"

"I do indeed. It's not very original, you know, it's the sort of picture that every dealer has a dozen of in his store-room, but you've never had a lesson in your life and it's a very creditable piece of work. You've evidently inherited some of your grandfather's talent. You have seen his pictures, haven't you?"

"I hadn't for years. Mummy wanted to find something in the box-room and she showed them to me. They're awful."

"I suppose they are. But they weren't thought so in his own day. They were highly praised and they were bought. Remember that a lot of stuff that we admire now will be thought just as awful in fifty years' time. That's the worst of art; there's no room for the second-rate."

"One can't tell what one'll be till one tries."

"Of course not, and if you want to take up painting professionally your mother and I are the last people who'd stand in your way. You know how much art means to us."

"There's nothing I want to do in the world more than paint."

"With the share of the Mason Estate that'll come to you eventually you'll always have enough to live on in a modest way, and there've been several amateurs who've made quite a nice little reputation for themselves."

"Oh, but I don't want to be an amateur."

"It's not so easy to be anything else with a thousand to fifteen hundred a year behind you. I don't mind telling you it'll be a bit of a disappointment to me. I

16

was keeping this job as secretary to the Estate warm for you, but I daresay some of the cousins will jump at it. I should have thought myself it was better to be a competent business man than a mediocre painter, but that's neither here nor there. The great thing is that you should be happy and we can only hope that you'll turn out a better artist than your grandfather."

There was a pause. Leslie looked at his son with kindly eyes.

"There's only one thing I'm going to ask you to do. My grandfather started life as a gardener and his wife was a cook. I only just remember him, but I have a notion that he was a pretty rough diamond. They say it takes three generations to make a gentleman, and at all events I don't eat peas with a knife. You're a member of the fourth. You may think it's just snobbishness on my part, but I don't much like the idea of you sinking in the social scale. I'd like you to go to Cambridge and take your degree, and after that if you want to go to Paris and study painting you shall go with my blessing."

That seemed a very generous offer to Charley and he accepted it with gratitude. He enjoyed himself very much at Cambridge. He did not find much opportunity to paint, but he got into a set interested in the drama and in his first year wrote a couple of one-act plays. They were acted at the A.D.C. and the Leslie Masons went to Cambridge to see them. Then he made the acquaintance of a don who was a distinguished musician. Charley played the piano better than most undergraduates, and he and the don played duets together. He studied harmony and counterpoint. After consideration he decided that he would rather be a musician than a painter. His father with great good humour consented to this, but when Charley had taken his degree, he carried him off to Norway for a fortnight's fishing. Two or three days before they were due to return Venetia Mason received a telegram from Leslie containing the one word Eureka. Notwithstanding their culture neither of them knew what it meant, but its significance was perfectly clear to the recipient and that is the primary use of language. She gave a sigh of relief. In September Charley went for four months into the firm of accountants employed by the Mason Estate to learn something of book-keeping and at the New Year joined his father in Lincoln's Inn Fields. It was to reward the application he had shown during his first year in business that his father was now sending him, with twenty-five pounds in his pocket, to have a lark in Paris. And a great lark Charley was determined to have.

II

THEY were nearly there. The attendants were collecting the luggage and piling it up inside the door so that it could be conveniently handed down to the porters. Women put a last dab of lipstick on their mouths and were helped into their furs. Men struggled into their great-coats and put on their hats. The propinquity in which these persons had sat for a few hours, the pleasant warmth of the Pullman, had made a corporate unity of them, separated as occupants of a coach with its own number from the occupants of other coaches; but now they fell asunder, and each one, or each group of two or three, regained the discreet individuality which for a while had been merged in that of all the others. In the smoke-laden air, rank with stale tobacco, strong scent, the odour of human bodies and the frowst of steam-heating, they acquired on a sudden an air of mystery. Strangers once more, they looked at one another with preoccupied, unseeing eyes. Each one felt in himself a vague hostility to his neighbour. Some were already queuing up in the passage so that they might get out quickly. The heat of the Pullman had coated the windows with vapour and Charley wiped them a bit clean with his hand to look out. He could see nothing.

The train ran into the station. Charley gave his bag to a porter and with long steps walked up the platform; he was expecting his friend Simon Fenimore to meet him. He was disappointed not to see him at once; but there was a great mob at the barrier and he supposed that he was waiting there. He scanned eagerly the eager faces; he passed through; persons struggled through the crowd to seize a new arrival's hand; women kissed one another; he could not see his friend. He was so convinced he must be there that he lingered for a little, but he was intimidated by his porter's obvious impatience and presently followed him out to the courtyard. He felt vaguely let down. The porter got him a taxi and Charley gave the driver the name of the hotel where Simon had taken a room for him. When the Leslie Masons went to Paris they always stayed at an hotel in the Rue St. Honoré. It was exclusively patronized by English and Americans, but after twenty years they still cherished the delusion that it was a discovery of their own, essentially French, and when they saw American luggage on a landing or went up in the lift with persons who could be nothing but English, they never ceased to be surprised.

"I wonder how on earth *they* happen to be here," they said.

For their own part they had always been careful never to speak about it to their friends; when they had hit upon a little bit of old France they weren't going to risk its being spoilt. Though the director and the porter talked English fluently they always spoke to them in their own halting French, convinced that this was the only language they knew. But the mere fact that he had so often been to this hotel with his family was a sufficient reason for Charley not to stay there when he was going to Paris by himself. He was bent on adventure, and a respectable family hotel, where, according to his parents, nobody went but the French provincial nobility, was hardly the right place for the glorious, wild and romantic experiences with which his imagination for the last month had been distracting his mind. So he had written to Simon asking him to get him a room somewhere in the Latin Quarter; he wasn't particular about sanitary conveniences and didn't mind how grubby it was so long as it had the right atmosphere; and Simon in due course had written back to tell him that he had engaged a room at a hotel near the Gare Montparnasse. It was in a quiet street just off the Rue de Rennes and conveniently near the Rue Campagne Première where he himself lived.

Charley quickly got over his disappointment that Simon had not come to meet him, he was sure either to be at the hotel or to have telephoned to say that he would be round immediately, and driving through the crowded streets that lead from the Gare du Nord to the Seine his spirits rose. It was wonderful to arrive in Paris by night. A drizzling rain was falling and it gave the streets an exciting mystery. The shops were brightly lit. The pavements were multitudinous with umbrellas and the water dripping on them glistened dimly under the street lamps. Charley remembered one of Renoir's pictures. Sometimes a gust of wind made women crouch under their umbrellas and their skirts swirled round their legs. His taxi drove furiously to his prudent English idea and he gasped whenever with a screeching of brakes it pulled up suddenly to avoid a collision. The red lights held them up at a crossing and in both directions a great stream of persons surged over like a panic-stricken mob flying before a police charge. To Charley's excited gaze they seemed quite different from an English crowd, more alert, more eager; when by chance his eyes fell on a girl walking by herself, a sempstress or a typist going home after the day's work, it delighted him to fancy that she was hurrying to meet her lover; and when he saw a pair walking arm in arm under an umbrella, a young man with a beard, in a broad-brimmed hat, and a girl with a fur round her neck, walking as though it were such bliss to be together they did not mind the rain and were unconscious of the jostling throng, he thrilled with a poignant and sympathetic joy. At one corner owing to a block his taxi was side by side with a handsome limousine. There sat in it a woman in a sable coat, with painted cheeks and painted lips, and a profile of incredible distinction. She might have been the Duchesse de Guermantes driving back after a tea party to her house in the Boulevard St. Germain. It was wonderful to be twenty-three and in Paris on one's own.

"By God, what a time I'm going to have."

The hotel was grander than he had expected. Its façade, with its architectural embellishments, suggested the flamboyant taste of the late Baron Haussmann. He found that a room had been engaged for him, but Simon had left neither letter nor message. He was taken upstairs not as he had anticipated by a slovenly boots in a dirty apron, with a sinister look on his ill-shaven face, but by an affable director who spoke perfect English and wore a morning coat. The room was furnished with hygienic severity, and there were two beds in it, but the director assured him that he would only charge him for the use of one. He showed Charley with pride the communicating bath-room. Left to himself Charley looked about him. He had expected a little room with heavy curtains of dull rep, a wooden bed with a huge eiderdown and an old mahogany wardrobe with a large mirror; he had expected to find used hairpins on the dressing-table and in the drawer of the table de nuit half a lipstick and a broken comb in which a few dyed hairs were still entangled. That was the idea his romantic fancy had formed of a student's room in the Latin Quarter. A bath-room! That was the last thing he had bargained for. This room might have been a room in one of the cheaper hotels in Switzerland to which he had sometimes been with his parents. It was clean, threadbare and sordid. Not even Charley's ardent imagination could invest it with mystery. He unpacked his bag disconsolately. He had a bath. He thought it rather casual of Simon, even if he could not be bothered to meet him, not to have left a message. If he made no sign of life he would have to dine by himself. His father and mother and Patsy would have got down to Godalming by now; there was going to be a jolly party, Sir Wilfred's two sons and their wives and two nieces of Lady Terry-Mason's. There would be music, games and dancing. He half wished now that he hadn't jumped at his father's offer to spend the holiday in Paris. It suddenly occurred to him that Simon had perhaps had to go off somewhere for his paper and in the hurry of an unexpected departure had forgotten to let him know. His heart sank.

Simon Fenimore was Charley's oldest friend and indeed it was to spend a few days with him that he had been so eager to come to Paris. They had been at a private school together and together at Rugby; they had been at Cambridge together too, but Simon had left without taking a degree, at the end of his second year in fact, because he had come to the conclusion that he was wasting time; and it was Charley's father who had got him on to the London newspaper for which for the last year he had been one of the Paris correspondents. Simon was alone in the world. His father was in the

Indian Forest Department and while Simon was still a young child had divorced his mother for promiscuous adultery. She had left India and Simon, by order of the Court in his father's custody, was sent to England and put into a clergyman's family till he was old enough to go to school. His mother vanished into obscurity. He had no notion whether she was alive or dead. His father died of cirrhosis of the liver when Simon was twelve and he had but a vague recollection of a thin, slightly-built man with a sallow, lined face and a tight-lipped mouth. He left only just enough money to educate his son. The Leslie Masons had been touched by the poor boy's loneliness and had made a point of asking him to spend good part of his holidays with them. As a boy he was thin and weedy, with a pale face in which his black eyes looked enormous, a great quantity of straight dark hair which was always in need of a brush, and a large, sensual mouth. He was talkative, forward for his age, a great reader, and clever. He had none of the diffidence which was in Charley such an engaging trait. Venetia Mason, though from a sense of duty she tried hard, could not like him. She could not understand why Charley had taken a fancy to someone who was in every way so unlike him. She thought Simon pert and conceited. He was insensible to kindness and took everything that was done for him as a matter of course. She had a suspicion that he had no very high opinion either of her or of Leslie. Sometimes when Leslie was talking with his usual good sense and intelligence about something interesting Simon would look at him with a glimmer of irony in those great black eyes of his and his sensual lips pursed in a sarcastic pucker. You would have thought Leslie was being prosy and a trifle stupid. Now and then when they were spending one of their pleasant quiet evenings together, chatting of one thing and another, he would go into a brown study; he would sit staring into vacancy, as though his thoughts were miles away, and perhaps, after a while, take up a book and start reading as though he were by himself. It gave you the impression that their conversation wasn't worth listening to. It wasn't even polite. But Venetia Mason chid herself.

"Poor lamb, he's never had a chance to learn manners. I *will* be nice to him. I *will* like him."

Her eyes rested on Charley, so good-looking, with his slim body, ("it's awful the way he grows out of his clothes, the sleeves of his dinner-jacket are too short for him already,") his curling brown hair, his blue eyes, with long lashes, and his clear skin. Though perhaps he hadn't Simon's showy brilliance, he was good, and he was artistic to his fingers' ends. But who could tell what he might have become if she had run away from Leslie and Leslie had taken to drink, and if instead of enjoying a cultured atmosphere and the influence of a nice home he had had, like Simon, to fend for himself? Poor Simon! Next day she went out and bought him half a dozen ties. He seemed pleased.

"I say, that's jolly decent of you. I've never had more than two ties at one time in my life."

Venetia was so moved by the spontaneous generosity of her pretty gesture that she was seized with a sudden wave of sympathy.

"You poor lonely boy," she cried, "it's so dreadful for you to have no parents."

"Well, as my mother was a whore, and my father a drunk, I daresay I don't miss much."

He was seventeen when he said this.

It was no good, Venetia simply couldn't like him.

25

He was harsh, cynical and unscrupulous. It exasperated her to see how much Charley admired him; Charley thought him brilliant and anticipated a great career for him. Even Leslie was impressed by the extent of his reading and the clearness with which even as a boy he expressed himself. At school he was already an ardent socialist and at Cambridge he became a communist. Leslie listened to his wild theories with good-humoured tolerance. To him it was all talk, and talk, he had an instinctive feeling, was just talk; it didn't touch the essential business of life.

"And if he does become a well-known journalist or gets into the House, there'll be no harm in having a friend in the enemy's camp."

Leslie's ideas were liberal, so liberal that he didn't mind admitting the Socialists had several notions that no reasonable man could object to; theoretically he was all in favour of the nationalization of the coal-mines, and he didn't see why the state shouldn't run the public services as well as private companies; but he didn't think they should go too far. Ground rents, for instance, that was a matter that was really no concern of the state; and slum property; in a great city you had to have slums, in point of fact the lower classes preferred them to model dwelling-houses, not that the Mason Estate hadn't done what it could in this direction; but you couldn't expect a landlord to let people live in his houses for nothing, and it was only fair that he should get a decent return on his capital.

Simon Fenimore had decided that he wanted to be a foreign correspondent for some years so that he could gain a knowledge of Continental politics which would enable him when he entered the House of Commons to be an expert on a subject of which most Labour members were necessarily ignorant; but when Leslie took him to see the proprietor of the newspaper who was prepared to give a brilliant young man his chance, he warned him that the proprietor was a very rich man, and that he could not expect to create a favourable impression if he delivered himself of revolutionary sentiments. Simon, however, made a very good impression on the magnate by the modesty of his demeanour, his air of energy and his easy conversation.

"He was as good as gold," Leslie told his wife afterwards. "He's got his head screwed on his shoulders all right, that young fellow. It's what I always told you, talk doesn't amount to anything really. When it comes down to getting a job with a living wage attached to it, like every sensible man he's prepared to put his theories in his pocket."

Venetia agreed with him. It was quite possible, their own experience proved it, to have a real love for beauty and at the same time to realize the importance of material things. Look at Lorenzo de' Medici; he'd been a successful banker and an artist to his finger-tips. She thought it very good of Leslie to have taken so much trouble to do a service for someone who was incapable of gratitude. Anyhow the job he had got him would take Simon to Vienna and thus remove Charley from an influence which she had always regarded with misgiving. It was that wild talk of his that had put it into the boy's head that he wanted to be an artist. It was all very well for Simon, he hadn't a penny in the world and no connections; but Charley had a snug berth to go into. There were enough artists in the world. Her consolation had been that Charley had so much candour of soul and a disposition of such sweetness that no evil communications could corrupt his good manners.

At this moment Charley was dressing himself and wondering, forlorn, how he should spend the evening. When he had got his trousers on he rang up the office of Simon's newspaper, and it was Simon himself who answered.

"Simon."

"Hulloa, have you turned up? Where are you?"

Simon seemed so casual that Charley was taken aback.

"At the hotel."

"Oh, are you? Doing anything to-night?"

"No."

"We'd better dine together, shall we? I'll stroll around and fetch you."

He rang off. Charley was dashed. He had expected Simon to be as eager to see him as he was to see Simon, but from Simon's words and from his manner you would have thought that they were casual acquaintances and that it was a matter of indifference to him if they met or not. Of course it was two years since they'd seen one another and in that time Simon might have changed out of all recognition. Charley had a sudden fear that his visit to Paris was going to be a failure and he awaited Simon's arrival with a nervousness that annoyed him. But when at last he walked into the room there was in his appearance at least little alteration. He was now twenty-three and he was still the lanky fellow, though only of average height, that he had always been. He was shabbily dressed in a brown jacket and gray flannel trousers and wore neither hat nor great-coat. His long face was thinner and paler than ever and his black eyes seemed larger. They were never still. Hard, shining, inquisitive, suspicious, they seemed to indicate the quality of the brain behind. His mouth was large and ironical, and he had small irregular teeth that somewhat reminded you of one of the smaller beasts of prey. With his pointed chin and prominent cheek-bones he was not good-looking, but his expression was so high-strung, there was in it so strange a disquiet, that you could hardly have passed him in the street without taking notice of him. At fleeting moments his face had a sort of tortured beauty, not a beauty of feature but the beauty of a restless, striving spirit. A disturbing thing about him was that there was no gaiety in his smile, it was a sardonic grimace, and when he laughed his face was contorted as though he were suffering from an agony of pain. His voice was high-pitched; it did not seem to be quite under his control, and when he grew excited often rose to shrillness.

Charley, restraining his natural impulse to run to the door and wring his hand with the eager friendliness of his happy nature, received him coolly. When there was a knock he called "come in," and went on filing his nails. Simon did not offer to shake hands. He nodded as though they had met already in the course of the day.

"Hulloa!" he said. "Room all right?"

"Oh, yes. The hotel's a bit grander than I expected."

"It's convenient and you can bring anyone in you like. I'm starving. Shall we go along and eat?"

"O.K."

"Let's go to the Coupole."

They sat down opposite one another at a table upstairs and ordered their dinner. Simon gave Charley an appraising look.

"I see you haven't lost your looks, Charley," he said with his wry smile.

"Luckily they're not my fortune."

Charley was feeling a trifle shy. The separation had for the moment at all events destroyed the old intimacy there had so long been between them. Charley was a good listener, he had indeed been trained to be so from early childhood, and he was never unwilling to sit silent while Simon poured out his ideas with eloquent confusion. Charley had always disinterestedly admired him; he was convinced he was a genius so that it seemed quite natural to play second fiddle to him. He had an affection for Simon because he was alone in the world and nobody much liked him, whereas he himself had a happy home and was in easy circumstances; and it gave him a sense of comfort that Simon, who cared for so few people, cared for him. Simon was often bitter and sarcastic, but with him he could also be strangely gentle. In one of his rare moments of expansion he had told him that he was the only person in the world that he gave a damn for. But now Charley felt with malaise that there was a barrier between them. Simon's restless eyes darted from his face to his hands, paused for an instant on his new suit and then glanced rapidly at his collar and tie; he felt that Simon was not surrendering himself as he had to him alone in the old days, but was holding back, critical and aloof; he seemed to be taking stock of him as if he were a stranger and he were making up his mind what sort of a person this was. It made Charley uncomfortable and he was sore at heart.

"How d'you like being a business man?" asked Simon.

Charley faintly coloured. After all the talks they had had in the past he was prepared for Simon to treat him with derision because he had in the end fallen in with his father's wishes, but he was too honest to conceal the truth.

"I like it much better than I expected. I find the work very interesting and it's not hard. I have plenty of time to myself."

"I think you've shown a lot of sense," Simon answered, to his surprise. "What did you want to be a painter or a pianist for? There's a great deal too much art in the world. Art's a lot of damned rot anyway."

"Oh, Simon!"

"Are you still taken in by the artistic pretensions of your excellent parents? You must grow up, Charley. Art! It's an amusing diversion for the idle rich. Our world, the world we live in, has no time for such nonsense."

"I should have thought . . ."

"I know what you would have thought; you would have thought it gave a beauty, a meaning to existence; you would have thought it was a solace to the weary and heavy-laden and an inspiration to a nobler and fuller life. Balls! We may want art again in the future, but it won't be your art, it'll be the art of the people."

"Oh, Lord!"

"The people want dope and it may be that art is the best form in which we can give it them. But they're not ready for it yet. At present it's another form they want."

"What is that?"

"Words."

It was extraordinary, the sardonic vigour he put into the monosyllable. But he smiled, and though his lips grimaced Charley saw in his eyes for a moment that

31

same look of good-humoured affection that he had been accustomed to see in them.

"No, my boy," he continued, "you have a good time, go to your office every day and enjoy yourself. It can't last very long now and you may just as well get all the fun out of it that you can."

"What d'you mean by that?"

"Never mind. We'll talk about it some other time. Tell me, what have you come to Paris for?"

"Well, chiefly to see you."

Simon flushed darkly. You would have thought that a word of kindness, and when Charley spoke you could never doubt that it was from the heart, horribly embarrassed him.

"And besides that?"

"I want to see some pictures, and if there's anything good in the theatre I'd like to go. And I want to have a bit of a lark generally."

"I suppose you mean by that that you want to have a woman."

"I don't get much opportunity in London, you know."

"Later on I'll take you to the Sérail."

"What's that?"

"You'll see. It's not bad fun."

They began to talk of Simon's experiences in Vienna, but he was reticent about them.

"It took me some time to find my feet. You see, I'd never been out of England before. I learnt German. I read a great deal. I thought. I met a lot of people who interested me."

"And since then, in Paris?"

"I've been doing more or less the same thing; I've been putting my ideas in order. I'm young. I've got plenty of time. When I'm through with Paris I shall go to Rome, Berlin or Moscow. If I can't get a job with the paper, I shall get some other job; I can always teach English and earn enough to keep body and soul together. I wasn't born in the purple and I can do without things. In Vienna, as an exercise in self-denial, I lived for a month on bread and milk. It wasn't even a hardship. I've trained myself now to do with one meal a day."

"D'you mean to say this is your first meal to-day?"

"I had a cup of coffee when I got up and a glass of milk at one."

"But what's the object of it? You're adequately paid in your job, aren't you?"

"I get a living wage. Certainly enough to have three meals a day. Who can achieve mastery over others unless he first achieves mastery over himself?"

Charley grinned. He was beginning to feel more at his ease.

"That sounds like a tag out of a dictionary of quotations."

"It may be," Simon replied indifferently. "Je prends mon bien où je le trouve. A proverb distils the wisdom of the ages and only a fool is scornful of the common-place. You don't suppose I intend to be a foreign correspondent for a London paper or a teacher of English all my life. These are my Wanderjahre. I'm going to spend them in acquiring the education I never got at the stupid school we both went to or in that suburban cemetery they call the University of Cambridge. But it's not only knowledge of men and books that I want to acquire; that's only an instrument; I want to acquire something much harder to come by and more important: an unconquerable will. I want to mould myself as the Jesuit novice is moulded by the iron discipline of the Order. I think I've always known myself; there's nothing that teaches you what you are, like being alone in the world, a stranger everywhere, and living all your life with people to whom you mean nothing. But my knowledge was instinctive. In these two years I've been abroad I've learnt to know myself as I know the fifth proposition of Euclid. I know my strength and my weakness and I'm ready to spend the next five or six years cultivating my strength and ridding myself of my weakness. I'm going to take myself as a trainer takes an athlete to make a champion of him. I've got a good brain. There's no one in the world who can see to the end of his nose with such perspicacity as I can, and believe me, in the world we live in that's a great force. I can talk. You have to persuade men to action not by reasoning, but by rhetoric. The general idiocy of mankind is such that they can be swayed by words, and however mortifying, for the present you have to accept the fact as you accept it in the cinema that a film to be a success must have a happy ending. Already I can do pretty well all I like with words; before I'm through I shall be able to do anything."

Simon took a long draught of the white wine they were drinking and sitting back in his chair began to laugh. His face writhed into a grimace of intolerable suffering.

"I must tell you an incident that happened a few months ago here. They were having a meeting of the British Legion or something like that, I forget what for, war graves or something; my chief was going to speak, but he had a cold in the head and he sent me instead. You know what our paper is, bloody patriotic as long as it helps our circulation, all the dirt we can get, and a high moral tone. My chief's the right man in the right place. He hasn't had an idea in his head for twenty years. He never opens his mouth without saying the obvious and when he tells a dirty story it's so stale that it doesn't even stink any more. But he's as shrewd as they make 'em. He knows what the proprietor wants and he gives it to him. Well, I made the speech he would have made. Platitudes dripped from my mouth. I made the welkin ring with claptrap. I gave them jokes so hoary that even a judge would have been ashamed to make them. They roared with laughter. I gave them pathos so shaming that you would have thought they would vomit. The tears rolled down their cheeks. I beat the big drum of patriotism like a Salvation Lass sublimating her repressed sex. They cheered me to the echo. It was the speech of the evening. When it was all over the big-wigs wrung my hand still overwhelmed with emotion. I got them all right. And d'you know, I didn't say a single word that I didn't know was contemptible balderdash. Words, words, words! Poor old Hamlet."

"It was a damned unscrupulous thing to do," said Charley. "After all, I daresay they were just a lot of ordinary, decent fellows who were only wanting to do what they thought was the right thing, and what's more they were probably prepared to put their hands in their pockets to prove the sincerity of their convictions."

"You would think that. In point of fact more money was raised for whatever the damned cause was than had ever been raised before at one of their meetings and the organizers told my chief it was entirely due to my brilliant speech."

Charley in his candour was distressed. This was not

the Simon he had known so long. Formerly, however wild his theories were, however provocatively expressed, there was a sort of nobility in them. He was disinterested. His indignation was directed against oppression and cruelty. Injustice roused him to fury. But Simon did not notice the effect he had on Charley or if he did was indifferent to it. He was absorbed in himself.

"But brain isn't enough and eloquence, even if it's necessary, is after all a despicable gift. Kerensky had them both and what did they avail him? The important thing is character. It's my character I've got to mould. I'm sure one can do anything with oneself if one tries. It's only a matter of will. I've got to train myself so that I'm indifferent to insult, neglect and ridicule. I've got to acquire a spiritual aloofness so complete that if they put me in prison I shall feel myself as free as a bird in the air. I've got to make myself so strong that when I make mistakes I am unshaken, but profit by them to act rightly. I've got to make myself so hard that not only can I resist the temptation to be pitiful, but I don't even feel pity. I've got to wring out of my heart the possibility of love."

"Why?"

"I can't afford to let my judgement be clouded by any feeling that I might have for a human being. You are the only person I've ever cared for in the world, Charley. I shan't rest till I know in my bones that if it were necessary to put you against a wall and shoot you with my own hands I could do it without a moment's hesitation and without a moment's regret."

Simon's eyes had a dark opaqueness which reminded you of an old mirror, in a deserted house, from which the quick-silver was worn away, so that when you looked in it you saw, not yourself, but a sombre depth in which seemed to lurk the reflections of long-past events and passions long since dead and yet in some terrifying way tremulous still with a borrowed and mysterious life.

"Did you wonder why I didn't come to the station to meet you?"

"It would have been nice if you had. I supposed you couldn't get away."

"I knew you'd be disappointed. It's our busy time at the office, we have to be on tap then to telephone to London the news that's come through in the course of the day, but it's Christmas Eve, the paper doesn't come out to-morrow and I could have got away easily. I didn't come because I wanted to so much. Ever since I got your letter saying you were coming over I've been sick with the desire to see you. When the train was due and I knew you'd be wandering up the platform looking for me and rather lost in that struggling crowd, I took a book and began to read. I sat there, forcing myself to attend to it, and refusing to let myself listen for the telephone that I expected every moment to ring. And when it did and I knew it was you, my joy was so intense that I was enraged with myself. I almost didn't answer. For more than two years now I've been striving to rid myself of the feeling I have for you. Shall I tell you why I wanted you to come over? One idealizes people when they're away, it's true that absence makes the heart grow fonder, and when one sees them again one's often surprised that one saw anything in them at all. I thought that if there were anything left in me of the old feeling I had for you the few days you're spending here now would be enough to kill it."

"I'm afraid you'll think me very stupid," said Charley, with his engaging smile, "but I can't for the life of me see why you want to."

"I do think you're very stupid."

"Well, taking that for granted, what is the reason?"

Simon frowned a little and his restless eyes darted here and there like a hare trying to escape a pursuer.

"You're the only person who ever cared for me."

"That's not true. My father and mother have always been very fond of you."

"Don't talk such nonsense. Your father was as indifferent to me as he is to art, but it gave him a warm, comfortable feeling of benevolence to be kind to the orphan penniless boy whom he could patronize and impress. Your mother thought me unscrupulous and self-seeking. She hated the influence she thought I had over you and she was affronted because she saw that I thought your father an old humbug, the worst sort of humbug, the one who humbugs himself; the only satisfaction I ever gave her was that she couldn't look at me without thinking how nice it was that you were so very different from me."

"You're not very flattering to my poor parents," said Charley, mildly.

Simon took no notice of the interruption.

"We clicked at once. What that old bore Goethe would have called elective affinity. You gave me what I'd never had. I, who'd never been a boy, could be a boy with you. I could forget myself in you. I bullied you and ragged you and mocked you and neglected you, but all the time I worshipped you. I felt wonderfully at home with you. With you I could be just myself. You were so unassuming, so easily pleased, so gay and so good-natured, merely to be with you rested my tortured nerves and released me for a moment from that driving force that urged me on and on. But I don't want rest and I don't want release. My will falters when I look at your sweet and diffident smile. I can't afford to be soft, I can't afford to be tender. When I look into those blue eyes of yours, so friendly, so confiding in human nature, I waver, and I daren't waver. You're my enemy and I hate you."

Charley had flushed uncomfortably at some of the things that Simon had said to him, but now he chuckled good-humouredly.

"Oh, Simon, what stuff and nonsense you talk."

Simon paid no attention. He fixed Charley with his glittering, passionate eyes as though he sought to bore into the depths of his being.

"Is there anything there?" he said, as though speaking to himself. "Or is it merely an accident of expression that gives the illusion of some quality of the soul?" And then to Charley: "I've often asked myself what it was that I saw in you. It wasn't your good looks, though I daresay they had something to do with it; it wasn't your intelligence, which is adequate without being remarkable; it wasn't your guileless nature or your good temper. What is it in you that makes people take to you at first sight? You've won half your battle before ever you take the field. Charm? What is charm? It's one of the words we all know the meaning of, but we can none of us define. But I know if I had that gift of yours, with my brain and my determination there's no obstacle in the world I couldn't surmount. You've got vitality and that's part of charm. But I have just as much vitality as you; I can do with four hours' sleep for days on end and I can work for sixteen hours a day without getting tired.

When people first meet me they're antagonistic, I have to conquer them by sheer brain-power, I have to play on their weaknesses, I have to make myself useful to them, I have to flatter them. When I came to Paris my chief thought me the most disagreeable young man and the most conceited he'd ever met. Of course he's a fool. How can a man be conceited when he knows his defects as well as I know mine? Now he eats out of my hand. But I've had to work like a dog to achieve what you can do with a flicker of your long eyelashes. Charm is essential. In the last two years I've got to know a good many prominent politicians and they've all got it. Some more and some less. But they can't all have it by nature. That shows it can be acquired. It means nothing, but it arouses the devotion of their followers so that they'll do blindly all they're bidden and be satisfied with the reward of a kind word. I've examined them at work. They can turn it on like water from a tap. The quick, friendly smile; the hand that's so ready to clasp yours. The warmth in the voice that seems to promise favours, the show of interest that leads you to think your concerns are your leader's chief preoccupation, the intimate manner which tells you nothing, but deludes you into thinking you are in your master's confidence. The clichés, the hundred varieties of dear old boy that are so flattering on influential lips. The ease and naturalness, the perfect acting that imitates nature, and the sensitiveness that discerns a fool's vanity and takes care never to affront it. I can learn all that, it only means a little more effort and a little more self-control. Sometimes of course they overdo it, the pros, their charm becomes so mechanical that it ceases to work; people see through it, and feeling they've been duped are resentful." He gave Charley another of his piercing

40

glances. "Your charm is natural, that's why it's so devastating. Isn't it absurd that a tiny wrinkle should make life so easy for you?"

"What on earth do you mean?"

"One of the reasons why I wanted you to come over was to see exactly in what your charm consisted. As far as I can tell it depends on some peculiar muscular formation of your lower orbit. I believe it to be due to a little crease under your eyes when you smile."

It embarrassed Charley to be thus anatomized, and to divert the conversation from himself; he asked:

"But all this effort of yours, what is it going to lead you to?"

"Who can tell? Let's go and have our coffee at the Dôme."

"All right. I'll get hold of a waiter."

"I'm going to stand you your dinner. It's the first meal that we've had together that I've ever paid for."

When he took out of his pocket some notes to settle up with he found with them a couple of cards.

"Oh, look, I've got a ticket for you for the Midnight Mass at St. Eustache. It's supposed to be the best church music in Paris and I thought you'd like to go."

"Oh, Simon, how nice of you. I should love to. You'll come with me, won't you?"

"I'll see how I feel when the time comes. Anyhow take the tickets."

Charley put them in his pocket. They walked to the Dôme. The rain had stopped, but the pavement was still wet and when the light of a shop window or a street lamp fell upon it, palely glistened. A lot of people were wandering to and fro. They came out of the shadow of the leafless trees as though from the wings of a theatre, passed across the light and then were lost again in another patch of night. Cringing but persistent, the Algerian peddlers, their eyes alert for a possible buyer, passed with a bundle of Eastern rugs and cheap furs over their arms. Coarse-faced boys, a fez on their heads, carried baskets of monkey-nuts and monotonously repeated their raucous cry: cacaouettes, cacaouettes! At a corner stood two negroes, their dark faces pinched with cold, as though time had stopped and they waited because there was nothing in the world to do but wait. The two friends reached the Dôme. The terrace where in summer the customers sat in the open was glassed in. Every table was engaged, but as they came in a couple got up and they took the empty places. It was none too warm, and Simon wore no coat.

"Won't you be cold?" Charley asked him. "Wouldn't you prefer to sit inside?"

"No, I've taught myself not to mind cold."

"What happens when you catch one?"

"I ignore it."

Charley had often heard of the Dôme, but had never been there, and he looked with eager curiosity at the people who sat all round them. There were young men in turtle-neck sweaters, some of them with short beards, and girls bare-headed, in raincoats; he supposed they were painters and writers, and it gave him a little thrill to look at them.

"English or American," said Simon, with a scornful shrug of the shoulders. "Wasters and rotters most of them, pathetically dressing up for a role in a play that has long ceased to be acted."

Over there was a group of tall, fair-haired youths who looked like Scandinavians, and at another table a swarthy, gesticulating, loquacious band of Levantines. But the greater number were quiet French people,

respectably dressed, shopkeepers from the neighbour-
hood who came to the Dôme because it was convenient,
with a sprinkling of provincials who, like Charley, still
thought it the resort of artists and students.

"Poor brutes, they haven't got the money to lead the
Latin Quarter life any more. They live on the edge of
starvation and work like galley-slaves. I suppose you've
read the *Vie de Bohême?* Rodolphe now wears a neat
blue suit that he's bought off the nail and puts his
trousers under his mattress every night to keep them
in shape. He counts every penny he spends and takes
care to do nothing to compromise his future. Mimi and
Musette are hard-working girls, trade unionists, who
spend their spare evenings attending party meetings,
and even if they lose their virtue, keep their heads."

"Don't you live with a girl?"

"No."

"Why not? I should have thought it would be very
pleasant. In the year you've been in Paris you must
have had plenty of chances of picking someone up."

"Yes, I've had one or two. Strange when you come
to think of it. D'you know what my place consists of?
A studio and a kitchen. No bath. The concierge is
supposed to come and clean up every day, but she has
varicose veins and hates climbing the stairs. That's
all I have to offer and yet there've been three girls who
wanted to come and share my squalor with me. One
was English, she's got a job here in the International
Communist Bureau, another was a Norwegian, she's
working at the Sorbonne, and one was French—you'd
have thought she had more sense; she was a dressmaker
and out of work. I picked her up one evening when
I was going out to dinner, she told me she hadn't had
a meal all day and I stood her one. It was a Saturday

night and she stayed till Monday. She wanted to stay on, but I told her to get out and she went. The Norwegian was rather a nuisance. She wanted to darn my socks and cook for me and scrub the floor. When I told her there was nothing doing she took to waiting for me at street corners, walking beside me in the street and telling me that if I didn't relent she'd kill herself. She taught me a lesson that I've taken to heart. I had to be rather firm with her in the end."

"What d'you mean by that?"

"Well, one day I told her that I was sick of her pestering. I told her that next time she addressed me in the street I'd knock her down. She was rather stupid and she didn't know I meant it. Next day when I came out of my house, it was about twelve and I was just going to the office, she was standing on the other side of the street. She came up to me, with that hang-dog look of hers, and began to speak. I didn't let her get more than two or three words out, I hit her on the chin and she went down like a ninepin."

Simon's eyes twinkled with amusement.

"What happened then?"

"I don't know. I suppose she got up again. I walked on and didn't look round to see. Anyhow she took the hint and that's the last I saw of her."

The story made Charley very uncomfortable and at the same time made him want to laugh. But he was ashamed of this and remained silent.

"The comic one was the English communist. My dear, she was the daughter of a dean. She'd been to Oxford and she'd taken her degree in economics. She was terribly genteel, oh, a perfect lady, but she looked upon promiscuous fornication as a sacred duty. Every time she went to bed with a comrade she felt she was

44

helping the Cause. We were to be good pals, fight the good fight together, shoulder to shoulder, and all that sort of thing. The dean gave her an allowance and we were to pool our resources, make my studio a Centre, have the comrades in to afternoon tea and discuss the burning questions of the day. I just told her a few home truths and that finished her.''

He lit his pipe again, smiling to himself quietly, with that painful smile of his, as though he were enjoying a joke that hurt him. Charley had several things to say, but did not know how to put them so that they should not sound affected and so arouse Simon's irony.

"But is it your wish to cut human relations out of your life altogether?" he asked, uncertainly.

"Altogether. I've got to be free. I daren't let another person get a hold over me. That's why I turned out the little sempstress. She was the most dangerous of the lot. She was gentle and affectionate. She had the meekness of the poor who have never dreamt that life can be other than hard. I could never have loved her, but I knew that her gratitude, her adoration, her desire to please, her innocent cheerfulness, were dangerous. I could see that she might easily become a habit of which I couldn't break myself. Nothing in the world is so insidious as a woman's flattery; our need for it is so enormous that we become her slave. I must be as impervious to flattery as I am indifferent to abuse. There's nothing that binds one to a woman like the benefits one confers on her. She would have owed me everything, that girl, I should never have been able to escape from her.''

"But, Simon, you have human passions like the rest of us. You're twenty-three."

"And my sexual desires are urgent? Less urgent than

45

you imagine. When you work from twelve to sixteen hours a day and sleep on an average six, when you content yourself with one meal a day, much as it may surprise you, your desires are much attenuated. Paris is singularly well arranged for the satisfaction of the sexual instinct at moderate expense and with the least possible waste of time, and when I find that my appetite is interfering with my work I have a woman just as when I'm constipated I take a purge."

Charley's clear blue eyes twinkled with amusement and a charming smile parting his lips displayed his strong white teeth.

"Aren't you missing a lot of fun? You know, one's young for such a little while."

"I may be. I know one can do nothing in the world unless one's single-minded. Chesterfield said the last word about sexual congress: the pleasure is momentary, the position is ridiculous, and the expense is damnable. It may be an instinct that one can't suppress, but the man's a pitiful fool who allows it to divert him from his chosen path. I'm not afraid of it any more. In a few more years I shall be entirely free from its temptation."

"Are you sure you can prevent yourself from falling in love one of these days? Such things do happen, you know, even to the most prudent men."

Simon gave him a strange, one might even have thought a hostile, look.

"I should tear it out of my heart as I'd wrench out of my mouth a rotten tooth."

"That's easier said than done."

"I know. Nothing that's worth doing is done easily, but that's one of the odd things about man, if his self-preservation is concerned, if he has to do something on

46

which his being depends, he can find in himself the strength to do it."

Charley was silent. If anyone else had spoken to him as Simon had done that evening he would have thought it a pose adopted to impress. Charley had heard during his three years at Cambridge enough extravagant talk to be able, with his common sense and quiet humour, to attach no more importance to it than it deserved. But he knew that Simon never talked for effect. He was too contemptuous of his fellows' opinion to extort their admiration by taking up an attitude in which he did not believe. He was fearless and sincere. When he said that he thought this and that, you could be certain that he did, and when he said he had done that and the other you need not hesitate to believe that he had. But just as the manner of life that Simon had described seemed to Charley morbid and unnatural, so the ideas he expressed with a fluency that showed they were well considered seemed to him outrageous and horrible. He noticed that Simon had avoided saying what was the end for which he was thus so sternly disciplining himself; but at Cambridge he had been violently communist and it was natural to suppose that he was training himself to play his part in the revolution they had then, all of them, anticipated in the near future. Charley, much more concerned with the arts, had listened with interest, but without feeling that the matter was any particular affair of his, to the heated arguments he heard in Simon's rooms. If he had been obliged to state his views on a subject to which he had never given much thought, he would have agreed with his father: whatever might happen on the Continent there was no danger of communism in England; the hash they'd made in Russia showed it was impracticable;

there always had been rich and poor in the world and there always would be; the English working man was too shrewd to let himself be led away by a lot of irresponsible agitators; and after all he didn't have a bad time.

Simon went on. He was eager to deliver himself of thoughts that he had bottled up for many months and he had been used to impart them to Charley for as long as he could remember. Though he reflected upon them with the intensity which was one of his great gifts, he found that they gained in clearness and force when he had this perfect listener to put them to.

"An awful lot of hokum is talked about love, you know. An importance is ascribed to it that is entirely at variance with fact. People talk as though it were self-evidently the greatest of human values. Nothing is less self-evident. Until Plato dressed his sentimental sensuality in a captivating literary form the ancient world laid no more stress on it than was sensible; the healthy realism of the Muslims has never looked upon it as anything but a physical need; it was Christianity, buttressing its emotional claims with neo-Platonism, that made it into the end and aim, the reason, the justification of life. But Christianity was the religion of slaves. It offered the weary and the heavy-laden heaven to compensate them in the future for their misery in this world and the opiate of love to enable them to bear it in the present. And like every drug it enervated and destroyed those who became subject to it. For two thousand years it's suffocated us. It's weakened our wills and lessened our courage. In this modern world we live in we know that almost everything is more important to us than love, we know that only the soft and the stupid allow it to affect their

48

actions, and yet we pay it a foolish lip-service. In books, on the stage, in the pulpit, on the platform the same old sentimental rubbish is talked that was used to hoodwink the slaves of Alexandria."

"But, Simon, the slave population of the ancient world was just the proletariat of to-day."

Simon's lips trembled with a smile and the look he fixed on Charley made him feel that he had said a silly thing.

"I know," said Simon quietly.

For a while his restless eyes were still, but though he looked at Charley his gaze seemed fixed on something in the far distance. Charley did not know of what he thought, but he was conscious of a faint malaise.

"It may be that the habit of two thousand years has made love a human necessity and in that case it must be taken into account. But if dope must be administered the best person to do so is surely not a dope-fiend. If love can be put to some useful purpose it can only be by someone who is himself immune to it."

"You don't seem to want to tell me what end you expect to attain by denying yourself everything that makes life pleasant. I wonder if any end can be worth it."

"What have you been doing with yourself for the last year, Charley?"

The sudden question seemed inconsequent, but he answered it with his usual modest frankness.

"Nothing very much, I'm afraid. I've been going to the office pretty well every day; I've spent a certain amount of time on the Estate getting to know the properties and all that sort of thing: I've played golf with father. He likes to get in a round two or three days a week. And I've kept up with my piano-playing.

49

I've been to a good many concerts. I've seen most of the picture shows. I've been to the opera a bit and seen a certain number of plays."

"You've had a thoroughly good time?"

"Not bad. I've enjoyed myself."

"And what d'you expect to do next year?"

"More or less the same, I should think."

"And the year after, and the year after that?"

"I suppose in a few years I shall get married and then my father will retire and hand over his job to me. It brings in a thousand a year, not so bad in these days, and of course eventually I shall get my half of my father's share in the Mason Estate."

"And then you'll lead the sort of life your father has led before you?"

"Unless the Labour party confiscate the Mason Estate. Then of course I shall be in the cart. But until then I'm quite prepared to do my little job and have as much fun as I can on the income I've got."

"And when you die will it have mattered a damn whether you ever lived or not?"

For a moment the unexpected question disconcerted Charley and he flushed.

"I don't suppose it will."

"Are you satisfied with that?"

"To tell you the truth I've never thought about it. But if you ask me point-blank, I think I should be a fool if I weren't. I could never have become a great artist. I talked it over with father that summer after I came down when we went fishing in Norway. He put it awfully nicely. Poor old dear, he was very anxious not to hurt my feelings, but I couldn't help admitting that what he said was true. I've got a natural facility for doing things, I can paint a bit and write a bit and play

50

a bit, perhaps I might have had a chance if I'd only been able to do one thing; but it was only a facility. Father was quite right when he said that wasn't enough, and I think he was right too when he said it was better to be a pretty good business man than a second-rate artist. After all, it's a bit of luck for me that old Sibert Mason married the cook and started growing vegetables on a bit of land that the growth of London turned into a valuable property. Don't you think it's enough if I do my duty in that state of life in which providence or chance, if you like, has placed me?"

Simon gave him a smile more indulgent than any that had tortured his features that evening.

"I daresay, Charley. But not for me. I would sooner be smashed into a mangled pulp by a bus when we cross the street than look forward to a life like yours."

Charley looked at him calmly.

"You see, Simon, I have a happy nature and you haven't."

Simon chuckled.

"We must see if we can't change that. Let's stroll along. I'll take you to the Sérail."

III

THE front door, a discreet door in a house of respectable appearance, was opened for them by a negro in Turkish dress and as they entered a narrow ill-lit passage a woman came out of an ante-room. She took them in with a quick, cool glance, but then recognizing Simon, immediately assumed an air of geniality. They shook hands warmly.

"This is Mademoiselle Ernestine," he said to Charley and then to her: "My friend has arrived from London this evening. He wishes to see life."

"You've brought him to the right place."

She gave Charley an appraising look. Charley saw a woman who might have been in the later thirties, good-looking in a cold, hard way, with a straight nose, thin painted lips and a firm chin; she was neatly dressed in a dark suit of somewhat masculine cut. She wore a collar and tie and as a pin the crest of a famous English regiment.

"He's good-looking," she said. "These ladies will be pleased to see him."

"Where is Madame to-night?"

"She's gone home to spend the holidays with her family. I am in charge."

"We'll go in, shall we?"

"You know your way."

The two young men passed along the passage and opening a door found themselves in a vast room garishly decorated in the pinchbeck style of a Turkish bath.

There were settees round the walls and in front of them little tables and chairs. A fair sprinkling of people were sitting about, mostly in day clothes, but a few in dinner-jackets; men in twos and threes; and at one table a mixed party, the women in evening frocks, who had evidently come to see one of the sights of Paris. Waiters in Turkish dress stood about and attended to orders. On a platform was an orchestra consisting of a pianist, a fiddler and a man who played the saxophone. Two benches facing one another jutted out on to the dance floor and on these sat ten or twelve young women. They wore Turkish slippers, but with high heels, baggy trousers of some shimmering material that reached to their ankles, and small turbans on their heads. The upper part of their bodies was naked. Other girls similarly dressed were seated with men who were standing a drink. Simon and Charley sat down and ordered a bottle of champagne. The band started up. Three or four men rose to their feet and going over to the benches chose partners to dance with. The rest of the girls listlessly danced together. They talked in a desultory way to one another and threw inquisitive glances at the men who were sitting at the various tables. It was apparent that the party of sight-seers, with the smart women from a different world, excited their curiosity. On the face of it, except that the girls were half naked, there was nothing to distinguish the place from any night club but the fact that there was room to dance in comfort. Charley noticed that at a table near theirs two men with dispatch-cases, from which in the course of conversation they extracted papers, were talking business as unconcernedly as if they were in a café. Presently one of the men from the group of sight-seers went and spoke to two girls who were dancing together, whereupon they stopped and went up to the table from which he had come; one of the women, beautifully dressed in black, with a string of emeralds round her neck, got up and began dancing with one of the two girls. The other went back to the bench and sat down. The sous-maîtresse, the woman in the coat and skirt, came up to Simon and Charley.

"Well, does your friend see any of these ladies who takes his fancy?"

"Sit down with us a minute and have a drink. He's having a look round. The night's young yet."

She sat down and when Simon called the waiter ordered an orangeade.

"I'm sorry he's come here for the first time on such a quiet night. You see, on Christmas Eve a lot of people have to stay at home. But it'll get more lively presently. A crowd of English have come over to Paris for the holidays. I saw in the paper that they're running the Golden Arrow in three sections. They're a great nation, the English; they have money."

Charley, feeling rather shy, was silent, and she asked Simon if he understood French.

"Of course he does. He spent six months in Touraine to learn it."

"What a beautiful district! Last summer when I took my holiday I motored all through the Châteaux country. Angèle comes from Tours. Perhaps your friend would like to dance with her." She turned to Charley. "You do dance, don't you?"

"Yes, I like it."

"She's very well educated and she comes from an excellent family. I went to see them when I was in Tours and they thanked me for all that I had done for

their daughter. They were persons of the greatest respectability. You mustn't think that we take anyone here. Madame is very particular. We have our name and we value it. All these ladies here come from families who are highly esteemed in their own town. That is why they like to work in Paris. Naturally they don't want to cause embarrassment to their relations. Life is hard and one has to earn one's living as best one can. Of course I don't pretend that they belong to the aristocracy, but the aristocracy in France is thoroughly corrupt, and for my part I set much greater value on the good French bourgeois stock. That is the backbone of the country."

Mademoiselle Ernestine gave you the impression of a sensible woman of sound principle. You could not but feel that her views on the social questions of the day would be well worth listening to. She patted Simon's hand and again speaking to Charley said:

"It always gives me pleasure to see Monsieur Simon. He's a good friend of the house. He doesn't come very often, but when he does he behaves like a gentleman. He is never drunk like some of your compatriots and one can talk to him of interesting subjects. We are always glad to see journalists here. Sometimes I think the life we lead is a little narrow and it does one good to talk to someone who is in the centre of things. It takes one out of one's rut. He's sympathetic."

In those surroundings, as though he felt himself strangely at home, Simon was easy and genial. If he was acting it was a very good performance that he was giving. You would have thought that he felt some queer affinity between himself and the sous-maîtresse of the brothel.

"Once he took me to a répétition générale at the Français. All Paris was there. Academicians, ministers, generals. I was dazzled."

"And I may add that not one of the women looked more distinguished than you. It did my reputation a lot of good to be seen with you."

"You should have seen the faces of some of the bigwigs who come here, when they saw me in the foyer walking on the arm of Monsieur Simon."

Charley knew that to go to a great social function with such a companion was the kind of joke that appealed to Simon's sardonic humour. They talked a little more and then Simon said:

"Listen, my dear, I think we ought to do our young friend proud as it's the first time he's been here. What about introducing him to the Princess? Don't you think he'd like her?"

Mademoiselle Ernestine's strong features relaxed into a smile and she gave Charley an amused glance.

"It's an idea. It would at least be an experience that he hasn't had before. She has a pretty figure."

"Let's have her along and stand her a drink."

Mademoiselle Ernestine called a waiter.

"Tell the Princess Olga to come here." Then to Charley: "She's Russian. Of course since the revolution we have been swamped with Russians, we're fed to the teeth with them and their Slav temperament; for a time the clients were amused by it, but they're tired of them now. And then they're not serious. They're noisy and quarrelsome. The truth is, they're barbarians, and they don't know how to behave. But Princess Olga is different. She has principles. You can see that she's been well brought up. She has something, there's no denying it."

While she was speaking Charley saw the waiter go up to a girl who was sitting on one of the benches and speak to her. His eyes had been wandering and he had noticed her before. She sat strangely still, and you would have thought that she was unconscious of her surroundings. She got up now, gave a glance in their direction, and walked slowly towards them. There was a singular nonchalance in her gait. When she came up she gave Simon a slight smile and they shook hands.

"I saw you come in just now," she said, as she sat down.

Simon asked her if she would drink a glass of champagne.

"I don't mind."

"This is a friend of mine who wants to know you."

"I'm flattered." She turned an unsmiling glance on Charley. She looked at him for a time that seemed to him embarrassingly long, but her eyes held neither welcome nor invitation; their perfect indifference was almost nettling. "He's handsome." Charley smiled shyly and then the faintest suspicion of a smile trembled on her lips. "He looks good-natured."

Her turban, her baggy trousers were of gauze, pale blue and thickly sprinkled with little silver stars. She was not very tall; her face was heavily made up, her cheeks extravagantly rouged, her lips scarlet and her eyelids blue; eyebrows and eyelashes were black with mascara. She was certainly not beautiful, she was only prettyish, with rather high cheek-bones, a fleshy little nose and eyes not set deep in their sockets, not prominent either, but on a level as it were with her face, like windows set flush with a wall. They were large and blue, and their blue, emphasized both by the colour of her turban and by the mascara, was like a flame. She had a neat, trim, slight figure, and the skin of her body, pale amber in hue, had a look of silky softness. Her breasts were small and round, virginal, and the well-shaped nipples were rosy.

"Why don't you ask the Princess to dance with you, Charley?" said Simon.

"Will you?" said he.

She gave the very faintest shrug of one shoulder and without a word rose to her feet. At the same time Mademoiselle Ernestine, saying she had affairs to attend to, left them. It was a new and thrilling experience for Charley to dance with a girl with nothing on above the waist. It made him rather breathless to put his hand on her naked body and to feel her bare breasts against him. The hand which he held in his was small and soft. But he was a well-brought-up young man, with good manners, and feeling it was only decent to make polite conversation, talked in the same way as he would have to any girl at a dance in London whom he did not know. She answered civilly enough, but he had a notion that she was not giving much heed to what he said. Her eyes wandered vaguely about the room, but there was no indication that they found there anything to excite her interest. When he clasped her a little more closely to him she accepted the more intimate hold without any sign that she noticed it. She acquiesced. The band stopped playing and they returned to their table. Simon was sitting there alone.

"Well, does she dance well?" he asked.

"Not very."

Suddenly she laughed. It was the first sign of animation she had given and her laugh was frank and gay.

"I'm sorry," she said, speaking English, "I wasn't

attending. I can dance better than that and next time I will."

Charley flushed.

"I didn't know you spoke English. I wouldn't have said that."

"But it was quite true. And you dance so well. you deserve a partner who can dance too."

Hitherto they had spoken French. Charley's was not very accurate, but it was fluent enough, and his accent was good. She spoke it very well, but with the sing-song Russian intonation which gives the language an alien monotony. Her English was not bad.

"The Princess was educated in England," said Simon.

"I went there when I was two and stayed till I was fourteen. I haven't spoken it much since then and I've forgotten."

"Where did you live?"

"In London. In Ladbroke Grove. In Charlotte Street. Wherever it was cheap."

"I'm going to leave you young things now," said Simon. "I'll see you to-morrow, Charley."

"Aren't you going to the Mass?"

"No."

He left them with a casual nod.

"Have you known Monsieur Simon long?" asked the Princess.

"He's my oldest friend."

"Do you like him?"

"Of course."

"He's very different from you. I should have thought he was the last person you would have taken to."

"He's brilliantly clever. He's been a very good friend to me."

She opened her mouth to speak, but then seemed to

think better of it, and kept silent. The music began to play once more.

"Will you dance with me again?" she asked. "I want to show you that I *can* dance when I want to."

Perhaps it was because Simon had left them and she felt less constraint, perhaps it was something in Charley's manner, maybe his confusion when he had realized that she spoke English, that had made her take notice of him, there was a difference in her attitude. It had now a kindliness which was unexpected and attractive. While they danced she talked with something approaching gaiety. She went back to her childhood and spoke with a sort of grim humour of the squalor in which she and her parents had lived in cheap London lodgings. And now, taking the trouble to follow Charley's steps, she danced very well. They sat down again and Charley glanced at his watch; it was getting on towards midnight. He was in a quandary. He had often heard them speak at home of the church music at St. Eustache, and the opportunity of hearing Mass there on Christmas Eve was one that he could not miss. The thrill of arriving in Paris, his talk with Simon, the new experience of the Sérail and the champagne he had drunk, had combined to fill him with a singular exaltation and he had an urgent desire to hear music; it was as strong as his physical desire for the girl he had been dancing with. It seemed silly to go at this particular juncture and for such a purpose; but there it was, he wanted to, and after all nobody need know.

"Look," he said, with an engaging smile, "I've got a date. I must go away now, but I shall be back in an hour. I shall still find you here, shan't I?"

"I'm here all night."

"But you won't get fixed up with anybody else?"

"Why have you got to go away?"

He smiled a trifle shyly.

"I'm afraid it sounds absurd, but my friend has given me a couple of tickets for the Mass at St. Eustache, and I may never have another opportunity of hearing it."

"Who are you going with?"

"Nobody."

"Will you take me?"

"You? But how could you get away?"

"I can arrange that with Mademoiselle. Give me a couple of hundred francs and I'll fix it."

He gave her a doubtful glance. With her naked body, her powder-blue turban and trousers, her painted face, she did not look the sort of person to go to church with. She saw his glance and laughed.

"I'd give anything in the world to go. Do, do. I can change in ten minutes. It would give me so much pleasure."

"All right."

He gave her the money and telling him to wait for her in the entrance, she hurried away. He paid for the wine and after ten minutes, counted on his watch, went out.

As he stepped into the passage a girl came up to him.

"I haven't kept you waiting, you see. I've explained to Mademoiselle. Anyway she thinks Russians are mad."

Until she spoke he had not recognized her. She wore a brown coat and skirt and a felt hat. She had taken off her make-up, even the red on her lips, and her eyes under the thin fair line of her shaven eyebrows looked neither so large nor so blue. In her brown clothes, neat but cheap, she looked nondescript. She might have been a workgirl such as you see pouring along side

61

streets from the back door of a department store at the luncheon hour. She was hardly even pretty, but she looked very young; and there was something humble in her bearing that gave Charley a pang.

"Do you like music, Princess?" he asked, when they got into a taxi.

He did not quite know what to call her. Even though she was a prostitute, he felt it would be rude, with her rank, on so short an acquaintance to call her Olga, and if she had been reduced to so humiliating a position by the stress of circumstances it behoved him all the more to treat her with respect.

"I'm not a princess, you know, and my name isn't Olga. They call me that at the Sérail because it flatters the clients to think they are going to bed with a princess and they call me Olga because it's the only Russian name they know besides Sasha. My father was a professor of economics at the University at Leningrad and my mother was the daughter of a customs official."

"What is your name then?"

"Lydia."

They arrived just as the Mass was beginning. There were crowds of people and no chance of getting a seat. It was bitterly cold and Charley asked her if she would like his coat. She shook her head without answering. The aisles were lit by naked electric globes and they threw harsh beams on the vaulting, the columns and the dark throng of worshippers. The choir was brilliantly lit. They found a place by a column where, protected by its shadow, they could feel themselves isolated. There was an orchestra on a raised platform. At the altar were priests in splendid vestments. The music seemed to Charley somewhat florid, and he listened to it with a faint sense of disappointment.

It did not move him as he had expected it would and the soloists, with their metallic, operatic voices, left him cold. He had a feeling that he was listening to a performance rather than attending a religious ceremony, and it excited in him no sensation of reverence. But for all that he was glad to have come. The darkness into which the light from the electric globes cut like a bright knife, making the Gothic lines grimmer; the soft brilliance of the altar, with its multitude of candles, with the priests performing actions whose meaning was unknown to him; the silent crowd that seemed not to participate but to wait anxiously like a crowd at a station barrier waiting for the gate to open; the stench of wet clothes and the aromatic perfume of incense; the bitter cold that lowered like a threatening unseen presence; it was not a religious emotion that he got from all this, but the sense of a mystery that had its roots far back in the origins of the human race. His nerves were taut, and when on a sudden the choir to the full accompaniment of the orchestra burst with a great shout into the Adeste Fidelis he was seized with an exultation over he knew not what. Then a boy sang a canticle; the thin, silvery voice rose in the silence and the notes trickled, with a curious little hesitation at first, as though the singer were not quite sure of himself, trickled like water crystal-clear trickling over the white stones of a brook; and then, the singer gathering assurance, the sounds were caught up, as though by great dark hands, and borne into the intricate curves of the arches and up to the night of the vaulted roof. Suddenly Charley was conscious that the girl by his side, Lydia, was crying. It gave him a bit of a turn, but with his polite English reticence he pretended not to notice; he thought that the dark church and the pure sound of the boy's voice had filled her with a sudden sense of shame. He was an imaginative youth and he had read many novels. He could guess, he fancied, what she was feeling and he was seized with a great pity for her. He found it curious, however, that she should be so moved by music that was not of the best quality. But now she began to be shaken by heavy sobs and he could pretend no longer that he did not know she was in trouble. He put out a hand and took hers, thinking to offer her thus the comfort of his sympathy, but she snatched away her hand almost roughly. He began to be embarrassed. She was now crying so violently that the bystanders could not but notice it. She was making an exhibition of herself and he went hot with shame.

"Would you like to go out?" he whispered.

She shook her head angrily. Her sobbing grew more and more convulsive and suddenly she sank down on her knees and, burying her face in her hands, gave herself up to uncontrolled weeping. She was heaped up on herself strangely, like a bundle of cast-off clothes, and except for the quivering shoulders you would have thought her in a dead faint. She lay crouched at the foot of the tall pillar, and Charley, miserably self-conscious, stood in front of her trying to protect her from view. He saw a number of persons cast curious glances at her and then at him. It made him angry to think what they must suppose. The musicians were hushed, the choir was mute, and the silence had a thrilling quality of awe. Communicants, serried row upon row, pressed up to the altar steps to take in their mouths the Sacred Host that the priest offered them. Charley's delicacy prevented him from looking at Lydia and he kept his eyes fixed on the bright-lit chancel. But when she raised herself a little he was conscious of her movement. She turned to the pillar and putting her arm against it hid her face in the crook of her elbow. The passion of her weeping had exhausted her, but the way in which she now sprawled, leaning against the hard stone, her bent legs on the stone paving, expressed such a hopelessness of woe that it was even more intolerable than to see her crushed and bowed on the floor like a person thrown into an unnatural attitude by a violent death.

The service reached its close. The organ joined with the orchestra for the voluntary, and an increasing stream of people, anxious to get to their cars or to find taxis, streamed to the doors. Then it was finished, and a great throng swept down the length of the church. Charley waited till they were alone in the place they had chosen and the last thick wedge of people seemed to be pressing to the doors. He put his hand on her shoulder.

"Come. We must go now."

He put his arm round her and lifted her to her feet. Inert, she let him do what he liked. She held her eyes averted. Linking her arm in his he led her down the aisle and waited again a little till all but a dozen people had gone out.

"Would you like to walk a few steps?"

"No, I'm so tired. Let's get into a taxi."

But they had to walk a little after all, for they could not immediately find one. When they came to a street lamp she stopped and taking a mirror from her bag looked at herself. Her eyes were swollen. She took out a puff and dabbed it over her face.

"There's not much to be done," he said, with a kindly smile. "We'd better go and have a drink somewhere. You can't go back to the Sérail like that."

"When I cry my eyes always swell. It'll take hours to go down."

Just then a taxi passed and Charley hailed it.

"Where shall we go?"

"I don't care. The Select. Boulevard Montparnasse."

He gave the address and they drove across the river. When they arrived he hesitated, for the place she had chosen seemed crowded, but she stepped out of the taxi and he followed her. Notwithstanding the cold a lot of people were sitting on the terrace. They found a table within.

"I'll go into the ladies' room and wash my eyes."

In a few minutes she returned and sat down by his side. She had pulled down her hat as far as she could to hide her swollen lids and had powdered herself, but she had put on no rouge and her face was white. She was quite calm. She said nothing about the passion of weeping that had overcome her and you might have thought she took it as a natural thing that needed no excuse.

"I'm very hungry," she said. "You must be hungry, too."

Charley was ravenous and while he waited for her had wondered whether in the circumstances it would seem very gross if he ordered himself bacon and eggs. Her remark relieved his mind. It appeared that bacon and eggs were just what she fancied. He wanted to order a bottle of champagne, thinking she needed the stimulant, but she would not let him.

"Why should you waste your money? Let's have some beer."

They ate their simple meal with appetite. They talked little. Charley, with his good manners, tried to make polite conversation, but she did not encourage him and presently they fell into silence. When they had finished and had had coffee, he asked Lydia what she would like to do.

"I should like to sit here. I'm fond of this place. It's cosy and intimate. I like to look at the people who come here."

"All right, we'll sit here."

It was not exactly how he had proposed to pass his first night in Paris. He wished he hadn't been such a fool as to take her to the Midnight Mass. He had not the heart to be unkind to her. But perhaps there was some intonation in his reply that struck her, for she turned a little to look him in the face. She gave him once more the smile he had already seen two or three times on her. It was a queer sort of smile. It hardly moved the lips; it held no gaiety, but was not devoid of kindliness; there was more irony in it than amusement and it was rare and unwilling, patient and disillusioned.

"This can't be very amusing for you. Why don't you go back to the Sérail and leave me here?"

"No, I won't do that."

"I don't mind being alone, you know. I sometimes come here by myself and sit for hours. You've come to Paris to enjoy yourself. You'd be a fool not to."

"If it doesn't bore you I'd like to sit here with you."

"Why?" She gave him on a sudden a disdainful glance. "Do you look upon yourself as being noble and self-sacrificing? Or are you sorry for me or only curious?"

Charley could not imagine why she seemed angry with him or why she said these wounding things.

"Why should I feel sorry for you? Or curious?"

He meant her to understand that she was not the first prostitute he had met in his life and he was not likely to be impressed with a life-story which was probably sordid and in all likelihood untrue. Lydia stared at him with an expression which to him looked like incredulous surprise.

"What did your friend Simon tell you about me?"

"Nothing."

"Why do you redden when you say that?"

"I didn't know I reddened," he smiled.

In fact Simon had told him that she was not a bad romp, and would give him his money's worth, but that was not the sort of thing he felt inclined to tell her just then. With her pale face and swollen eyelids, in that poor brown dress and the black felt hat, there was nothing to remind one of the creature, in her blue Turkish trousers, with a naked body, who had had a curious, exotic attractiveness. It was another person altogether, quiet, respectable, demure, with whom Charley could as little think of going to bed as with one of the junior mistresses at Patsy's old school. Lydia relapsed into silence. She seemed to be sunk in reverie. When at last she spoke it was as though she were continuing her train of thought rather than addressing him.

"If I cried just now in church it wasn't for the reason that you thought. I've cried enough for that, heaven knows, but just then it was for something different. I felt so lonely. All those people, they have a country, and in that country, homes; to-morrow they'll spend Christmas Day together, father and mother and children; some of them, like you, went only to hear the music, and some have no faith, but just then, all of them, they were joined together by a common feeling; that ceremony, which they've known all their lives, and whose meaning is in their blood, every word spoken, every action of the priests, is familiar to them, and even if they don't believe with their minds, the awe, the mystery, is in their bones and they believe with their hearts; it is part of the recollections of their childhood, the gardens they played in, the countryside, the streets of the towns. It binds them together, it makes them one, and some deep instinct tells them that they belong to one another. But I am a stranger. I have no country, I have no home, I have no language. I belong nowhere. I am outcast."

She gave a mournful little chuckle.

"I'm a Russian and all I know of Russia is what I've read. I yearn for the broad fields of golden corn and the forests of silver beech that I've read of in books and though I try and try, I can't see them with my mind's eye. I know Moscow from what I've seen of it at the cinema. I sometimes rack my brain to picture to myself a Russian village, the straggling village of log houses with their thatched roofs that you read about in Chekov, and it's no good, I know that what I see isn't that at all. I'm a Russian and I speak my native language worse than I speak English and French. When I read Tolstoi and Dostoievsky it is easier for me to read them in a translation. I'm just as much a foreigner to my own people as I am to the English and French. You who've got a home and a country, people who love you, people whose ways are your ways, whom you understand without knowing them—how can you tell what it is to belong nowhere?"

"But have you no relations at all?"

"Not one. My father was a socialist, but he was a quiet, peaceable man absorbed in his studies, and he took no active part in politics. He welcomed the revolution and thought it was the opening of a new era for Russia. He accepted the Bolsheviks. He only asked to be allowed to go on with his work at the university. But they turned him out and one day he got news that he was going to be arrested. We escaped through Finland, my father, my mother and me. I was two. We lived in England for twelve years. How, I don't know. Sometimes my father got a little work to do, sometimes people helped us, but my father was homesick. Except when he was a student in Berlin he'd never been out of Russia before; he couldn't accustom himself to English life, and at last he felt he had to go back. My mother implored him not to. He couldn't help himself, he had to go, the desire was too strong for him; he got into touch with people at the Russian embassy in London, he said he was prepared to do any work the Bolsheviks gave him; he had a good reputation in Russia, his books had been widely praised, and he was an authority on his subject. They promised him everything and he sailed. When the ship docked he was taken off by the agents of the Cheka. We heard that he'd been taken to a cell on the fourth floor of the prison and thrown out of the window. They said he'd committed suicide."

She sighed a little and lit another cigarette. She had been smoking incessantly since they finished supper.

"He was a mild gentle creature. He never did anyone harm. My mother told me that all the years they'd been married he'd never said a harsh word to her. Because he'd made his peace with the Bolsheviks the people who'd helped us before wouldn't help us any more. My mother thought we'd be better off in Paris. She had friends there. They got her work addressing letters. I was apprenticed to a dressmaker. My mother died because there wasn't enough to eat for both of us and she denied herself so that I shouldn't go hungry. I found a job with a dressmaker who gave me half the usual wages because I was Russian. If those friends of my mother's, Alexey and Evgenia, hadn't given me a bed to sleep in I should have starved too. Alexey played the violin in an orchestra at a Russian restaurant and Evgenia ran the ladies' cloak-room. They had three children and the six of us lived in two rooms. Alexey was a lawyer by profession, he'd been one of my father's pupils at the university."

"But you have them still?"

"Yes, I have them still. They're very poor now. You see, everyone's sick of the Russians, they're sick of Russian restaurants and Russian orchestras. Alexey hasn't had a job for four years. He's grown bitter and quarrelsome and he drinks. One of the girls has been taken charge of by an aunt who lives at Nice, and another has gone into service, the son has become a gigolo and he does the night clubs at Montmartre; he's often here, I don't know why he isn't here this evening, perhaps he's clicked. His father curses him and beats him when he's drunk, but the hundred francs he brings home when he's found a friend helps to keep things going. I live there still."

"Do you?" said Charley in surprise.

"I must live somewhere. I don't go to the Sérail till night and when trade is slack I often get back by four or five. But it's terribly far away."

For a while they sat in silence.

"What did you mean when you said just now you hadn't been crying for the reason I thought?" asked Charley at length.

She gave him once more a curious, suspicious look.

"Do you really mean that you don't know who I am? I thought that was why your friend Simon sent for me."

71

"He told me nothing except—except that you'd give me a good time."

"I'm the wife of Robert Berger. That is why, although I'm a Russian, they took me at the Sérail. It gives the clients a kick."

"I'm afraid you'll think me very stupid, but I honestly don't know what you're talking about."

She gave a short, hard laugh.

"Such is fame. A day's journey and the name that's on every lip means nothing. Robert Berger murdered an English bookmaker called Teddie Jordan. He was condemned to fifteen years' penal servitude. He's at St. Laurent in French Guiana."

She spoke in such a matter-of-fact way that Charley could hardly believe his ears. He was startled, horrified and thrilled.

"And you really didn't know?"

"I give you my word I didn't. Now you speak of it I remember reading about the case in the English papers. It created rather a sensation because the—the victim was English, but I'd forgotten the name of the—of your husband."

"It created a sensation in France, too. The trial lasted three days. People fought to get to it. The papers gave it the whole of their front page. No one talked of anything else. Oh, it was a sensation all right. That was when I first saw your friend Simon, at least that's when he first saw me, he was reporting the case for his paper and I was in court. It was an exciting trial, it gave the journalists plenty of opportunity. You must get him to tell you about it. He's proud of the articles he wrote. They were so clever, bits of them got translated and were put in the French papers. It did him a lot of good."

Charley did not know what to say. He was angry with Simon; he recognized his puckish humour in putting him in the situation in which he now found himself.

"It must have been awful for you," he said lamely.

She turned a little and looked into his eyes. He, whose life had been set in pleasant places, had never before seen on a face a look of such hideous despair. It hardly looked like a human face, but like one of those Japanese masks which an artist has fashioned to portray a certain emotion. He shivered. Lydia till now, for Charley's sake, had been talking mostly in English, breaking into French now and then when she found it too difficult to say what she wanted in the unfamiliar language, but now she went on in French. The sing-song of her Russian accent gave it a strange plaintiveness, but at the same time lent a sense of unreality to what she said. It gave you the impression of a person talking in a dream.

"I'd only been married six months. I was going to have a baby. Perhaps it was that that saved his neck. That and his youth. He was only twenty-two. The baby was born dead. I'd suffered too much. You see, I loved him. He was my first love and my last love. When he was sentenced they wanted me to divorce him, transportation is a sufficient reason in French law; they told me that the wives of convicts always divorced and they were angry with me when I wouldn't. The lawyer who defended him was very kind to me. He said that I'd done everything I could, and that I'd had a bad time, but I'd stood by him to the end and now I ought to think of myself, I was young and must remake my life, I was making it even more difficult if I stayed tied to a convict. He was impatient with me when I said that I loved Robert and Robert was

73

the only thing in the world that mattered to me, and that whatever he did I'd love him, and that if ever I could go out to him, and he wanted me, I'd go and gladly. At last he shrugged his shoulders and said there was nothing to be done with us Russians, but if ever I changed my mind and wanted a divorce I was to come to him and he'd help me. And Evgenia and Alexey, poor drunken, worthless Alexey, they gave me no peace. They said Robert was a scoundrel, they said he was wicked, they said it was disgraceful that I should love him. As if one could stop loving because it's disgraceful to love! It's so easy to call a man a scoundrel. What does it mean? He murdered and he suffered for his crime. None of them knew him as I knew him. You see, he loved me. They didn't know how tender he was, how charming, how gay, how boyish. They said he came near killing me as he killed Teddie Jordan; they didn't see that it only made me love him more."

It was almost impossible for Charley, knowing nothing of the circumstances, to get anything coherent out of what she was saying.

"Why should he have killed you?" he asked.

"When he came home—after he'd killed Jordan, it was very late and I'd gone to bed, but his mother was waiting up for him. We lived with her. He was in high spirits, but when she looked at him she knew he'd done something terrible. You see, for weeks she'd been expecting it and she'd been frantic with anxiety.

"Where have you been all this time?" she asked him.

"'I? Nowhere,' he said. 'Round with the boys.' He chuckled and gently patted her cheek. 'It's so easy to kill a man, mother,' he said. 'It's quite ridiculous, it's so easy.'

"Then she knew what he'd done and she burst out crying.

74

" 'Your poor wife,' she said. 'Oh, how desperately unhappy you're going to make her.'

"He looked down and sighed.

" 'Perhaps it would be better if I killed her too,' he said.

" 'Robert!' she cried.

"He shook his head.

" 'Don't be afraid, I shouldn't have the courage,' he said. 'And yet, if I did it in her sleep, she'd know nothing.'

" 'My God, why did you do it?' she cried.

"Suddenly he laughed. He had a wonderfully gay, infectious laugh. You couldn't hear it without feeling happy.

" 'Don't be so silly, mother, I was only joking,' he said. 'I've done nothing. Go to bed and to sleep.'

"She knew he was lying. But that's all he would say. At last she went to her room. It was a tiny house, in Neuilly, but it had a bit of garden and there was a little pavilion at the end of it. When we married she gave us the house and moved in there so that she could be with her son and yet not on the top of us. Robert came up to our room and he waked me with a kiss on my lips. His eyes were shining. He had blue eyes, not so blue as yours, gray rather, but they were large and very brilliant. There was almost always a smile in them. They were wonderfully alert."

But Lydia had gradually slowed down the pace of her speech as she came to these sentences. It was as though a thought had struck her and she was turning it over in her mind while she talked. She looked at Charley with a curious expression.

"There *is* something in your eyes that reminds me of him, and your face is the same shape as his. He wasn't

75

so tall as you and he hadn't got your English complexion. He was very good-looking." She was silent for a moment. "What a malicious fool that Simon of yours is."

"What do you mean by that?"

"Nothing."

She leant forward, with her elbows on the table, her face in her hands, and went on, in a rather monotonous voice, as though she were reciting under hypnosis something that was passing before her vacant eyes.

"I smiled when I woke.

" 'How late you are,' I said. 'Be quick and come to bed.'

" 'I can't sleep now,' he said. 'I'm too excited. I'm hungry. Are there any eggs in the kitchen?'

"I was wide awake by then. You can't think how charming he looked sitting on the side of the bed in his new gray suit. He was always well-dressed and he wore his clothes wonderfully well. His hair was very beautiful, dark brown and waving, and he wore it long, brushed back on his head.

" 'I'll put on a dressing-gown and we'll go and see,' I said.

"We went into the kitchen and I found eggs and onions. I fried the onions and scrambled them with the eggs. I made some toast. Sometimes when we went to the theatre or had been to a concert we used to make ourselves something to eat when we got home. He loved scrambled eggs and onions, and I cooked them just in the way he liked. We used to love those modest suppers that we had by ourselves in the kitchen. He went into the cellar and brought out a bottle of champagne. I knew his mother would be cross, it was the last of half a dozen bottles that Robert had had given him by one of his racing friends, but he said he felt like champagne just then and he opened the bottle. He ate the eggs greedily and he emptied his glass at a gulp. He was in tearing spirits. When we first got into the kitchen I'd noticed that though his eyes were shining so brightly his face was pale, and if I hadn't known that nothing was more unlikely I should have thought he'd been drinking, but now the colour came back to his cheeks. I thought he'd been just tired and hungry. He'd been out all day, tearing about, I was sure, and it might be that he hadn't had a bite to eat. Although we'd only been parted a few hours he was almost crazy with joy at being with me again. He couldn't stop kissing me and while I was scrambling the eggs I had to push him away because he wanted to hug me and I was afraid he'd spoil the cooking. But I couldn't help laughing. We sat side by side at the kitchen table as close as we could get. He called me every sweet, endearing name he could think of, he couldn't keep his hands off me, you would have thought we'd only been married a week instead of six months. When we'd finished I wanted to wash everything up so that when his mother came in for breakfast she shouldn't find a mess, but he wouldn't let me. He wanted to get to bed quickly.

"He was like a man possessed of a god. I never thought it was possible for a man to love a woman as he loved me that night. I never knew a woman was capable of such adoration as I was filled with. He was insatiable. It seemed impossible to slake his passion. No woman ever had such a wonderful lover as I had that night. And he was my husband. Mine! Mine! I worshipped him. If he'd let me I would have kissed his feet. When at last he fell asleep exhausted, the dawn was already peeping through a chink in the curtains. But I couldn't sleep. I looked at his face as the light grew stronger; it was the unlined face of a boy. He slept, holding me in his arms, and there was a tiny smile of happiness on his lips. At last I fell asleep too.

"He was still sleeping when I woke and I got out of bed very quietly so as not to disturb him. I went into the kitchen to make his coffee for him. We were very poor. Robert had worked in a broker's office, but he'd had a quarrel with his employer and had walked out on him, and since then he hadn't found anything regular to do. He was crazy about racing and sometimes he made a bit that way, though his mother hated it, and occasionally he earned a little money by selling second-hand cars on commission, but all we really had to depend on was his mother's pension, she was the widow of an army doctor, and the little money she had besides. We didn't keep a servant and my mother-in-law and I did the housework. I found her in the kitchen, peeling potatoes for lunch.

" 'How is Robert?' she asked me.

" 'He's still asleep. I wish you could see him. With his hair all tousled he looks as if he was sixteen.'

"The coffee was on the hob and the milk was warm. I put it on to boil and had a cup, then I crept upstairs to get Robert's clothes. He was a dressy fellow and I'd learnt how to press them. I wanted to have them all ready for him and neatly laid out on a chair when he woke. I brought them down into the kitchen and gave them a brush and then I put an iron on to heat. When I put the trousers on the kitchen table I noticed there were stains on one of the legs.

" 'What on earth is that?' I cried. 'Robert *has* got his trousers in a mess.'

78

"Madame Berger got up from her chair so quickly that she upset the potatoes. She snatched up the trousers and looked at them. She began to tremble.

" 'I wonder what it is,' I said. 'Robert will be furious. His new suit.'

"I saw she was upset, but you know, the French are funny in some ways, they don't take things like that as casually as we Russians do. I don't know how many hundred francs Robert had paid for the suit, and if it was ruined she wouldn't sleep for a week thinking of all the money that had been wasted.

" 'It'll clean,' I said.

" 'Take Robert up his coffee,' she said sharply. 'It's after eleven and quite time he woke. Leave me the trousers. I know what to do with them.'

"I poured him out a cup and was just going upstairs with it when we heard Robert clattering down in his slippers. He nodded to his mother and asked for the paper.

" 'Drink your coffee while it's hot,' I said to him.

"He paid no attention to me. He opened the paper and turned to the latest news.

" 'There's nothing,' said his mother.

"I didn't know what she meant. He cast his eyes down the columns and then took a long drink of coffee. He was unusually silent. I took his coat and began to give it a brush.

" 'You made your trousers in an awful mess last night,' I said. 'You'll have to wear your blue suit to-day.'

"Madame Berger had put them over the back of a chair. She took them to him and showed him the stains. He looked at them for a minute while she watched him in silence. You would have thought he couldn't take his eyes off them. I couldn't understand their silence. It was strange. I thought they were taking a trivial accident in an absurdly tragic way. But of course the French have thrift in their bones.

" 'We've got some petrol in the house,' I said. 'We can get the stains out with that. Or they can go to the cleaner's.'

"They didn't answer. Robert, frowning, looked down. His mother turned the trousers round, I suppose to look if there were stains on the back, and then, I think, felt that there was something in the pockets.

" 'What have you got here?'

"He sprang to his feet.

" 'Leave it alone. I won't have you look ın my pockets.'

"He tried to snatch the trousers from her, but before he could do so she had slipped her hand into the hip-pocket and taken out a bundle of bank-notes. He stopped dead when he saw that she had them. She let the trousers drop to the ground and with a groan put her hand to her breast as though she'd been stabbed. I saw then that they were both of them as pale as death. A sudden thought seized me; Robert had often said to me that he was sure his mother had a little hoard hidden away somewhere in the house. We'd been terribly short of money lately. Robert was crazy to go down to the Riviera; I'd never been there and he'd been saying for weeks that if he could only get a bit of cash we'd go down and have a honeymoon at last. You see, at the time we married, he was working at that broker's and couldn't get away. The thought flashed through my mind that he'd found his mother's hoard. I blushed to the roots of my hair at the idea that he'd stolen it and yet I wasn't surprised. I hadn't lived with him for six months without knowing that he'd think it rather a lark. I saw that they were thousand-franc notes that she held in her hand. Afterwards I knew there were seven of them. She looked at him as though her eyes would start out of her head.

" 'When did you get them, Robert?' she asked.

"He gave a laugh, but I saw he was nervous.

" 'I made a lucky bet yesterday,' he answered.

" 'Oh, Robert,' I cried, 'you promised your mother you'd never play the horses again.'

" 'This was a certainty,' he said, 'I couldn't resist. We shall be able to go down to the Riviera, my sweet. You take them and keep them or they'll just slip through my fingers.'

" 'No, no, she mustn't have them,' cried Madame Berger. She gave Robert a look of real horror, so that I was astounded, then she turned to me. 'Go and do your room. I won't have the rooms left unmade all day long.'

"I saw she wanted to get rid of me and I thought I'd be better out of the way if they were going to quarrel. The position of a daughter-in-law is delicate. His mother worshipped Robert, but he was extravagant and it worried her to death. Now and then she made a scene. Sometimes they'd shut themselves up in her pavilion at the end of the garden and I'd hear their voices raised in violent discussions. He would come away sulky and irritable and when I saw her I knew she'd been crying. I went upstairs. When I came down again they stopped talking at once and Madame Berger told me to go out and buy some eggs for lunch. Generally Robert went out about noon and didn't come back till night, often very late, but that day he stayed in. He read and played the piano. I asked him what had passed between him and his mother, but he wouldn't tell me, he told me to mind my own business. I think neither of them spoke more than a dozen sentences all day. I thought it would never end. When we went to bed I snuggled up to Robert and put my arms round his neck, for of course I knew he was worried and I wanted to console him, but he pushed me away.

" 'For God's sake leave me alone,' he said. 'I'm in no mood for love-making to-night. I've got other things to think about.'

"I was bitterly wounded, but I didn't speak. I moved away from him. He knew he'd hurt me, for in a little while he put out his hand and lightly touched my face.

" 'Go to sleep, my sweet,' he said. 'Don't be upset because I'm in a bad humour to-day. I drank too much yesterday. I shall be all right to-morrow.'

" 'Was it your mother's money?' I whispered.

"He didn't answer at once.

" 'Yes,' he said at last.

" 'Oh, Robert, how could you?' I cried.

"He paused again before he said anything. I was wretched. I think I began to cry.

" 'If anyone should ask you anything you never saw me with the money. You never knew that I had any.'

" 'How can you think I'd betray you?' I cried.

" 'And the trousers. Maman couldn't get the stains out. She's thrown them away.'

"I suddenly remembered that I'd smelt something burning that afternoon while Robert was playing and I was sitting with him. I got up to see what it was.

" 'Stay here,' he said.

" 'But something's burning in the kitchen,' I said

" 'Maman's probably burning old rags. She's in a dirty temper to-day, she'll bite your head off if you go and interfere with her.'

"I knew now that it wasn't old rags she was burning; she hadn't thrown the trousers away, she'd burnt them. I began to be horribly frightened, but I didn't say anything. He took my hand.

" 'If anyone should ask you about them,' he said, 'you must say that I got them so dirty cleaning a car that they had to be given away. My mother gave them to a tramp the day before yesterday. Will you swear to that?'

" 'Yes,' I said, but I could hardly speak.

"Then he said a terrifying thing.

" 'It may be that my head depends on it.'

"I was too stunned, I was too horrified, to say anything. My head began to ache so that I thought it would burst. I don't think I closed my eyes all night. Robert slept fitfully. He was restless even in his sleep and turned from side to side. We went downstairs early, but my mother-in-law was already in the kitchen. As a rule she was very decently dressed and when she went out she looked quite smart. She was a doctor's widow and the daughter of a staff officer; she had a feeling about her position and she would let no one know to what economies she was reduced to make the show she did when she went to pay visits on old army friends. Then, with her waved hair and her manicured hands, with rouge on her cheeks, she didn't look more than forty; but now, her hair tousled, without any make-up, in a dressing-gown, she looked like an old procuress who'd retired to live on her savings. She didn't say good morning to Robert. Without a word she handed him the paper. I watched him while he read it and I saw his expression change. He felt my eyes upon him and looked up. He smiled.

" 'Well, little one,' he said gaily, 'what about this coffee? Are you going to stand there all the morning looking at your lord and master or are you going to wait on him?'

"I knew there was something in the paper that would tell me what I had to know. Robert finished his breakfast and went upstairs to dress. When he came down again, ready to go out, I had a shock, for he was wearing the light gray suit that he had worn two days before, and the trousers that went with it. But then of course I remembered that he'd had a second pair made when he ordered the suit. There had been a lot of discussion about it. Madame Berger had grumbled at the expense, but he had insisted that he couldn't hope to get a job unless he was decently dressed and at last she gave in as she always did, but she insisted that he should have a second pair of trousers, she said it was always the trousers that grew shabby first and it would be an economy in the end if he had two pairs. Robert went out and said he wouldn't be in to lunch. My mother-in-law went out soon afterwards to do her marketing and the moment I was alone I seized the paper. I saw that an English bookmaker, called Teddie Jordan, had been found dead in his flat. He had been stabbed in the back. I had often heard Robert speak of him. I knew it was he who had killed him. I had such a sudden pain in my heart that I thought I should die. I was terrified. I don't know how long I sat there. I couldn't move. At last I heard a key in the door and I knew it was Madame Berger coming in again. I put the paper back where she'd left it and went on with my work."

Lydia gave a deep sigh. They had not got to the restaurant till one or after and it was two by the time they finished supper. When they came in the tables were full and there was a dense crowd at the bar. Lydia had been talking a long time and little by little people had been going. The crowd round the bar thinned out. There were only two persons sitting at it now and only one table besides theirs was occupied. The waiters were getting restive.

"I think we ought to be going," said Charley. "I'm sure they want to be rid of us."

At that moment the people at the other table got up to go. The woman who brought their coats from the cloak-room brought Charley's too and put it on the table beside him. He called for the bill.

"I suppose there's some place we could go to now?"

"We could go to Montmartre. Graaf's is open all night. I'm terribly tired."

"Well, if you like I'll drive you home."

"To Alexey and Evgenia's? I can't go there to-night. He'll be drunk. He'll spend the whole night abusing Evgenia for bringing up the children to be what they are and weeping over his own sorrows. I won't go to the Sérail. We'd better go to Graaf's. At least it's warm there."

She seemed so woebegone, and really so exhausted, that Charley with hesitation made a proposal. He remembered that Simon had told him that he could take anyone into the hotel.

"Look here, I've got two beds in my room. Why don't you come back with me there?"

She gave him a suspicious look, but he shook his head smiling.

"Just to sleep, I mean," he added. "You know, I've

85

had a journey to-day and what with the excitement and one thing and another I'm pretty well all in."

"All right."

There was no cab to be found when they got out into the street, but it was only a little way to the hotel and they walked. A sleepy night watchman opened the door for them and took them upstairs in the lift. Lydia took off her hat. She had a broad, white brow. He had not seen her hair before. It was short, curling round the neck, and pale brown. She kicked off her shoes and slipped out of her dress. When Charley came back from the bathroom, having got into his pyjamas, she was not only in bed but asleep. He got into his own bed and put out the light. They had not exchanged a word since they left the restaurant.

Thus did Charley spend his first night in Paris.

IV

IT was late when he woke. For a moment he had no notion where he was. Then he saw Lydia. They had not drawn the curtains and a gray light filtered through the shutters. The room with its pitchpine furniture looked squalid. She lay on her back in the twin bed with her eyes open, staring up at the dingy ceiling. Charley glanced at his watch. He felt shy of the strange woman in the next bed.

"It's nearly twelve," he said. "We'd better just have a cup of coffee and then I'll take you to lunch somewhere if you like."

She looked at him with grave, but not unkindly, eyes.

"I've been watching you sleep. You were sleeping as peacefully, as profoundly, as a child. You had such a look of innocence on your face, it was shattering."

"My face badly needs a shave," said he.

He telephoned down to the office for coffee and it was brought by a stout, middle-aged maid, who gave Lydia a glance, but whose expression heavily conveyed nothing. Charley smoked a pipe and Lydia one cigarette after another. They talked little. Charley did not know how to deal with the singular situation in which he found himself and Lydia seemed lost in thoughts unconcerned with him. Presently he went into the bathroom to shave and bath. When he came back he found Lydia sitting in an armchair at the window in his dressing-gown. The window looked into the courtyard and all there was to see was the windows, storey above storey, of the rooms opposite. On the gray Christmas morning it looked incredibly cheerless. She turned to him.

"Couldn't we lunch here instead of going out?"

"Downstairs, d'you mean? If you like. I don't know what the food's like."

"The food doesn't matter. No, up here, in the room. It's so wonderful to shut out the world for a few hours. Rest, peace, silence, solitude. You would think they were luxuries that only the very rich can afford, and yet they cost nothing. Strange that they should be so hard to come by."

"If you like I'll order you lunch here and I'll go out."

Her eyes lingered on him and there was a slightly ironic smile in them.

"I don't mind you. I think probably you're very sweet and nice. I'd rather you stayed; there's something cosy about you that I find comforting."

Charley was not a youth who thought very much about himself, but at that moment he could not help a slight sense of irritation because really she seemed to be using him with more unconcern than was reasonable. But he had naturally good manners and did not betray his feeling. Besides, the situation was odd, and though it was not to find himself in such a one that he had come to Paris, it could not be denied that the experience was interesting. He looked round the room. The beds were unmade; Lydia's hat, her coat and skirt, her shoes and stockings were lying about, mostly on the floor; his own clothes were piled up untidily on a chair.

"The place looks terribly frowsy," he said. "D'you think it would be very nice to lunch in all this mess?"

"What does it matter?" she answered, with the first

laugh he had heard from her. "But if it upsets your prim English sense of decorum, I'll make the beds, or the maid can while I'm having a bath."

She went into the bathroom and Charley telephoned for a waiter. He ordered some eggs, some meat, cheese and fruit, and a bottle of wine. Then he got hold of the maid. Though the room was heated there was a fireplace and he thought a fire would be cheerful. While the maid was getting the logs he dressed himself, and then, when she got busy setting things to rights, he sat down and looked at the grim courtyard. He thought disconsolately of the jolly party at the Terry-Masons'. They would be having a glass of sherry now before sitting down to their Christmas dinner of turkey and plum pudding, and they would all be very gay, pleased with their Christmas presents, noisy and jolly. After a while Lydia came back. She had no make-up on her face, but she had combed her hair neatly, the swelling of her eyelids had gone down, and she looked young and pretty; but her prettiness was not the sort that excites carnal desires and Charley, though naturally susceptible, saw her come in without a flutter of his pulse.

"Oh, you've dressed," she said. "Then I can keep on your dressing-gown, can't I? Let me have your slippers. I shall float about in them, but it doesn't matter."

The dressing-gown had been a birthday present from his mother, and it was of blue patterned silk; it was much too long for her, but she arranged herself in it so that it was not unbecoming. She was glad to see the fire and she sat down in the chair he had drawn up for her. She smoked a cigarette. What seemed to him strange was that she took the situation as though there were nothing strange in it. She was as casual in her behaviour as though she had known him all her life; if anything more was needed to banish any ideas he might have cherished about her, nothing could have been more efficacious than the impression he so clearly got from her that she had put out of her mind for good and all the possibility of his wanting to go to bed with her. He was surprised to see with what good appetite she ate. He had a notion after what she had told him the night before that she was too distraught to eat but sparingly, and it was a shock to his romantic sensibility to see that she ate as much as he did and with obvious satisfaction.

They were drinking their coffee when the telephone rang. It was Simon.

"Charley? Would you like to come round and have a talk?"

"I'm afraid I can't just now."

"Why not?" Simon asked sharply.

It was characteristic of him to think that everyone should be ready to drop whatever he was doing if he wanted him. However little something mattered to him, if he had a whim for it and he was crossed, it immediately assumed consequence.

"Lydia's here."

"Who the devil's Lydia?"

Charley hesitated an instant.

"Well, Princess Olga."

There was a pause and then Simon burst into a harsh laugh.

"Congratulations, old boy. I knew you'd click. Well, when you have a moment to spare for an old friend, let me know."

He rang off. When Charley turned back to Lydia she

was staring into the fire. Her impassive face gave no sign that she had heard the conversation. Charley pushed back the little table at which they had lunched and made himself as comfortable as he could in a shallow armchair. Lydia leaned over and put another log on the fire. There was a sort of intimacy in the action that did not displease Charley. She was settling herself down as a small dog turns round two or three times on a cushion and having made a suitable hollow curls up in it. They stayed in all the afternoon. The joyless light of the winter day gradually failed and they sat by the light of the wood-fire. In the rooms on the opposite side of the court lights were turned on here and there, and the pale, uncurtained windows had a false strange look like lighted windows in the stage-set of a street. But they were not more unreal than the position in which he found himself seemed to Charley, sitting in that sordid bedroom, by the fitful blazing of the log fire, while that woman whom he did not know told him her terrible story. It seemed not to occur to her that he might be unwilling to listen. So far as he could tell she had no inkling that he might have anything else to do, nor that in baring her heart to him, in telling him her anguish, she was putting a burden on him that a stranger had no right to exact. Was it that she wanted his sympathy? He wasn't even sure of that. She knew nothing about him and wanted to know nothing. He was only a convenience, and but for his sense of humour, he would have found her indifference exasperating. Towards evening she fell silent, and presently by her quiet breathing Charley knew she had fallen asleep. He got up from his chair, for he had sat in it so long that his limbs ached, and went to the window, on tiptoe so as not to wake her, and sitting down on a stool looked out into the courtyard. Now and again he saw someone pass behind the lighted windows; he saw an elderly woman watering a flower-pot; he saw a man in his shirt-sleeves lying on his bed reading; he wondered who and what these people were. They looked like ordinary middle-class persons in modest circumstances, for after all the hotel was cheap and the quarter dowdy; but seen like that, through the windows, as though in a peep-show, they looked strangely unreal. Who could tell what people were really and what grim passions, what crimes, their commonplace aspect concealed? In some of the rooms the curtains were drawn and only a chink of light between them showed that there was anyone there. Some of the windows were black; they were not empty, for the hotel was full, but their occupants were out. On what mysterious errands? Charley's nerves were shaken and he had a sudden feeling of horror for all those unknown persons whose lives were so strange to him; below the smooth surface he seemed to sense something confused, dark, monstrous and terrible.

He pondered, his brow knit in concentration, the long, unhappy story to which he had listened all the afternoon. Lydia had gone back and forth, now telling him of her struggle to live when she was working for a pittance at a dressmaker's and after that some incident of her poverty-stricken childhood in London; then more of those agonizing days that followed the murder, the terror of the arrest and the anguish of the trial. He had read detective stories, he had read the papers, he knew that crimes were committed, he knew that people lived in penury, but he had known it all, as it were from the outside; it gave him a strange, a frightening sensation to find himself thrown into personal contact

with someone to whom horrible things had actually happened. He remembered suddenly, he did not know why, a picture of Manet's of somebody's execution—was it Maximilian's?—by a shooting squad. He had always thought it a striking picture. Now it came to him as a shock to realize that it portrayed an incident that had occurred. The Emperor had in fact stood in that place, and as the soldiers levelled their rifles, it must have seemed incredible to him that he should stand there and in a moment cease to live.

And now that he knew Lydia, now that he had listened to her last night and that day, now that he had eaten with her, and danced with her, now that for so many hours they had lived together in such close proximity, it seemed unbelievable that such things should have befallen her.

If ever anything looked like pure chance it was that Lydia and Robert Berger met at all. Through the friends she lived with, who worked in a Russian restaurant, Lydia sometimes got a ticket for a concert, and when she couldn't and there was something she very much wanted to hear, she scraped together out of her weekly earnings enough to buy herself standing-room. This was her only extravagance and to go to a concert her only recreation. It was chiefly Russian music she liked. Listening to that she felt that somehow she was getting to the heart of the country she had never seen, but which drew her with a yearning that must ever remain unsatisfied. She knew nothing of Russia but what she had heard from the lips of her father and mother, from the conversations between Evgenia and Alexey when they talked of old times, and from the novels she had read. It was when she was listening to the music of Rimsky-Korsakov and

Glazounov, to the racy and mordant compositions of
Stravinsky, that the impressions she had thus gained
gathered form and substance. Those wild melodies,
those halting rhythms, in which there was something
so alien from Europe, took her out of herself and
her sordid existence and overwhelmed her with such
a passion of love that happy, releasing tears flowed down
her cheeks. But because nothing of what she saw with
the mind's eye had she seen with a bodily eye, because
it was a product of hearsay and a fevered imagination,
she saw it in a strangely distorted fashion; she saw the
Kremlin, with its gilt and star-sprinkled domes, the
Red Square and the Kitai Gorod, as though they were
the setting of a fairy tale; for her Prince Andrey and
the charming Natasha still went their errands in the
busy streets of Moscow, Dmitri Karamazov, after a wild
night with the gipsies, still met the sweet Alyosha on
the Mostbaretsk Bridge, the merchant Rogozhin dashed
past in his sled with Nastasya Filippovna by his side,
and the wan characters of Chekov's stories drifted hither
and yon at the breath of circumstance like dead leaves
before the wind; the Summer Garden and the Nevsky
Prospekt were magic names, and Anna Karenina still
drove in her carriage, Vronsky elegant in his new
uniform climbed the stairs of the great houses on the
Fontanka Canal, and the misbegotten Raskolnikov
walked the Liteiny. In the passion and nostalgia of
that music, with Turgeniev at the back of her mind,
she saw the spacious, dilapidated country houses where
they talked through the scented night, and the marshes,
pale in the windless dawn, where they shot the wild
duck; with Gorki, the wretched villages where they
drank furiously, loved brutally and killed; the turbid
flow of the Volga, the interminable steppes of the

Caucasus, and the enchanting garish Crimea. Filled with longing, filled with regret for a life that had passed for ever, homesick for a home she had never known, a stranger in a hostile world, she felt at that moment one with the great, mysterious country. Even though she spoke its language haltingly, she was Russian, and she loved her native land; at such moments she felt that there was where after all she belonged and she understood how it was that her father, despite the warnings, was obliged, even at the risk of death, to return to it.

It was at a concert, one where all the music was Russian, that she found herself standing next to a young man who, she noticed, now and then looked at her curiously. Once she happened to turn her eyes on him and was struck by the passionate absorption with which he seemed to be listening; his hands were clasped and his mouth slightly open as though he were out of breath. He was rapt in ecstasy. He had clean-cut features and looked well-bred. Lydia gave him but a passing glance and once more returned to the music and the crowding dreams it awoke in her. She too was carried away and she was hardly aware that a little sob broke from her lips. She was startled when she felt a small, soft hand take hers and give it a slight pressure. She quickly drew her hand away. The piece was the last before the interval and when it ended the young man turned to her. He had lovely eyes, gray under bushy eyebrows, and they were peculiarly gentle.

"You're crying, Mademoiselle."

She had thought he might be Russian like herself, but his accent was purely French. She understood that that quick pressure of her hand was one of instinctive sympathy, and was touched by it.

"Not because I am unhappy," she answered, with a faint smile.

He smiled back and his smile was charming.

"I know. This Russian music, it's strangely thrilling and yet it tears one's heart to pieces."

"But you're French. What can it mean to you?"

"Yes. I'm French. I don't know what it means to me. It's the only music I want to listen to. It is power and passion, blood and destruction. It makes every nerve in my body tingle." He gave a little laugh at himself. "Sometimes when I listen to it I feel there is nothing that man is capable of that I cannot do."

She did not answer. It was singular that the same music could say such different things to different people. To her the music they had just heard spoke of the tragedy of human destiny, the futility of striving against fate, and the joy, the peace of humility and resignation.

"Are you coming to next week's concert?" he asked then. "That's to be all Russian too."

"I don't think so."

"Why not?"

He was very young, he could be no older than herself, and there was an ingenuousness in him that made it impossible for her to answer too stiffly a question which in a stranger was indiscreet. There was something in his manner that made her sure he was not trying to pick her up. She smiled.

"I'm not a millionaire. They're rare now, you know, the Russians who are."

"I know some of the people who are running these concerts. I have a pass that admits two. If you like to meet me next Sunday in the doorway, you can come in on it."

"I don't think I could quite do that."

"Do you think it would be compromising?" he smiled. "The crowd would surely be a sufficient chaperon."

"I work in a dressmaker's shop. It would be hard to compromise me. I don't know that I can put myself under an obligation to a total stranger."

"I am sure you are a very well-brought-up young lady, but you should not have unreasonable prejudices."

She did not want to argue the point.

"Well, we'll see. In any case I thank you for the suggestion."

They talked of other things till the conductor once more raised his baton. At the end of the concert he turned to say good-bye to her.

"Till next Sunday then?" he said.

"We'll see. Don't wait for me."

They lost one another in the crowd that thronged towards the exits. During the next week she thought from time to time of the good-looking young man with the large gray eyes. She thought of him with pleasure. She had not arrived at her age without having had to resist now and then the advances of men. Both Alexey and his son the gigolo had made a pass at her, but she had not found it difficult to deal with them. A smart box on the ear had made the lachrymose drunkard understand that there was nothing doing, and the boy she had kept quiet by a judicious mingling of ridicule and plain speech. Often enough men had tried to pick her up in the street, but she was always too tired and often too hungry to be tempted by their advances; it caused her a grim amusement to reflect that the offer of a square meal would have tempted her much more than the offer of a loving heart. She had felt, with her woman's instinct, that the young man of the concert was not quite like that. Doubtless, like any other youth of his age, he would not miss an opportunity for a bit of fun if he could get it, but it was not for the sake of that that he had offered to take her to the concert on Sunday. She had no intention of going, but she was touched that he had asked her. There was something very nice about him, something ingenuous and frank. She felt that she could trust him. She looked at the programme. They were giving the Symphonie Pathétique, she didn't much care about that, Tchaikovsky was too Europeanized for her taste, but they were giving also the *Sacre du Printemps* and Borodin's string quartet. She wondered whether the young man had really meant what he said. It might very well be that his invitation had been issued on the spur of the moment and in half an hour completely forgotten. When Sunday came she had half a mind to go and see, she did very much want to hear the concert, and she had not a penny more in her pocket than she needed for her Metro and her lunches during the week, she had had to give everything else to Evgenia to provide the household with food; if he was not there no harm would have been done, and if he was and really had a pass for two, well, it would cost him nothing and committed her to nothing.

Finally an impulse took her to the Salle Pleyel and there he was, where he had said he would be, waiting for her. His eyes lit up and he shook her warmly by the hand as though they were old friends.

"I'm so glad you've come," he said. "I've been waiting for twenty minutes. I was so afraid I'd miss you."

She blushed and smiled. They went into the concert room and she found he had seats in the fifth row.

"Did you get these given you?" she asked with surprise.

"No, I bought them. I thought it would be nice to be comfortable."

"What folly! I'm so used to standing."

But she was flattered by his generosity and when presently he took her hand did not withdraw it. She felt that if it gave him pleasure to hold it, it did her no harm, and she owed him that. During the interval he told her his name, Robert Berger, and she told him hers. He added that he lived with his mother at Neuilly and that he worked in a broker's office. He talked in an educated way, with a boyish enthusiasm that made her laugh, and there was an animation about him that Lydia could not but feel attractive. His shining eyes, the mobility of his face, suggested an ardent nature. To sit next to him was like sitting in front of a fire; his youth glowed with a physical warmth. When the concert was over they walked along the Champs-Élysées together and then he asked her if she would like some tea. He would not let her refuse. It was a luxury Lydia had never known to sit in a smart tea-shop among well-dressed people, and the appetizing smell of cakes, the heady smell of women's perfume, the warmth, the comfortable chairs, the noisy talk, went to her head. They sat there for an hour. Lydia told him about herself, what her father had been and what had happened to him, how she lived now and how she earned her living; he listened as eagerly as he talked. His gray eyes were tender with sympathy. When it was time for her to go he asked her whether she would come to a cinema one evening. She shook her head.

"Why not?"

"You are a rich young man, and . . ."

"Oh, no, I'm not. Far from it. My mother has little more than her pension and I have only the little I make."

"Then you shouldn't have tea at expensive tea-rooms. Anyhow I am a poor working girl. Thank you for all your kindness to me, but I am not a fool; you have been sweet to me, I don't think it would be very nice of me to accept more of your kindness when I can make no return for it."

"But I don't want a return. I like you. I like to be with you. Last Sunday, when you were crying, you looked so touching, it broke my heart. You're alone in the world, and I—I'm alone too in my way. I was hoping we could be friends."

She looked at him coolly for a moment. They were the same age, but of course really she was years older than he; his mien was so candid she had no doubt that he believed what he said, but she was wise enough to know that he was talking nonsense.

"Let me be quite frank with you," she said. "I know I'm not a raving beauty, but after all I'm young and there are people who think me prettyish, people who like the Russian type, it's asking too much of me to believe that you are seeking my society just for the pleasure of my conversation. I've never been to bed with a man. I don't think it would be very honest of me if I let you go on wasting your time and your money on me when I have no intention of going to bed with you."

"That is frank enough in all conscience," he smiled, oh, so charmingly, "but you see, I knew that. I haven't lived in Paris all my life without learning something. I know instinctively whether a girl is ready for a little fun or if she isn't. I saw at once that you were good.

100

If I held your hand at the concert it was because you were feeling the music as deeply as I was, and the touch of your hand—I hardly know how to explain it—I felt that your emotion flowed into me and gave mine a richer intensity. Anyhow there was in my feeling nothing of desire."

"And yet we were feeling very different things," she said thoughtfully. "Once I looked at your face and I was startled by its expression. It was cruel and ruthless. It was not like a human face any more, it was a mask of triumphant malice. It frightened me."

He laughed gaily and his laugh was so young, so musical and care-free, the look of his eyes so tenderly frank, it was impossible to believe that for a moment under the influence of that emotional music his features had borne an expression of such cold ferocity.

"What fancies you have! You don't think I am a white-slaver, like at the cinema, and that I am trying to get you into my clutches and shall then ship you out to Buenos Aires?"

"No," she smiled, "I don't think that."

"How can it hurt you to come to the pictures with me? You've made the position quite clear and I accept it."

She laughed now. It was absurd to make so much fuss. She had little enough amusement in her life, and if he liked to give her a treat and was content merely to sit beside her and to talk, she would be a fool to forgo it. After all, she was nothing. She need answer for her actions to nobody. She could take care of herself and she had given him full warning.

"Oh, very well," she said.

They went to the pictures several times and after the

show Robert accompanied Lydia to whichever was the nearest station for her to get a train home. During the little walk he took her arm and for a part of the performance he held her hand, once or twice when they parted he kissed her lightly on both cheeks, but these were the only familiarities he permitted himself. He was good company. He had a chaffing, ironic way of talking about things that pleased her. He did not pretend to have read very much, he had no time, he said, and life was more entertaining than books, but he was not stupid and he could speak intelligently of such books as he had read. It interested Lydia to discover that he had a peculiar admiration for André Gide. He was an enthusiastic tennis-player and he told her that at one time he had been encouraged to take it seriously; people of importance in the game, thinking he had the making of a champion, had interested themselves in him. But nothing came of it.

"One needs more money and more time to get into the first rank than I could dispose of," he said.

Lydia had a notion that he was in love with her, but she would not allow herself to be certain of it, for she could not but fear that her own feelings made her no safe judge of his. He occupied her thoughts more and more. He was the first friend of her own age that she had ever had. She owed him happy hours at the concerts he took her to on Sunday afternoons, and happy evenings at the cinema. He gave her life an interest and excitement it had never had before. For him she took pains to dress more prettily. She had never been in the habit of making up, but on the fourth or fifth time she met him she rouged her cheeks a little and made up her eyes.

"What have you done to yourself?" he said, when

102

they got into the light. "Why have you been putting all that stuff on your face?"

She laughed and blushed under her rouge.

"I wanted to be a little more of a credit to you. I couldn't bear that people should think you were with a little kitchen-maid who'd just come up to Paris from her native province."

"But almost the first thing I liked in you was that you were so natural. One gets so tired of all these painted faces. I don't know why, I found it touching that you had nothing on your pale cheeks, nothing on your lips, nothing on your eyebrows. It was refreshing, like a little wood that you come into after you've been walking in the glare of the road. Having no make-up on gives you a look of candour and one feels it is a true expression of the uprightness of your soul."

Her heart began to beat almost painfully, but it was that curious sort of pain which is more blissful than pleasure.

"Well, if you don't like it, I'll not do it again. After all, I only did it for your sake."

She looked with an inattentive mind at the picture he had brought her to see. She had mistrusted the tenderness in his musical voice, the smiling softness of his eyes, but after this it was almost impossible not to believe that he loved her. She had been exercising all the self-control she possessed to prevent herself from falling in love with him. She had kept on saying to herself that it was only a passing fancy on his part and that it would be madness if she let her feelings run away with her. She was determined not to become his mistress. She had seen too much of that sort of thing among the Russians, the daughters of refugees who had so much difficulty in making any sort of a living; often enough, because they were bored, because they were sick of grinding poverty, they entered upon an affair, but it never lasted; they seemed to have no capacity for holding a man, at least not the Frenchmen whom they generally fell for; their lovers grew tired of them, or impatient, and chucked them; then they were even worse off than they had been before, and often nothing remained but the brothel. But what else was there that she could hope for? She knew very well he had no thought of marriage. The possibility of such a thing would never have crossed his head. She knew French ideas. His mother would not consent to his marrying a Russian sewing-woman, which was all she was really, without a penny to bless herself with. Marriage in France was a serious thing; the position of the respective families must be on a par and the bride had to bring a dowry conformable with the bride-groom's situation. It was true that her father had been a professor of some small distinction at the university, but in Russia, before the revolution, and since then Paris swarmed with princes and counts and guardsmen who were driving taxis or doing manual labour. Every-one looked upon the Russians as shiftless and undepend-able. People were sick of them. Lydia's mother, whose grandfather had been a serf, was herself hardly more than a peasant, and the professor had married her in accordance with his liberal principles; but she was a pious woman and Lydia had been brought up with strict principles. It was in vain that she reasoned with herself; it was true that the world was different now and one must move with the times: she could not help it, she had an instinctive horror of becoming a man's mistress. And yet. And yet. What else was there to look forward to? Wasn't she a fool to miss the oppor-tunity that presented itself? She knew that her prettiness was only the prettiness of youth, in a few years she would be drab and plain; perhaps she would never have another chance. Why shouldn't she let herself go? Only a little relaxation of her self-control and she would love him madly, it would be a relief not to keep that constant rein on her feelings, and he loved her, yes, he loved her, she knew it, the fire of his passion was so hot it made her gasp, in the eagerness of his mobile face she read his fierce desire to possess her; it would be heavenly to be loved by someone she loved to desperation, and if it didn't last, and of course it couldn't, she would have had the ecstasy of it, she would have the recollection, and wouldn't that be worth all the anguish, the bitter anguish she must suffer when he left her? When all was said and done, if it was intolerable there was always the Seine or the gas oven.

But the curious, the inexplicable, thing was that he didn't seem to want her to be his mistress. He used her with a consideration that was full of respect. He could not have behaved differently if she had been a young girl in the circle of his family acquaintance whose situation and fortune made it reasonable to suppose that their friendship would eventuate in a marriage satisfactory to all parties. She could not understand it. She knew that the notion was absurd, but in her bones she had a queer inkling that he wished to marry her. She was touched and flattered. If it was true he was one in a thousand, but she almost hoped it wasn't, for she couldn't bear that he should suffer the pain that such a wish must necessarily bring him; whatever crazy ideas he harboured, there was his mother in the background, the sensible, practical, middle-class French-woman, who would never let him jeopardize his future and to whom he was devoted as only a Frenchman can be to his mother.

But one evening, after the cinema, when they were walking to the Metro station he said to her:

"There's no concert next Sunday. Will you come and have tea at home? I've talked about you so much to my mother that she'd like to make your acquaintance."

Lydia's heart stood still. She realized the situation at once. Madame Berger was getting anxious about this friendship that her son had formed, and she wanted to see her, the better to put an end to it.

"My poor Robert, I don't think your mother would like me at all. I think it's much wiser we shouldn't meet."

"You're quite wrong. She has a great sympathy for you. The poor woman loves me, you know, I'm all she has in the world, and it makes her happy to think that I've made friends with a young girl who is well brought up and respectable."

Lydia smiled. How little he knew women if he imagined that a loving mother could feel kindly towards a girl that her son had casually picked up at a concert! But he pressed her so strongly to accept the invitation, which he said he issued on his mother's behalf, that at last she did. She thought indeed that it would only make Madame Berger look upon her with increased suspicion if she refused to meet her. They arranged that he should pick her up at the Porte St. Denis at four on the following Sunday and take her to his mother's. He drove up in a car.

"What luxury!" said Lydia, as she stepped in.

"It's not mine, you know. I borrowed it from a friend."

Lydia was nervous of the ordeal before her and

not even Robert's affectionate friendliness sufficed to give her confidence.

They drove to Neuilly.

"We'll leave the car here," said Robert, drawing up to the kerb in a quiet street. "I don't want to leave it outside our house. It wouldn't do for the neighbours to think I had a car and of course I can't explain that it's only lent."

They walked a little.

"Here we are."

It was a tiny detached villa, rather shabby from want of paint and smaller than, from the way Robert had talked, she expected. He took her into the drawing-room. It was a small room crowded with furniture and ornaments, with oil pictures in gold frames on the walls, and opened by an archway on to the dining-room in which the table was set for tea. Madame Berger put down the novel she was reading and came forward to greet her guest. Lydia had pictured her as a rather stout, short woman in widow's weeds, with a mild face and the homely, respectable air of a person who has given up all thought of earthly vanity; she was not at all like that; she was thin, and in her high-heeled shoes as tall as Robert; she was smartly dressed in black flowered silk and she wore a string of false pearls round her neck; her hair, permanently waved, was very dark brown and though she must have been hard on fifty there was not a white streak in it. Her sallow skin was somewhat heavily powdered. She had fine eyes, Robert's delicate, straight nose, and the same thin lips, but in her, age had given them a certain hardness. She was in her way and for her time of life a good-looking woman, and she evidently took pains over her appearance, but there was in her expression nothing of the charm that made Robert so attractive. Her eyes, so bright and dark, were cool and watchful. Lydia felt the sharp, scrutiñizing look with which Madame Berger took her in from head to foot as she entered the room, but it was immediately superseded by a cordial and welcoming smile. She thanked Lydia effusively for coming so long a distance to see her.

"You must understand how much I wanted to see a young girl of whom my son has talked to me so much. I was prepared for a disagreeable surprise. I have, to tell you the truth, no great confidence in my son's judgement. It is a relief to me to see that you are as nice as he told me you were."

All this she said with a good deal of facial expression, with smiles and little nods of the head, flatteringly, in the manner of a hostess accustomed to society trying to set a stranger at her ease. Lydia, watchful too, answered with becoming diffidence. Madame Berger gave an emphatic, slightly forced laugh and made an enthusiastic little gesture.

"But you are charming. I'm not surprised that this son of mine should neglect his old mother for your sake."

Tea was brought in by a stolid-looking young maid whom Madame Berger, while continuing her gesticulative, complimentary remarks, watched with sharp, anxious eyes, so that Lydia guessed that a tea-party was an unusual event in the house and the hostess not quite sure that the servant knew how to set about things. They went into the dining-room and sat down. There was a small grand piano in it.

"It takes up room," said Madame Berger, "but my son is passionately devoted to music. He plays for hours at a time. He tells me that you are a musician of the first class."

"He exaggerates. I'm very fond of it, but very ignorant."

"You are too modest, mademoiselle."

There was a dish of little cakes from the confectioner's and a dish of sandwiches. Under each plate was a doyley and on each a tiny napkin. Madame Berger had evidently taken pains to do things in a modish way. With a smile in her cold eyes she asked Lydia how she would like her tea.

"You Russians always take lemon, I know, and I got a lemon for you specially. Will you begin with a sandwich?"

The tea tasted of straw.

"I know you Russians smoke all through your meals. Please do not stand on any ceremony with me. Robert, where are the cigarettes?"

Madame Berger pressed sandwiches on Lydia, she pressed cakes; she was one of those hostesses who look upon it as a mark of hospitality to make their guests eat however unwilling they may be. She talked without ceasing, well, in a high-pitched, metallic voice, smiling a great deal, and her politeness was effusive. She asked Lydia a great many questions, which had a casual air so that on the face of it they looked like the civil inquiries a woman of the world would put out of sympathy for a friendless girl, but Lydia realized that they were cleverly designed to find out everything she could about her. Lydia's heart sank; this was not the sort of woman who for love of her son would allow him to do an imprudent thing; but the certainty of this gave her back her own assurance. It was obvious that she had nothing to lose; she certainly had nothing to hide; and she answered the questions with frankness.

She told Madame Berger, as she had already told Robert, about her father and mother, and what her life had been in London and how she had lived since her mother's death. It even amused her to see behind Madame Berger's warm sympathy, through her shocked commiserating answers, the shrewdness that weighed every word she heard and drew conclusions upon it. After two or three unavailing attempts to go, which Madame Berger would not hear of, Lydia managed to tear herself away from so much friendliness. Robert was to see her home. Madame Berger seized both her hands when she said good-bye to her and her fine dark eyes glittered with cordiality.

"You are delicious," she said. "You know your way now, you must come and see me often, often; you will be always sure of a hearty welcome."

When they were walking along to the car Robert took her arm with an affectionate gesture which seemed to ask for protection rather than to offer it and which charmed her.

"Well, my dear one, it went off very well. My mother liked you. You made a conquest of her at once. She'll adore you."

Lydia laughed.

"Don't be so silly. She detested me."

"No, no, you're wrong. I promise you. I know her, I saw at once that she took to you."

Lydia shrugged her shoulders, but did not answer. When they parted they arranged to go to the cinema on the following Tuesday. She agreed to his plan, but she was pretty sure that his mother would put a stop to it. He knew her address now.

"If anything should happen to prevent you, you'll send me a petit bleu?"

"Nothing will happen to prevent me," he said fondly.

She was very sad that evening. If she could have got by herself she would have cried. But perhaps it was just as well that she couldn't; it was no good making oneself bad blood. It had been a foolish dream. She would get over her unhappiness; after all, she was used to it. It would have been much worse if he had been her lover and thrown her over.

Monday passed, Tuesday came; but no petit bleu. She was certain that it would be there when she got back from work. Nothing. She had an hour before she need think of getting ready, and she passed it waiting with sickening anxiety for the bell to ring; she dressed with the feeling that she was foolish to take the trouble, for the message would arrive before she was finished. She wondered if it were possible that he would let her go to the cinema and not turn up. It would be heartless, it would be cruel, but she knew that he was under his mother's thumb, she suspected he was weak, and it might be that to let her go to a meeting-place and not come himself would seem to him the best way, brutal though it was, to show her that he was done with her. No sooner had this notion occurred to her than she was sure of it and she nearly decided not to go. Nevertheless she went. After all, if he could be so beastly it would prove that she was well rid of him.

But he was there all right and when he saw her walking along he came towards her with the springy gait which marked his eager vitality. On his face shone his sweet smile. His spirits seemed even higher than usual.

"I'm not in the mood for the pictures this evening," he said. "Let us have a drink at Fouquet's and then go for a drive. I've got a car just round the corner."

"If you like."

It was fine and dry, though cold, and the stars in the frosty night seemed to laugh with a good-natured malice at the gaudy lights of the Champs-Élysées. They had a glass of beer, Robert meanwhile talking nineteen to the dozen, and then they walked up the Avenue George V to where he had parked his car. Lydia was puzzled. He talked quite naturally, but she had no notion what were his powers of dissimulation, and she could not help asking herself whether he proposed the drive in order to break unhappy news to her. He was an emotional creature, sometimes, she had discovered, even a trifle theatrical, (but that amused rather than offended her), and she wondered whether he were setting the stage for an affecting scene of renunciation.

"This isn't the same car that you had on Sunday," she said, when they came to it.

"No. It belongs to a friend who wants to sell. I said I wanted to show it to a possible purchaser."

They drove to the Arc de Triomphe and then along the Avenue Foch till they came to the Bois. It was dark there except when they met the head-lights of a car coming towards them, and deserted except for a car parked here and there in which one surmised a couple was engaged in amorous conversation. Presently Robert drew up at the kerb.

"Shall we stop here and smoke a cigarette?" he said. "You're not cold?"

"No."

It was a solitary spot and in other circumstances Lydia might have felt a trifle nervous. But she thought she knew Robert well enough to know that he was incapable of taking advantage of the situation. He had too nice a nature. Moreover she had an intuition that he had something on his mind, and was curious to know what it was. He lit her cigarette and his and for a moment kept silent. She realized that he was embarrassed and did not know how to begin. Her heart began to beat anxiously.

"I've got something to say to you, my dear," he said at last.

"Yes?"

"Mon Dieu, I hardly know how to put it. I'm not often nervous, but at the moment I have a curious sensation that is quite new to me."

Lydia's heart sank, but she had no intention of showing that she was suffering.

"If one has something awkward to say," she answered lightly, "it's better to say it quite plainly, you know. One doesn't do much good by beating about the bush."

"I'll take you at your word. Will you marry me?"

"Me?"

It was the last thing she had expected him to say.

"I love you passionately. I think I fell in love with you at first sight, when we stood side by side at that concert, and the tears poured down your pale cheeks."

"But your mother?"

"My mother is delighted. She's waiting now. I said that if you consented I would take you to her. She wants to embrace you. She's happy at the thought that I'm settling down with someone she entirely approves of, and the idea is that after we've all had a good cry together we should crack a bottle of champagne."

"Last Sunday when you took me to see your mother, had you told her that you wished to marry me?"

"But of course. She very naturally wanted to see

what you were like. She's not stupid, my mother; she made up her mind at once."

"I had an idea she didn't like me."

"You were wrong."

They smiled into one another's eyes, and she raised her face to his. For the first time he kissed her on the lips.

"There's no doubt," he said, "that a right-hand drive is much more convenient for kissing a girl than a left-hand."

"You fool," she laughed.

"Then you do care for me a little?"

"I've worshipped you ever since I first saw you."

"But with the reserve of a well-brought-up young woman who will not give free rein to her emotions until she's quite sure it's prudent?" he answered, tenderly chaffing her.

But she answered seriously:

"I've suffered so much in my short life, I didn't want to expose myself to a suffering perhaps greater than I could bear."

"I adore you."

She had never known such happiness; indeed, she could hardly bring herself to believe it: at that moment her heart overflowed with gratitude to life. She would have liked to sit there, nestling in his arms, for ever; at that moment she would have liked to die. But she bestirred herself.

"Let us go to your mother," she said.

She felt on a sudden warm with love for that woman who but just knew her, and yet, contrary to all expectation, because her son loved her, because with her sharp eyes she had seen that she deeply loved her son, had consented, even gladly, to their marriage. Lydia did

114

not think there could be another woman in France who was capable of such a sacrifice.

They drove off. Robert parked the car in a street parallel to the one in which he lived. When they reached the little house he opened the front door with his latch-key and excitedly preceded Lydia into the sitting-room.

"O.K., mother."

Lydia immediately followed him in and Madame Berger, in the same black dress of flowered silk as she had worn on Sunday, came forward and took her in her arms.

"My dear child," she cried. "I'm so happy."

Lydia burst into tears. Madame Berger kissed her tenderly.

"There, there, there! You mustn't cry. I give you my son with all my heart. I know you'll make him a good wife. Come, sit down. Robert will open a bottle of champagne."

Lydia composed herself and dried her eyes.

"You are too good to me, Madame. I don't know what I've done to deserve so much kindness."

Madame Berger took her hand and gently patted it.

"You have fallen in love with my son and he has fallen in love with you."

Robert had gone out of the room. Lydia felt that she must at once state the facts as they were.

"But, Madame, I don't feel sure that you realize the circumstances. The little money that my father was able to get out of Russia went years ago. I have nothing but what I earn. Nothing, absolutely nothing. And only two dresses besides the one I'm wearing."

"But, my dear child, what does that matter? Oh, I don't deny it, I should have been pleased if you had been able to bring Robert a reasonable dot, but money isn't everything. Love is more important. And nowadays what is money worth? I flatter myself that I am a good judge of character and it didn't take me long to discover that you have a sweet and honest nature. I saw that you had been well brought up and I judged that you had good principles. After all that is what one wants in a wife, and you know, I know my Robert, he would never have been happy with a little French bourgeoise. He has a romantic disposition and it says something to him that you are Russian. And it isn't as if you were nobody; it is after all something one need not be ashamed of to be the daughter of a professor.

Robert came in with glasses and a bottle of champagne. They sat talking late into the night. Madame Berger had her plan cut and dried and they could do nothing but accept it; Lydia and Robert should live in the house while she would make herself comfortable in the little pavilion at the back of the garden. They would have their meals in common, but otherwise she would keep to her own quarters. She was decided that the young couple must be left to themselves and not exposed to interference from her.

"I don't want you to look upon me as a mother-in-law," she told Lydia. "I want to be the mother to you that you've lost, but I also want to be your friend."

She was anxious that the marriage should take place without delay. Lydia had a League of Nations passport and a Carte de Séjour; her papers were in order; so they had only to wait the time needed for notification to be made at the Mairie. Since Robert was Catholic and Lydia Orthodox, they decided, notwithstanding Madame Berger's reluctance, to waive a religious ceremony that neither of them cared about. Lydia was too excited and too confused to sleep that night.

The marriage took place very quietly. The only persons present were Madame Berger and an old friend of the family, Colonel Legrand, an army doctor who had been a brother officer of Robert's father; Evgenia and Alexey and their children. It took place on a Friday and since Robert had to go to work on the Monday morning their honeymoon was brief. Robert drove Lydia to Dieppe in a car that he had been lent and drove her back on Sunday night.

Lydia did not know that the car, like the cars in which he had on other occasions driven her, was not lent, but stolen; that was why he had always parked them a street or two from that in which he lived; she did not know that Robert had a few months before been sentenced to two years' imprisonment with sursis, that is, with a suspended sentence because it was his first conviction; she did not know that he had since been tried on a charge of smuggling drugs and had escaped conviction by the skin of his teeth; she did not know that Madame Berger had welcomed the marriage because she thought it would settle Robert and that it was indeed the only chance he had of leading an honest life.

V

CHARLEY had no idea how long he had been sitting at the window, absent-mindedly gazing out into the dark court, when he was called back from the perplexed welter of his thoughts by the sound of Lydia's voice.

"I believe I've been asleep," she said.

"You certainly have."

He turned on the light, which he had not done before for fear of waking her. The fire was almost out and he put on another log.

"I feel so refreshed. I slept without dreaming."

"D'you have bad dreams?"

"Fearful."

"If you'll dress we might go out to dinner."

There was an ironic, but not unkindly, quality in the smile she gave him.

"I don't suppose this is the way you usually spend Christmas Day."

"I'm bound to say it isn't," he answered, with a cheerful grin.

She went into the bathroom and he heard her having a bath. She came back still wearing his dressing-gown.

"Now if you'll go in and wash, I'll dress."

Charley left her. He accepted it as quite natural that though she had slept all night in the next bed to his she should not care to dress in his presence.

Lydia took him to a restaurant she knew in the Avenue du Maine where she said the food was good.

Though a trifle self-consciously old-world, with its panelled walls, chintz curtains and pewter plates, it was a friendly little place, and there was no one there but two middle-aged women in collars and ties and three young Indians who ate in moody silence. You had a feeling that, lonely and friendless, they dined there that evening because they had no place to go.

Lydia and Charley sat in a corner where their conversation could not be overheard. Lydia ate with hearty appetite. When he offered her a second helping of one of the dishes they had ordered she pushed forward her plate.

"My mother-in-law used to complain of my appetite. She used to say that I ate as though I had never had enough in my life. Which was true, of course."

It gave Charley a turn. It was a queer sensation to sit down to dinner with someone who year in and year out had never had quite enough to eat. And another thing: it disturbed his preconceived ideas to discover that one could undergo all the misery she had undergone and yet eat voraciously. It made her tragedy a little grotesque; she was not a romantic figure, but just a quite ordinary young woman, and that somehow made all that had happened to her more horrible.

"Did you get on well with your mother-in-law?" he asked.

"Yes. Reasonably. She wasn't a bad woman. She was hard, scheming, practical and avaricious. She was a good housekeeper and she liked everything in the house to be just so. I used to infuriate her with my Russian sloppiness, but she had a great control over her temper and never allowed an irritable word to escape her. After Robert, her great passion was for

119

respectability. She was proud of her father having been a staff officer and her husband a colonel in the Medical Service. They were both officers in the Legion of Honour. Her husband had lost a leg in the war. She was very proud of their distinguished record, and she had a keen sense of the social importance their position gave her. I suppose you'd say she was a snob, but in such a petty way that it didn't offend you, it only made you laugh. She had notions of morality that foreigners often think are unusual in France. For instance, she had no patience with women who were unfaithful to their husbands, but she looked upon it as natural enough that men should deceive their wives. She would never have dreamt of accepting an invitation unless she had the power to return it. Once she'd made a bargain she'd stick to it even though it turned out to be a bad one. Though she counted every penny she spent she was scrupulously honest, honest by principle and honest from loyalty to her family. She had a deep sense of justice. She knew she'd acted dishonourably in letting me marry Robert in the dark, and should at least have given me the chance of deciding whether, knowing all, I would marry him or not—and of course I would never have hesitated; but she didn't know that, and she thought that I should have good cause to blame her when I found out and all she could answer was that where Robert was concerned she was prepared to sacrifice anyone else; and because of that she forced herself to be tolerant of a great deal in me that she didn't like. She put all her determination, all her self-control, all her tact, into the effort of making the marriage a success. She felt it was the only chance that Robert had of reforming and her love was so great that she was prepared to lose him to me. She was even prepared to lose her influence over him, and that I think is what a woman values, whether it's a son or a husband or a lover or anything, even more than his love for her. She said that she wouldn't interfere with us and she never did. Except in the kitchen, later on when we gave up the maid, and at meal-times, we hardly saw her. When she wasn't out she spent the whole time in her little pavilion at the end of the garden and when, thinking she was lonely, we asked her to come and sit with us, she refused on the excuse that she had work to do, letters to write, or a book she wanted to finish. She was a woman whom it was difficult to love, but impossible not to respect."

"What has happened to her now?" asked Charley.

"The cost of the trial ruined her. Most of her small fortune had already gone to keep Robert out of prison and the rest went on lawyers. She had to sell the house which was the mainstay of her pride in her position as an officer's widow and she had to mortgage her pension. She was always a good cook, she's gone as general servant in the apartment of an American who has a studio at Auteuil."

"D'you ever see her?"

"No. Why should I? We have nothing in common. Her interest in me ceased when I could be no further use in keeping Robert straight."

Lydia went on to tell him about her married life. It was a pleasure for her to have a house of her own and heaven not to have to go to work every morning. She soon discovered that there was no money to waste, but compared with what she had been used to, the circumstances in which she now lived were affluent. And at least she had security. Robert was sweet to her, he was easy to live with, inclined to let her wait on him, but she loved him so much that this was a delight to her, gay with an impudent, happy-go-lucky cynicism that made her laugh, and brim-full of vitality. He was generous to a fault considering how poor they were. He gave her a gold wrist-watch and a vanity case that must have cost at least a couple of thousand francs and a bag in crocodile skin. She was surprised to find a tram ticket in one of the pockets, and when she asked Robert how it got there, he laughed. He said he had bought the bag off a girl who had had a bad day at the races. Her lover had only just given it her and it was such a bargain that he had not been able to resist buying it. Now and then he took her to the theatre and then they went to Montmartre to dance. When she wanted to know how he had the money for such extravagance he answered gaily that with the world full of fools it would be absurd if a clever man couldn't get on to a good thing now and again. But these excursions they kept secret from Madame Berger. Lydia would have thought it impossible to love Robert more than when she married him, but every day increased her passion. He was not only a charming lover, but also a delightful companion.

About four months after their marriage Robert lost his job. This created a disturbance in the household that she failed to understand, for his salary had been negligible; but he and his mother shut themselves up in the pavilion for a long time, and when Lydia saw her mother-in-law next it was obvious that she had been crying. Her face was haggard and she gave Lydia a look of sullen exasperation as though she blamed her. Lydia could not make it out. Then the old doctor, the friend of the family, Colonel Legrand, came and the three of them were again closeted in Madame Berger's room.

For two or three days Robert was silent and for the first time since she had known him somewhat irritable; when she asked him what was the matter he told her sharply not to bother. Then, thinking perhaps that he must offer some explanation, he said the whole trouble was that his mother was so avaricious. Lydia knew that though she was sparing, she was never so where her son was concerned, for him nothing was too good; but seeing that Robert was in a highly nervous state, she felt it better to say nothing. For two or three days Madame Berger looked dreadfully worried, but then, whatever the difficulty was, it was settled; she dismissed, however, the maid to keep whom had been almost a matter of principle, for so long as she had a servant Madame Berger could look upon herself as a lady. But now she told Lydia that it was a useless waste; the two of them could easily run the little house between them, and doing the marketing herself she could be sure of not being robbed; and besides, with nothing to do really, she would enjoy cooking. Lydia was only too willing to do the housework.

Life went on pretty much as it had before. Robert quickly regained his good humour and was as gay, loving and delightful as he had ever been. He got up late in the morning and went out to hunt for a job, and often he did not come back till late in the night. Madame Berger always had a good meal for Robert, but when the two women were alone they ate sparingly; a bowl of thin soup, a salad and a bit of cheese. It was plain that Madame Berger was harassed. More than once Lydia came into the kitchen and found her standing there, doing nothing, with her face distraught, as though an intolerable anxiety possessed her, but on Lydia's approach she chased the expression away and busied herself with the work upon which she was engaged. She still kept up appearances, and on the 'days' of old friends dressed herself in her best, faintly rouged her cheeks, and sallied forth, very upright and a pattern of middle-class respectability, to pay her visit. After a short while, though he was still without a job, Robert seemed to have no less spending-money than he had before. He told Lydia that he had managed to sell one or two secondhand cars on commission; and then that he had got in with some racing men at a bar he went to and got tips from them. Lydia did not know why a suspicion insinuated itself into her unwilling mind that something was going on that was not above board. On one occasion an incident occurred which troubled her. One Sunday Robert told his mother that a man who, he hoped, was going to give him a job had asked him to bring Lydia to lunch at his house near Chartres and he was going to drive her down; but when they had started, picking up the car two streets off the one in which they lived, he told Lydia that this was an invention. He had had a bit of luck at the races on the previous Thursday and was taking her to lunch at Jouy. He had told his mother this story because she would look upon it as an unjustified extravagance to go and spend money at a restaurant. It was a warm and beautiful day. Luncheon was served in the garden and the place was crowded. They found two seats at a table that was already occupied by a party of four. This party were finishing their meal and left while they were but half through theirs.

"Oh, look," said Robert, "one of those ladies has left her bag behind."

He took it and, to Lydia's surprise, opened it. She saw there was money inside. He looked quickly right

124

and left and then gave her a sharp, cunning, malicious glance. Her heart stood still. She had a conviction that he was just about to take the money out and put it in his pocket. She gasped with horror. But at that moment one of the men who had been at the table came back and saw Robert with the bag in his hands.

"What are you doing with that bag?" he asked.

Robert gave him his frank and charming smile.

"It was left behind. I was looking to see if I could find out to whom it belonged."

The man looked at him with stern, suspicious eyes.

"You had only to give it to the proprietor."

"And do you think you would ever have got it back?" Robert answered blandly, returning him the bag.

Without a word the man took it and went away.

"Women are criminally careless with their bags," said Robert.

Lydia gave a sigh of relief. Her suspicion was absurd. After all, with people all around, no one could have the effrontery to steal money out of a bag; the risk was too great. But she knew every expression of Robert's face and, unbelievable as it was, she was certain that he had intended to take it. He would have looked upon it as a capital joke.

She had resolutely put the occurrence out of her mind, but on that dreadful morning when she read in the paper that the English bookmaker, Teddie Jordan, had been murdered it returned to her. She remembered the look in Robert's eyes. She had known then, in a horrible flash of insight, that he was capable of anything. She knew now what the stain was on his trousers. Blood! And she knew where those thousand-franc notes had come from. She knew also why, when he had lost his job, Robert had worn that sullen look,

why his mother had been distracted and why Colonel
Legrand, the doctor, had been closeted with mother
and son for hours of agitated colloquy. Because Robert
had stolen money. And if Madame Berger had sent
away the maid and since then had skimped and saved,
it was because she had had to pay a sum she could ill
afford to save him from prosecution. Lydia read once
more the account of the crime. Teddie Jordan lived
alone in a ground-floor flat which the concierge kept
clean for him. He had his meals out, but the concierge
brought him his coffee every morning at nine. It was
thus she had found him. He was lying on the floor, in
his shirt-sleeves, a knife wound in his back, near the
gramophone, with a broken record under him so that
it looked as if he had been stabbed while changing it.
His empty pocket-book was on the chimney-piece.
There was a half-finished whiskey and soda on a table
by the side of an armchair and another glass, unused,
on a tray with the bottle of whiskey, a syphon and an
uncut cake. It was obvious that he had been expecting
a visitor, but the visitor had refused to drink. Death
had taken place some hours before. The reporter had
apparently conducted a small investigation of his own,
but how much fact there was in what he narrated and
how much fiction, it was hard to say. He had questioned
the concierge, and from her learnt that so far as she
knew no women ever came to the apartment, but a
certain number of men, chiefly young, and from this
she had drawn her own conclusions. Teddie Jordan was
a good tenant, gave no trouble, and when in funds, was
generous. The knife had been thrust into his back
with such violence that, according to the reporter,
the police were convinced that the murderer must have
been a man of powerful physique. There were no signs

of disorder in the room, which indicated that Jordan had been attacked suddenly and had had no chance to defend himself. The knife was not found, but stains on the window curtain showed that it had been wiped on it. The reporter went on to say that, though the police had looked with care, they had discovered no fingerprints; from this he concluded that the murderer had either wiped them away or worn gloves. In the first case it showed great coolness and in the second premeditation.

The reporter had then gone on to Jojo's Bar. This was a small bar in a back street behind the Boulevard de la Madeleine, frequented by jockeys, bookmakers and betting men. You could get simple fare, bacon and eggs, sausages and chops, and it was here that Jordan regularly had his meals. It was here too that he did much of his business. The reporter learnt that Jordan was popular among the bar's frequenters. He had his ups and downs, but when he had had a good day was open-handed. He was always ready to stand anyone a drink and was hail-fellow-well-met with everyone. All the same he had the reputation of being a pretty wily customer. Sometimes he was up against it and then would run up a fairly heavy bill, but in the end he always paid up. The reporter mentioned the concierge's suspicions to Jojo, the proprietor of the bar, but was assured by him that there was no foundation for them. He ended his graphic story by saying that the police were actively engaged in making inquiries and expected to make an arrest within twenty-four hours.

Lydia was terrified. She did not doubt for a moment that Robert was guilty of the crime; she was as sure of that as if she had seen him commit it.

"How could he? How could he?" she cried.

But she was startled at the sound of her own voice. Even though the kitchen was empty she must not let her thoughts find expression. Her first, her only feeling was that he must be saved from the terrible danger that faced him. Whatever he had done, she loved him; nothing he could do would ever make her love him less. When it occurred to her that they might take him from her she could have screamed with anguish. Even at that moment she was intoxicated by the thought of his soft lips on hers and the feel of his slim body, still a boy's body, in her arms. They said the knife-thrust had shown great violence, and they were looking for a big, powerful man. Robert was strong and wiry, but he was neither big nor powerful. And then there was what the concierge suspected. The police would hunt in the night-clubs and the cafés, in Montmartre and the Rue de Lappe, which the homosexuals frequented. Robert never went to such places and no one knew better than she how far he was from any abnormal inclination. It was true that he went a good deal to Jojo's Bar, but so did many others; he went to get tips from the jockeys and better odds from the bookmakers than he was likely to get at the tote. It was all above board. There was no reason why suspicion should ever fall on him. The trousers had been destroyed, and who would ever think that Madame Berger, with her thrift, had persuaded Robert to buy a second pair? If the police discovered that Robert knew Jordan (and Jordan knew masses of people) and made an examination of the house (it was unlikely, but it might be that they would make enquiries of everyone with whom the bookmaker was known to have been friendly) they would find nothing. Except that little packet of thou-

sand-franc notes. At the thought of them Lydia was panic-stricken. It would be easy to ascertain that they had been in straitened circumstances. Robert and she had always thought that his mother had a little hoard hidden away somewhere in her pavilion, but that doubtless had gone at the time Robert lost his job; if suspicion once fell on him it was inevitable that the police should discover what the trouble had been; and how then could she explain that she had several thousand francs? Lydia did not know how many notes there had been in the packet. Perhaps eight or ten. It was a substantial sum to poor people. It was a sum that Madame Berger, even though she knew how Robert had got the notes, would never have the courage to part with. She would trust in her own cunning to hide them where no one would think of looking. Lydia knew it would be useless to talk to her. No argument would move her in such a case. The only thing was to get at them herself and burn them. She would never have a moment's peace till then. Then the police might come and no incriminating evidence could be discovered. With frenzied anxiety she set her mind to think where Madame Berger would have been most likely to put them. She did not often go into the pavilion, for Madame Berger did the room herself, but she had in her mind's eye a pretty clear picture of it, and in her thought now she examined minutely every piece of furniture and every likely place of concealment. She determined to take the first opportunity to make a search.

The opportunity presented itself sooner than she could have foreseen. That very afternoon, after the meagre lunch which the two women had eaten in silence, Lydia was sitting in the parlour, sewing. She could not read, but she had to do something to calm the frightful disquietude that gnawed at her heart-strings. She heard Madame Berger come into the house and supposed she was going into the kitchen, but the door was opened.

"If Robert comes back tell him I shall be in soon after five."

To Lydia's profound astonishment she saw that her mother-in-law was dressed in all her best. She wore her black dress of flowered silk and a black satin toque, and she had a silver fox round her neck.

"Are you going out?" Lydia cried.

"Yes, it's the last day of la générale. She would think it very ill-mannered of me if I did not put in an appearance. Both she and the general had a great affection for my poor husband."

Lydia understood. She saw that in view of what might happen Madame Berger was determined that on that day of all others she must behave as she naturally would. To omit a social duty might be ascribed to fear that her son was implicated in the murder of the book-maker. To fulfil it, on the other hand, was proof that the possibility had never entered her head. She was a woman of indomitable courage. Beside her, Lydia could only feel herself weak and womanish.

As soon as she was gone Lydia bolted the front door so that no one could come in without ringing and crossed the tiny garden. She gave it a cursory glance; there was a patch of weedy grass surrounded by a gravel walk, and in the middle of the grass a bed in which chrysanthemums had been planted to flower in the autumn. She had a conviction that her mother-in-law was more likely to have hidden the notes in her own apartment than there. The pavilion consisted of one largish room with a closet adjoining which Madame

Berger had made into her dressing-room. The larger room was furnished with a highly carved bedroom suite in mahogany, a sofa, an armchair and a rosewood desk. On the walls were enlarged photographs of herself and her deceased husband, a photograph of his grave, under which hung his medals and his Legion of Honour, and photographs of Robert at various ages. Lydia considered where a woman of that sort would naturally hide something. She had doubtless a place that she always used, since for years she had had to keep her money where Robert could not find it. She was too cunning to choose such an obvious hiding-place as the bed, a secret drawer in the writing-desk, or the slits in the armchair and the sofa. There was no fireplace in the room, but a gas stove with an iron pipe. Lydia looked at it. She saw no possibility of concealing anything there; besides, in winter it was used, and Lydia thought her mother-in-law the sort of woman who, having found a safe place, would stick to it. She stared about her with perplexity. Because she could think of nothing better to do she unmade the bed and took the pillow out of its slip. She looked at it carefully and felt it over. The mattress was covered with a material so hard that she felt sure Madame Berger could not have cut one of the seams and re-sewn it. If she had used the same hiding-place for a long period it must be one that she could get at conveniently and such that, if she wanted to take money out, she could quickly efface all trace of her action. For form's sake Lydia looked through the chest of drawers and the writing-desk. Nothing was locked and everything was carefully arranged. She looked into the wardrobe. Her mind had been working busily all the time. She had heard innumerable stories of how the Russians hid things,

131

money and jewels, so that they might save them from the Bolsheviks. She had heard stories of extreme ingenuity that had been of no avail and of others in which by some miracle discovery had been averted. She remembered one of a woman who had been searched in the train between Moscow and Leningrad. She had been stripped to the skin, but she had sewn a diamond necklace in the hem of her fur-coat, and though it had been carefully examined the diamonds were overlooked. Madame Berger had a fur-coat too, an old astrakhan that she had had for years, and this was in the wardrobe. Lydia took it out and made a thorough search, but she could neither see nor feel anything. There was no sign of recent stitching. She replaced it and one by one took out the three or four dresses that Madame Berger possessed. There was no possibility that the notes could have been sewn up in any of them. Her heart sank. She was afraid that her mother-in-law had hidden the notes so well that she would never find them. A new idea occurred to her. People said that the best way to hide something was in a place so conspicuous that no one would think of looking there. A work basket, for instance, like the one Madame Berger had on a little table beside the armchair. Somewhat despondently, with a look at her watch, for time was passing and she could not afford to stay too long, she turned the things in it over. There was a stocking that Madame Berger had been mending, scissors, needles, various odds and ends, and reels of cotton and silk. There was a half-finished tippet in black wool that Madame Berger was making to put over her shoulders when she came from the pavilion to the house. Among the reels of black and white cotton Lydia was surprised to find one of yellow thread.

She wondered what her mother-in-law used that for. Her heart gave a great leap as her eyes fell on the curtains. The only light in the room came from the glass door, and one pair hung there; another pair served as a portière for the door that led to the dressing-room. Madame Berger was very proud of them, they had belonged to her father the colonel and she remembered them from her childhood. They were very rich and heavy, with a fringed and festooned pelmet, and they were of yellow damask. Lydia went up first to those at the window and turned back the lining. They had been made for a higher room than that in which they now were, and since Madame Berger had not had the heart to cut them, had been turned up at the bottom. Lydia examined the deep hem; it had been sewn by a professional sempstress and the thread was faded. Then she looked at the curtains on each side of the door. She gave a deep sigh. At the corner nearest to the front wall, and so in darkness, there was a little piece about four inches long which the clean thread showed to have been recently stitched. Lydia got the scissors out of the work-basket and quickly cut; she slipped her hand through the opening and pulled out the notes. She put them in her dress and then it did not take her more than a few minutes to get a needle and the yellow thread and sew up the seam so that no one could tell it had been touched. She looked round the room to see that no trace of her interference remained. She went back to the house, upstairs into the bathroom, and tore the notes into little pieces; she threw them into the pan of the closet and pulled the plug. Then she went downstairs again, drew back the bolt on the front door, and sat down once more to her sewing. Her heart was beating so madly that she could hardly endure it; but she was infinitely relieved. Now the police could come and they would find nothing.

Presently Madame Berger returned. She came into the drawing-room and sank down on a sofa. The effort she had made had taken it out of her and she was all in. Her face sagged and she looked an old woman. Lydia gave her a glance, but said nothing. In a few minutes, with a sigh of weariness, she raised herself to her feet and went to her room. When she came back she had taken off her smart clothes and wore felt slippers and a shabby black dress. Notwithstanding the marcelled hair, the paint on her lips and the rouge on her face, she looked like an old charwoman.

"I'll see about preparing dinner," she said.

"Shall I come and help you?" asked Lydia.

"No, I prefer to be alone."

Lydia went on working. The silence in the little house was sinister. It was so intense that the sound after a while of Robert inserting his latch-key in the lock had all the effect of a frightening noise. Lydia clenched her hands to prevent herself from crying out. He gave his little whistle as he entered the house, and Lydia, gathering herself together, went out into the passage. He had two or three papers in his hand.

"I've brought you the evening papers," he cried gaily. "They're full of the murder."

He went into the kitchen where he knew his mother would be and threw the papers on the table. Lydia followed him in. Without a word Madame Berger took one of them and began to read it. There were big headlines. It was front-page news.

"I've been to Jojo's Bar. They can talk of nothing else. Jordan was one of their regular clients and everybody knew him. I talked to him myself on the night

134

he was murdered. He'd not done so badly on the day's racing and he was standing everybody drinks."

His conversation was so easy and natural, you would have thought he had not a care in the world. His eyes glittered and there was a slight flush on the cheeks that were usually rather pasty. He was excited, but showed no sign of nervousness. Trying to make her tone as unconcerned as his, Lydia asked him:

"Have they any idea who the murderer was?"

"They suspect it was a sailor. The concierge says she saw Jordan come in with one about a week ago. But of course it may just as well have been someone disguised as a sailor. They're rounding up the frequenters of the notorious bars in Montmartre. From the condition of the skin round the wound it appears that the blow was struck with great force. They're looking for a husky, big man of powerful physique. Of course there are one or two boxers who have a funny reputation."

Madame Berger put down the paper without remark.

"Dinner will be ready in a few minutes," she said. "Is the cloth laid, Lydia?"

"I'll go and lay it."

When Robert was there they took the two principal meals of the day in the dining-room, even though it gave more work. But Madame Berger said:

"We can't live like savages. Robert has been well brought up and he's accustomed to having things done properly."

Robert went upstairs to change his coat and put on his slippers. Madame Berger could not bear him to sit about the house in his best clothes. Lydia set about laying the table. Suddenly a thought occurred to her and it was such a violent shock that she staggered and to support herself had to put her hand on the back of a chair. It was two nights before that Teddie Jordan had been murdered, and it was two nights before that Robert had awakened her, made her cook supper for him, and then hurried her to bed. He had come to her arms straight from committing the horrible crime; and his passion, his insatiable desire, the frenzy of his lust had their source in the blood of a human being.

"And if I conceived that night?"

Robert clattered downstairs in his slippers.

"I'm ready, mummy," he cried.

"I'm coming."

He entered the dining-room and sat down in his usual place. He took his napkin out of the ring and stretched over to take a piece of bread from the platter on which Lydia had put it.

"Is the old woman giving us a decent dinner to-night? I've got a beautiful appetite. I had nothing but a sandwich at Jojo's for lunch."

Madame Berger brought in the bowl of soup and taking her seat at the head of the table ladled out a couple of spoonfuls for the three of them. Robert was in high spirits. He talked gaily. But the two women hardly answered. They finished the soup.

"What's coming next?" he asked.

"Cottage pie."

"Not one of my favourite dishes."

"Be thankful you have anything to eat at all," his mother answered sharply.

He shrugged his shoulders and gave Lydia a gay wink. Madame Berger went into the kitchen to fetch the cottage pie.

"The old woman doesn't seem in a very good humour to-night. What's she been doing with herself?"

"It was the générale's last day of the season. She went there."

"The old bore! That's enough to put anyone out of temper."

Madame Berger brought in the dish and served it. Robert helped himself to some wine and water. He went on talking of one thing and another, in his usual ironical and rather amusing way, but at last he could ignore no longer the taciturnity of his companions.

"But what is the matter with you both to-night?" he interrupted himself angrily. "You sit there as glum as two mutes at a funeral."

His mother, forcing herself to eat, had been sitting with her eyes glued to her plate, but now she raised them and, silently, looked him full in the face.

"Well, what is it?" he cried flippantly.

She did not answer, but continued to stare at him. Lydia gave her a glance. In those dark eyes, as full of expression as Robert's, she read reproach, fear, anger, but also an unhappiness so poignant that it was intolerable. Robert could not withstand the intensity of that anguished gaze and dropped his eyes. They finished the meal in silence. Robert lit a cigarette and gave one to Lydia. She went into the kitchen to fetch the coffee. They drank it in silence.

There was a ring at the door. Madame Berger gave a little cry. They all sat still as though they were paralysed. The ring was repeated.

"Who is that?" whispered Madame Berger.

"I'll go and see," said Robert. Then, with a hard look on his face: "Pull yourself together, mother. There's nothing to get upset about."

He went to the front door. They heard strange

voices, but he had closed the parlour door after him and they could not distinguish what was said. In a minute or two he came back. Two men followed him into the room.

"Will you both go into the kitchen," he said. "These gentlemen wish to talk to me."

"What do they want?"

"That is precisely what they are going to tell me," Robert answered coolly.

The two women got up and went out. Lydia stole a glance at him. He seemed perfectly self-possessed. It was impossible not to guess that the two strangers were detectives. Madame Berger left the kitchen door open, hoping she would be able to hear what was being said, but across the passage, through a closed door, the words spoken were inaudible. The conversation went on for the best part of an hour, then the door was opened.

"Lydia, go and fetch me my coat and my shoes," cried Robert. "These gentlemen want me to accompany them."

He spoke in his light, gay voice, as though his assurance were unperturbed, but Lydia's heart sank. She went upstairs to do his bidding. Madame Berger said never a word. Robert changed his coat and put on his shoes.

"I shall be back in an hour or two," he said. "But don't wait up for me."

"Where are you going?" asked his mother.

"They want me to go to the Commissariat. The Commissaire de Police thinks I may be able to throw some light on the murder of poor Teddie Jordan."

"What has it got to do with you?"

"Only that, like many others, I knew him."

Robert left the house with the two detectives.

"You'd better clear the table and help me to wash up," said Madame Berger.

They washed up and put everything in its place. Then they sat on each side of the kitchen table to wait. They did not speak. They avoided one another's eyes. They sat for an interminable time. The only sound that broke the ominous silence was the striking of the cuckoo clock in the passage. When it struck three Madame Berger got up.

"He won't come back to-night. We'd better go to bed."

"I couldn't sleep. I'd rather wait here."

"What is the good of that? It's only wasting the electric light. You've got something to make you sleep, haven't you? Take a couple of tablets."

With a sigh Lydia rose to her feet. Madame Berger gave her a frowning glance and burst out angrily:

"Don't look as if the world was coming to an end. You've got no reason to pull a face like that. Robert's done nothing that can get him into trouble. I don't know what you suspect."

Lydia did not answer, but she gave her a look so charged with pain that Madame Berger dropped her eyes.

"Go to bed! Go to bed!" she cried angrily.

Lydia left her and went upstairs. She lay awake all night waiting for Robert, but he did not come. When in the morning she came down, Madame Berger had already been out to get the papers. The Jordan murder was still front-page news, but there was no mention of an arrest; the Commissaire was continuing his investigations. As soon as she had drunk her coffee Madame Berger went out. It was eleven before she came back.

139

Lydia's heart sank when she saw her drawn face. "Well?"

"They won't tell me anything. I got hold of the lawyer and he's gone to the Commissariat."

They were finishing a miserable luncheon when there was a ring at the front door. Lydia opened it and found Colonel Legrand and a man she had not seen before. Behind them were two other men, whom she at once recognized as the police officers who had come the night before, and a grim-faced woman. Colonel Legrand asked for Madame Berger. Her anxiety had brought her to the kitchen door, and seeing her, the man who was with him pushed past Lydia.

"Are you Madame Léontine Berger?"

"I am."

"I am Monsieur Lukas, Commissaire de Police. I have an order to search this house." He produced a document. "Colonel Legrand has been designated by your son, Robert Berger, to attend the search on his behalf."

"Why do you want to search my house?"

"I trust that you will not attempt to prevent me from fulfilling my duty."

She gave the Commissaire an angry, scornful look.

"If you have an order I have no power to prevent you."

Accompanied by the Colonel and the two detectives the Commissaire went upstairs, while the woman who had come with them remained in the kitchen with Madame Berger and Lydia. There were two rooms on the upper floor, a fairly large one which Robert and his wife used, and a smaller one in which he had slept as a bachelor. There was besides only a bathroom with a geyser. They spent nearly two hours there and when they came down the Commissaire had in his hand Lydia's vanity-case.

"Where did you get this?" he asked.

"My husband gave it me."

"Where did he get it?"

"He bought it off a woman who was down and out."

The Commissaire gave her a searching look. His eyes fell on the wrist-watch she was wearing and he pointed to it.

"Did your husband also give you that?"

"Yes."

He made no further observation. He put the vanity-case down and rejoined his companions who had gone into the double room which was part dining-room and part parlour. But in a minute or two Lydia heard the front door slam and looking out of the window saw one of the police officers go to the gate and drive off in the car that was standing at the kerb. She looked at the pretty vanity-case with sudden misgiving. Presently, so that a search might be made of the kitchen, Lydia and Madame Berger were invited to go into the parlour. Everything there was in disorder. It was plain that the search had been thorough. The curtains had been taken down and they lay on the floor. Madame Berger winced when her eyes fell on them, and she opened her mouth to speak, but by an effort of will kept silence. But when, after some time in the kitchen, the men crossed the tiny patch of garden to the pavilion, she could not prevent herself from going to the window and looking at them. Lydia saw that she was trembling, and was afraid the woman who was with them would see it too. But she was idly looking at a motor paper. Lydia went up to the window and took her mother-in-law's hand. She dared not even whisper that there was no danger. When Madame Berger saw the yellow brocade curtains being taken down she clutched Lydia's hand violently, and all Lydia could do was by an answering pressure to attempt to show her that she need not fear. The men remained in the room nearly as long as they had remained upstairs.

While they were there the officer who had gone away returned. After a little he went out again and fetched two shovels from the waiting car. The two underlings, with Colonel Legrand watching, proceeded to dig up the flower bed. The Commissaire came into the sitting-room.

"Have you any objection to letting this lady search you?" he asked.

"None."

"None."

He turned to Lydia.

"Then perhaps Madame would go to her room with this person."

When Lydia went upstairs she saw why they had been so long. It looked as though the room had been ransacked by burglars. On the bed were Robert's clothes and she guessed that they had been subjected to very careful scrutiny. The ordeal over, the Commissaire asked Lydia questions about her husband's wardrobe. They were not difficult to answer, for it was not extensive: two pairs of tennis trousers, two suits besides the one he had on, a dinner-jacket and plus-fours; and she had no reason not to reply truthfully. It was past seven o'clock when the search was at last concluded. But the Commissaire had not yet done. He took up Lydia's vanity-case which she had brought in from the kitchen and which was lying on a table.

142

"I am going to take this away with me and also your watch, Madame, if you will kindly give it me."

"Why?"

"I have reason to suspect that they are stolen goods."

Lydia stared at him in dismay. But Colonel Legrand stepped forward.

"You have no right to take them. Your warrant to search the house does not permit you to remove a single thing from it."

The Commissaire smiled blandly.

"You are quite right, Monsieur, but my colleague has, on my instructions, secured the necessary authority."

He made a slight gesture, whereupon the man who had gone away in the car—on an errand which was now patent—produced from his pocket a document which he handed to him. The Commissaire passed it on to Colonel Legrand. He read it and turned to Lydia.

"You must do as Monsieur le Commissaire desires."

She took the watch off her wrist. The Commissaire put it with the vanity-case in his pocket.

"If my suspicions prove to be unfounded the objects will of course be returned to you."

When at last they all left and Lydia had bolted the door behind them, Madame Berger hurried across the garden. Lydia followed her. Madame Berger gave a cry of consternation when she saw the condition in which the room was.

"The brutes!"

She rushed to the curtains. They were lying on the floor. She gave a piercing scream when she saw that the seams had been ripped up. She flopped on to the ground and turned on Lydia a face contorted with horror.

143

"Don't be afraid," said Lydia. "They didn't find the notes. I found them and destroyed them. I knew you'd never have the courage."

She gave her hand to Madame Berger and helped her to her feet. Madame Berger stared at her. They had never spoken of the subject that for forty-eight hours had obsessed their tortured thoughts. But now the time for silence was passed. Madame Berger seized Lydia's arm with a cruel grip and in a harsh, intense voice said:

"I swear to you by all the love I bear him that Robert didn't murder the Englishman."

"Why do you say that when you know as certainly as I do that he did?"

"Are you going to turn against him?"

"Does it look like it? Why do you suppose I destroyed those notes? You must have been mad to think they wouldn't find them. Could you think a trained detective would miss such an obvious hiding-place?"

Madame Berger released her hold of Lydia's arm. Her expression changed and a sob burst from her throat. Suddenly she stretched out her arms, took Lydia in them, and pressed her to her breast.

"Oh, my poor child, what trouble, what unhappiness I've brought upon you."

It was the first time Lydia had ever seen Madame Berger betray emotion. It was the first time she had ever known her show an uncalculated, disinterested affection. Hard, painful sobs rent her breast and she clung desperately to Lydia. Lydia was deeply moved. It was horrible to see that self-controlled woman, with her pride and her iron will, break down.

"I ought never to have let him marry you," she

wailed. "It was a crime. It was unfair to you. It seemed his only chance. Never, never, never should I have allowed it."

"But I loved him."

"I know. But will you ever forgive him? Will you ever forgive me? I'm his mother, it doesn't matter to me, but you're different; how can your love survive this?"

Lydia snatched herself away and seized Madame Berger by the shoulders. She almost shook her.

"Listen to me. I don't love for a month or a year. I love for always. He's the only man I've loved. He's the only man I shall ever love. Whatever he's done, whatever the future has in store, I love him. Nothing can make me love him less. I adore him."

Next day the evening papers announced that Robert Berger had been arrested for the murder of Teddie Jordan.

A few weeks later Lydia knew that she was with child and she realized with horror that she had received the fertilizing seed on the very night of the brutal murder.

Silence fell between Lydia and Charley. They had long since finished their dinner and the other diners had gone. Charley, listening without a word, absorbed as he had never been in his life, to Lydia's story, had, all the same, been conscious that the restaurant was empty and that the waitresses were anxious for them to go, and once or twice he had been on the point of suggesting to Lydia that they should move. But it was difficult, for she spoke as if in a trance, and though often her eyes met his he had an uncanny sensation that she did not see him. But then a party of Americans came in, six of them, three men and three girls, and asked if it was too late to have dinner. The patronne, foreseeing a lucrative order, since they were all very lively, assured them that her husband was the cook and if they didn't mind waiting, would cook them whatever they wished. They ordered champagne cocktails. They were out to enjoy themselves and their gaiety filled the little restaurant with laughter. But Lydia's tragic story seemed to encompass the table at which she and Charley sat with a mysterious and sinister atmosphere which the high spirits of that happy crowd could not penetrate; and they sat in their corner, alone, as though they were surrounded by an invisible wall.

"And do you love him still?" asked Charley at last.

"With all my heart."

She spoke with such a passionate sincerity that it was impossible not to believe her. It was strange, and Charley could not prevent the slight shiver of dismay that passed through him. She did not seem to belong to quite the same human species as he did. That violence of feeling was rather terrifying, and it made him a little uncomfortable to be with her. He might have felt like that if he had been talking quite casually to someone for an hour or two and then suddenly discovered it was a ghost. But there was one thing that troubled him. It had been on his mind for the last twenty-four hours, but not wishing her to think him censorious, he had not spoken of it.

"In that case I can't help wondering how you can bear to be in a place like the Sérail. Couldn't you have found some other means of earning your living?"

"Easily."

"Then I don't understand."

"People were very kind to me after the trial. I could have got a job as saleswoman in one of the big shops.

I'm a good needle-woman, I was apprenticed to a dress-maker, I could have got work in that business. There was even a man who wanted to marry me if I would divorce Robert."

There seemed nothing more to say, and Charley was silent. She planted her elbows on the red-and-white-checkered table-cloth and rested her face on her hands. Charley was sitting opposite to her and she gazed into his eyes with a long reflective look that seemed to bore into the depths of his being.

"I wanted to atone."

Charley stared at her uncomprehendingly. Her words, spoken hardly above a whisper, gave him a shock. He had a sensation that he had never had before; it seemed to him that a veil that painted the world in pleasant, familiar colours had been suddenly rent and he looked into a convulsed and writhing darkness.

"What in God's name do you mean?"

"Though I love Robert with all my heart, with all my soul, I know that he sinned. I felt that the only way I could serve Robert now was by submitting to a degradation that was the most horrible I could think of. At first I thought I would go to one of those brothels where soldiers go, and workmen, and the riff-raff of a great city, but I feared I should feel pity for those poor people whose hurried, rare visits to such places afford the only pleasure of their cruel lives. The Sérail is frequented by the rich, the idle, the vicious. There was no chance there that I should feel anything but hatred and contempt for the beasts who bought my body. There my humiliation is like a festering wound that nothing can heal. The brutal indecency of the clothes I have to wear is a shame that no habit can

147

dull. I welcome the suffering. I welcome the contempt these men have for the instrument of their lust. I welcome their brutality. I'm in hell as Robert is in hell and my suffering joins with his, and it may be that my suffering makes it more easy for him to bear his."

"But he's suffering because he committed a crime. You suffered enough for no fault of yours. Why should you expose yourself to suffering unnecessarily?"

"Sin must be paid for by suffering. How can you with your cold English nature know what the love is that is all my life? I am his and he is mine. I should be as vile as his crime was if I hesitated to share his suffering. I know that my suffering as well as his is necessary to expiate his sin."

Charley hesitated. He had no particular religious feelings. He had been brought up to believe in God, but not to think of him. To do that would be—well, not exactly bad form, but rather priggish. It was difficult for him now to say what he had in mind, but he found himself in a situation where it seemed almost natural to say the most unnatural things.

"Your husband committed a crime and was punished for it. I daresay that's all right. But you can't think that a—a merciful God demands atonement from you for somebody else's misdeeds."

"God? What has God to do with it? Do you suppose I can look at the misery in which the vast majority of the people live in the world and believe in God? Do you suppose I believe in God who let the Bolsheviks kill my poor, simple father? Do you know what I think? I think God has been dead for millions upon millions of years. I think when he took infinity and set in motion the process that has resulted in the universe, he died, and for ages and ages men have sought and worshipped a being who ceased to exist in the act of making existence possible for them."

"But if you don't believe in God I can't see the point of what you're doing. I could understand it if you believed in a cruel God who exacted an eye for an eye and a tooth for a tooth. Atonement, the sort of atonement you want to make, is meaningless if there's no God."

"You would have thought so, wouldn't you? There's no logic in it. There's no sense. And yet, deep down in my heart, no, much more than that, in every fibre of my body, I know that I must atone for Robert's sin. I know that that is the only way he can gain release from the evil that racks him. I don't ask you to think I'm reasonable. I only ask you to understand that I can't help myself. I believe that somehow—how I don't know—my humiliation, my degradation, my bitter, ceaseless pain, will wash his soul clean, and even if we never see one another again he will be restored to me."

Charley sighed. It was all strange to him, strange, morbid and disturbing. He did not know what to make of it. He felt more than ever ill-at-ease with that alien woman with her crazy fancies; and yet she looked ordinary enough, a prettyish little thing, not very well dressed; a typist or a girl in the post-office. Just then, at the Terry-Masons', they would probably have started dancing; they would be wearing the paper caps they'd got out of the crackers at dinner. Some of the chaps would be a bit tight, but hang it all, on Christmas Day no one could mind. There'd have been a lot of kissing under the mistletoe, a lot of fun, a lot of ragging, a lot of laughter; they were all having a grand time. It seemed very far away, but thank God, it was there, normal, decent, sane and real; this was a nightmare. A nightmare? He wondered if there was anything in what she said, this woman with her tragic history and her miserable life, that God had died when he created the wide world; and was he lying dead on some vast mountain range on a dead star or was he absorbed into the universe he had caused to be? It was rather funny, if you came to think of it, Lady Terry-Mason rounding up all the house party to go to church on Christmas morning. And his own father backing her up.

"I don't pretend I'm much of a church-goer myself, but I think one ought to go on Christmas Day. I mean, I think it sets a good example."

That's what he would say.

"Don't look so serious," said Lydia. "Let's go."

They walked along the forbidding, sordid street that leads from the Avenue du Maine to the Place de Rennes, and there Lydia suggested that they should go to the news reel for an hour. It was the last performance of the day. Then they had a glass of beer and went back to the hotel. Lydia took off her hat and the fur she wore round her neck. She looked at Charley thoughtfully.

"If you want to come to bed with me you can, you know," she said in just the same tone as she might have used if she had asked him if he would like to go to the Rotonde or the Dôme.

Charley caught his breath. All his nerves revolted from the idea. After what she had told him he could not have touched her. His mouth for a moment went grim with anger; he really was not going to have her mortify her flesh at his expense. But his native politeness prevented him from uttering the words that were on the tip of his tongue.

"Oh, I don't think so, thank you."

"Why not? I'm there for that and that's what you came to Paris for, isn't it? Isn't that why all you English come to Paris?"

"I don't know. Anyhow I didn't."

"What else did you come for?"

"Well, partly to see some pictures."

She shrugged her shoulders.

"It's just as you like."

She went into the bathroom. Charley was a trifle piqued that she accepted his refusal with so much unconcern. He thought at least she might have given him credit for his delicacy. Because perhaps she owed him something, at least board and lodging for twenty-four hours, he might well have looked upon it as a right to take what she offered; it wouldn't have been unbecoming if she had thanked him for his disinterestedness. He was inclined to sulk. He undressed, and when she came in from the bathroom, in his dressing-gown, he went in to wash his teeth. She was in bed when he returned.

"Will it bother you if I read a little before I go to sleep?" he asked.

"No. I'll turn my back to the light."

He had brought a Blake with him. He began to read. Presently from Lydia's quiet breathing in the next bed he knew she was asleep. He read on for a little and switched off the light.

Thus did Charley Mason spend Christmas Day in Paris.

VI

THEY did not wake till so late next morning that by the time they had had their coffee, read the papers (like a domestic couple who had been married for years), bathed and dressed, it was nearly one.

"We might go along and have a cocktail at the Dôme and then lunch," he said. "Where would you like to go?"

"There's a very good restaurant on the boulevard in the other direction from the Coupole. Only it's rather expensive."

"Well, that doesn't matter."

"Are you sure?" She looked at him doubtfully. "I don't want you to spend more than you can afford. You've been very sweet to me. I'm afraid I've taken advantage of your kindness."

"Oh, rot!" he answered, flushing.

"You don't know what it's meant to me, these two days. Such a rest. Last night's the first night for months that I've slept without waking and without dreams. I feel so refreshed. I feel quite different."

She did indeed look much better this morning. Her skin was clearer and her eyes brighter. She held her head more alertly.

"It's been a wonderful little holiday you've given me. It's helped me so much. But I mustn't be a burden to you."

"You haven't been."

She smiled with gentle irony.

"You've been very well brought up, my dear. It's nice of you to say that, and I'm so unused to having people say nice things to me that it makes me want to cry. But after all you've come to Paris to have a good time; you know now you're not likely to have it with me. You're young and you must enjoy your youth. It lasts so short a while. Give me lunch to-day if you like and this afternoon I'll go back to Alexey's."

"And to-night to the Sérail?"

"I suppose so."

She sighed, but she checked the sigh and with a little gay shrug of the shoulders gave him a bright smile. Frowning slightly in his uncertainty Charley looked at her with pained eyes. He felt awkward and big, and his radiant health, his sense of well-being, the high spirits that bubbled inside him, seemed to himself in an odd way an offence. He was like a rich man vulgarly displaying his wealth to a poor relation. She looked very frail, a slim little thing in a shabby brown dress, and after that good night so much younger that she seemed almost a child. How could you help being sorry for her? And when you thought of her tragic story, when you thought—oh, unwillingly, for it was ghastly and senseless, yet troubling so that it haunted you—of that crazy idea of hers of atoning for her husband's crime by her own degradation, your heart-strings were wrung. You felt that you didn't matter at all, and if your holiday in Paris, to which you'd looked forward with such excitement, was a wash-out—well, you just had to put up with it. It didn't seem to Charley that it was he who was uttering the halting words he spoke, but a power within him that acted independently of his will. When he heard them issue from his lips he didn't even then know why he said them.

"I don't have to get back to the office till Monday morning and I'm staying till Sunday. If you care to stay on here till then, I don't see why you shouldn't."

Her face lit up so that you might have thought a haphazard ray of the winter sun had strayed into the room.

"Do you mean that?"

"Otherwise I wouldn't have suggested it."

It looked as though her legs suddenly gave way, for she sank on to a chair.

"Oh, it would be such a blessing. It would be such a rest. It would give me new courage. But I can't, I can't."

"Why not? On account of the Sérail?"

"Oh, no, not that. I could send them a wire to say I had influenza. It's not fair to you."

"That's my business, isn't it?"

It seemed a bit grim to Charley that he should have to persuade her to do what it was quite plain she was only too anxious to do, and what he would just as soon she didn't. But he didn't see how else he could act now. She gave him a searching look.

"Why should you do this? You don't want me, do you?" He shook his head. "What can it matter to you if I live or die, what can it matter to you if I'm happy or not? You've not known me forty-eight hours yet. Friendship? I'm a stranger to you. Pity? What has one got to do with pity at your age?"

"I wish you wouldn't ask me embarrassing questions," he grinned.

"I suppose it's just natural goodness of heart. They always say the English are kind to animals. I remember one of our landladies who used to steal our tea took in a mangy mongrel because it was homeless."

"If you weren't so small I'd give you a smack on

the face for that," he retorted cheerfully. "Is it a go?"

"Let's go out and have lunch. I'm hungry."

During luncheon they spoke of indifferent things, but when they had finished and Charley, having paid the bill, was waiting for his change, she said to him:

"Did you really mean it when you said I could stay with you till you went away?"

"Definitely."

"You don't know what a boon it would be to me. I can't tell you how I long to take you at your word."

"Then why don't you?"

"It won't be much fun for you."

"No, it won't," he answered frankly, but with a charming smile. "But it'll be interesting."

She laughed.

"Then I'll go back to Alexey's and get a few things. At least a toothbrush and some clean stockings."

They separated at the station and Lydia took the Metro. Charley thought that he would see if Simon was in. After asking his way two or three times he found the Rue Campagne Première. The house in which Simon lived was tall and dingy, and the wood of the shutters showed gray under the crumbling paint. When Charley put in his head at the concierge's loge he was almost knocked down by the stink of fug, food and human body that assailed his nostrils. A little old woman in voluminous skirts, with her head wrapped in a dirty red muffler, told him in rasping, angry tones, as though she violently resented his intrusion, where exactly Simon lived, and when Charley asked if he was in bade him go and see. Charley, following her directions, went through the dirty courtyard and up a narrow staircase smelling of stale urine. Simon lived on the second floor and in answer to Charley's ring opened the door.

"H'm. I wondered what had become of you."

"Am I disturbing you?"

"No. Come in. You'd better keep on your coat. It's not very warm in here."

That was true. It was icy. It was a studio, with a large north light, and there was a stove in it, but Simon, who had apparently been working, for the table in the middle was littered with papers, had forgotten to keep it up and the fire was almost out. Simon drew a shabby armchair up to the stove and asked Charley to sit down.

"I'll put some more coke on. It'll soon get warmer. I don't feel the cold myself."

Charley found that the armchair, having a broken spring, was none too comfortable. The walls of the studio were a cold slate-gray, and they too looked as though they hadn't been painted for years. Their only ornament was large maps tacked up with drawing-pins. There was a narrow iron bed which hadn't been made.

"The concierge hasn't been up to-day yet," said Simon, following Charley's glance.

There was nothing else in the studio but the large dining-table, bought second-hand, which Simon wrote at, some shelves with books in them, a desk-chair such as they use in offices, two or three kitchen chairs piled up with books, and a strip of worn carpet by the bed. It was cheerless and the cold winter light coming in through the north window added its moroseness to the squalid scene. A third-class waiting-room at a wayside station could not have seemed more unfriendly.

Simon drew a chair up to the stove and lit a pipe. With his quick wits he guessed the impression his surroundings were making on Charley and smiled grimly.

156

"It's not very luxurious, is it? But then I don't want luxury." Charley was silent and Simon gave him a coolly disdainful look. "It's not even comfortable, but then I don't want comfort. No one should be dependent on it. It's a trap that's caught many a man who you would have thought had more sense."

Charley was not without a streak of malice and he was not inclined to let Simon put it over on him.

"You look cold and peaked and hungry, old boy. What about taking a taxi to the Ritz Bar and having some scrambled eggs and bacon in warmth and comfortable armchairs?"

"Go to hell. What have you done with Olga?"

"Her name's Lydia. She's gone home to get a toothbrush. She's staying with me at the hotel till I go back to London."

"The devil she is. Going some, aren't you?" The two young men stared at one another for a moment. Simon leant forward. "You haven't fallen for her, have you?"

"Why did you bring us together?"

"I thought it would be rather a joke. I thought it would be a new experience for you to go to bed with the wife of a notorious murderer. And to tell you the truth, I thought she might fall for you. I should laugh like a hyena if she has. After all, you're rather the same type as Berger, but a damned sight better-looking."

Charley suddenly remembered a remark that Lydia had made when they were having supper together after the Midnight Mass. He had not understood what she meant at the time, but now he did.

"It may surprise you to learn that she tumbled to that. I'm afraid you won't be able to laugh like a hyena."

157

"Have you been together ever since I left you with her on Christmas Eve?"

"Yes."

"It seems to agree with you. You look all right. A bit pale, perhaps."

Charley tried not to look self-conscious. He would not for the world have had Simon know that his relations with Lydia had been entirely platonic. It would only have aroused his derisive laughter. He would have looked upon Charley's behaviour as despicably sentimental.

"I don't think it was a very good joke to get me off with her without letting me know what I was in for," said Charley.

Simon gave him a tortured smile.

"It appealed to my sense of humour. It'll be something to tell your parents when you go home. Anyhow you've got nothing to grouse about. It's all panned out very well. Olga knows her job and will give you a damned good time in that way, and she's no fool; she's read a lot and she can talk much more intelligently than most women. It'll be a liberal education, my boy. D'you think she's as much in love with her husband as ever she was?"

"I think so."

"Curious, human nature is, isn't it? He was an awful rotter, you know. I suppose you know why she's at the Sérail? She wants to make enough money to pay for his escape; then she'll join him in Brazil."

Charley was disconcerted. He had believed her when she told him that she was there because she wanted to atone for Robert's sin, and even though the notion had seemed to him extravagant there was something about it that had strangely moved him. It was a shock to

158

think that she might have lied to him. If what Simon said were true she had just been making a fool of him.

"I covered the trial for our paper, you know," Simon went on. "It caused rather a sensation in England because the fellow that Berger killed was an Englishman, and they gave it a lot of space. It was a snip for me; I'd never been to a murder trial in France before and I was pretty keen to see one. I've been to the Old Bailey, and I was curious to compare their methods with ours. I wrote a very full account of it; I've got it here; I'll give it you to read if you like."

"Yes, I would."

"The murder created a great stir in France. You see, Robert Berger wasn't an apache or anything like that. He was by way of being a gent. His people were very decent. He was well-educated and he spoke English quite passably. One of the papers called him the Gentleman Gangster and it caught on; it took the public fancy and made him quite a celebrity. He was good-looking too, in his way, and young, only twenty-two, and that helped. The women all went crazy over him. God, the crush there was to get into the trial! It was a real thrill when he came into the court-room. He was brought in between two warders for the press photographers to have a go at him before the judges came in. I never saw anyone so cool. He was quite nicely dressed and he knew how to wear his clothes. He was freshly shaved and his hair was very neat. He had a fine head of dark brown hair. He smiled at the photographers and turned this way and that, as they asked him to, so that they could all get a good view of him. He looked like any young chap with plenty of money that you might see at the Ritz Bar having a drink with a girl. It tickled me to think that he was such a rogue. He was a born criminal. Of course his people weren't rich, but they weren't starving, and I don't suppose he ever really wanted for a hundred francs. I wrote a rather pretty article about him for one of the weekly papers, and the French press printed extracts from it. If did me a bit of good over here. I took the line that he engaged in crime as a form of sport. See the idea? It worked up quite amusingly. He'd been almost a first-class tennis-player and there was some talk of training him for championship play, but oddly enough, though he played a grand game in ordinary matches, he had a good serve and was quick at the net, when it came to tournaments he always fell down. Something went wrong then. He hadn't got power of resistance, determination or whatever it is, that the great tennis-player has got to have. An interesting psychological point, I thought. Anyhow his career as a tennis-player came to an end because money began to be missed from the changing-room when he was about, and though it was never actually proved that he'd taken it everyone concerned was pretty well convinced that he was the culprit."

Simon relit his pipe.

"One thing that peculiarly struck me in Robert Berger was his combination of nerve, self-possession and charm. Of course charm is an invaluable quality, but it doesn't often go with nerve and self-possession. Charming people are generally weak and irresolute, charm is the weapon nature gives them to cope with their disadvantages; I would never set much trust in anyone who had it."

Charley gave his friend a slightly amused glance; he knew that Simon was belittling a quality he did not think he possessed in order to assure himself that it was of no great consequence beside those he was convinced he had. But he did not interrupt.

"Robert Berger was neither weak nor irresolute. He very nearly got away with his murder. It was a damned smart bit of work on the part of the police that they got him. There was nothing sensational or spectacular in the way they went about the job; they were just thorough and patient. Perhaps accident helped them a little, but they were clever enough to take advantage of it. People must always be prepared to do that, you know, and they seldom are."

An absent look came into Simon's eyes, and once more Charley was aware that he was thinking of himself.

"What Lydia didn't tell me was how the police first came to suspect him," said Charley.

"When first they questioned him they hadn't the ghost of an idea that he had anything to do with the murder. They were looking for a much bigger man."

"What sort of a chap was Jordan?"

"I never ran across him. He was a bad hat, but he was all right in his way. Everybody liked him. He was always ready to stand you a drink, and if you were down and out he never minded putting his hand in his pocket. He was a little fellow, he'd been a jockey, but he'd got warned off in England, and it turned out later that he'd done nine months at Wormwood Scrubs for false pretences. He was thirty-six. He'd been in Paris ten years. The police had an idea that he was mixed up in the drug traffic, but they'd never been able to get the goods on him."

"But how did the police come to question Berger at all?"

"He was one of the frequenters of Jojo's Bar. That's where Jordan used to have his meals. It's rather a shady

161

place patronized by bookmakers and jockeys, touts, runners and the sort of people with the reputation that we journalists describe as unsavoury, and naturally the police interviewed as many of them as they could get hold of. You see, Jordan had a date with someone that night, that was shown by the fact that there were a couple of glasses on the tray and a cake, and they thought he might have dropped a hint about whom he was going to meet. They had a pretty shrewd suspicion that he was queer, and it was just possible one of the chaps at Jojo's had seen him about with someone. Berger had been rather pally with Jordan, and Jojo, the owner of the bar, told the police he'd seen him touch the bookie for money several times. Berger had been tried on a charge of smuggling heroin into France from Belgium, and the two men who were up with him went to jug, but he got off somehow. The police knew he was as guilty as hell, and if Jordan had been mixed up with dope and had met his death in connection with that, they thought Berger might very well know who was responsible. He was a bad lot. He'd been convicted on another charge, stealing motor-cars, and got a suspended sentence of two years."

"Yes, I know that," said Charley.

"His system was as simple as it was ingenious. He used to wait till he saw someone drive up to one of the big stores, the Printemps or the Bon Marché, in a Citroën, and go in, leaving it at the kerb. Then he'd walk up, as bold as brass, as though he'd just come out of the store, jump in and drive off."

"But didn't they lock the cars?"

"Seldom. And he had some Citroën keys. He always stuck to the one make. He'd use the car for two or three days and then leave it somewhere, and when he wanted another, he'd start again. He stole dozens. He never tried to sell them, he just borrowed them when he wanted one for a particular purpose. That was what gave me the idea for my article. He pinched them for the fun of the thing, for the pleasure of exercising his audacious cleverness. He had another ingenious dodge that came out at the trial. He'd hang around in his car about the bus stops just at the time the shops closed, and when he saw a woman waiting for a bus he'd stop and ask her if she'd like a lift. I suppose he was a pretty good judge of character and knew the sort of woman who'd be likely to accept a ride from a good-looking young man. Well, the woman got in and he'd drive off in the direction she wanted to go, and when they came to a more or less deserted street he stalled the car. He pretended he couldn't get it to start and he would ask the woman to get out, lift the hood and tickle the carburettor while he pressed the self-starter. The woman did so, leaving her bag and her parcels in the car, and just as she was going to get in again, when the engine was running, he'd shoot off and be out of sight before she realized what he was up to. Of course a good many women went and complained to the police, but they'd only seen him in the dark, and all they could say was that he was a good-looking, gentlemanly young man in a Citroën, with a pleasant voice, and all the police could do was to tell them that it was very unwise to accept lifts from good-looking, gentlemanly young men. He was never caught. At the trial it came out that he must often have done very well out of these transactions.

"Anyhow a couple of police officers went to see him. He didn't deny that he'd been at Jojo's Bar on the evening of the murder and had been with Jordan, but he said he'd left about ten o'clock and hadn't seen him after that. After some conversation they invited him to accompany them to the Commissariat. The Commissaire de Police who was in charge of the preliminary proceedings had no notion, mind you, that Berger was the murderer. He thought it was a toss-up whether Jordan had been killed by some tough that he'd brought to his flat or by a member of the drug-ring whom he might have double-crossed. If the latter, he thought he could wheedle, jockey, bully or frighten Berger into giving some indication that would enable the police to catch the man they were after.

"I managed to get an interview with the Commissaire. He was a chap called Lukas. He was not at all the sort of type you'd expect to find in a job like that. He was a big, fat, hearty fellow, with red cheeks, a heavy moustache and great shining black eyes. He was a jolly soul and you'd have bet a packet that there was nothing he enjoyed more than a good dinner and a bottle of wine. He came from the Midi and he had an accent that you could cut with a knife. He had a fat, jovial laugh. He was a friendly, back-slapping, good-natured man to all appearances and you felt inclined to confide in him. In point of fact he'd had wonderful success in getting confessions out of suspects. He had great physical endurance and was capable of conducting an examination for sixteen hours at a stretch. There's no third degree in France of the American sort, no knocking about, I mean, or tooth-drilling or anything like that, to extort a confession; they just bring a man into the room and make him stand, they don't let him smoke and they don't give him anything to eat, they just ask him questions; they go on and on, they smoke, and when they're hungry

164

they have a meal brought in to them; they go on all night, because they know that at night a man's powers of resistance are at their lowest; and if he's guilty he has to be very strong-minded if by morning for the sake of a cup of coffee and a cigarette he won't confess. The Commissaire got nothing out of Berger. He admitted that at one time he'd been friendly with the heroin smugglers, but he asserted his innocence of the charge on which he'd been tried and acquitted. He said he'd done stupid things in his youth, but he'd had his lesson; after all, he'd only borrowed cars for two or three days to take girls out, it wasn't a very serious crime, and now that he was married he was going straight. As far as the drug traffickers were concerned he'd had nothing to do with them since his trial and he had had no idea that Teddie Jordan was mixed up with them. He was very frank. He told the Commissaire that he was very much in love with his wife, and his great fear was that she would discover his past. For her sake as well as for his own and his mother's, he was determined to lead in future a decent and honourable life. The fat, jolly man went on asking questions, but in a friendly, sympathetic way so that you felt, I think, that he couldn't wish you any harm. He applauded Berger's good resolutions, he congratulated him on marrying a penniless girl for love, he hoped they would have children which were not only an ornament to a home, but a comfort to their parents. But he had Berger's dossier; he knew that in the heroin case, though the jury had refused to convict, he was undoubtedly guilty, and from enquiries he had made that day, that he had been discharged from the broker's firm and had only escaped prosecution because his mother had made restitution of the money he had embezzled. It was a lie that since his marriage he had been leading an honest life. He asked him about his financial circumstances. Berger confessed that they were difficult, but his mother had a little and soon he was bound to get a job and then they would be all right. And pocket money? Now and then he made a bit racing and he introduced clients to bookmakers, that was how he'd become friendly with Jordan, and got a commission. Sometimes he just went without.

" 'En effet,' said the Commissaire, 'the day before he was killed you said you were penniless and you borrowed fifty francs from Jordan.'

" 'He was good to me. Poor chap. I shall miss him.'

"The Commissaire was looking at Berger with his friendly, twinkling eyes, and it occurred to him that the young man was not ill-favoured. Was it possible? But no, that was nonsense. He had a notion that Berger was lying when he said he had given up all relations with the drug traffickers. After all, he was hard up and there was good money to be made there; Berger went about among the sort of people who were addicted to dope. The Commissaire had an impression, though he had no notion on what he founded it, that Berger, if he didn't know for certain who'd committed the murder, had his suspicions: of course he wouldn't tell, but if they found heroin hidden away in the house at Neuilly they might be able to force him to. The Commissaire was a shrewd judge of character and he was pretty sure that Berger would give a friend away to save his own skin. He made up his mind that he would hold Berger and have the house searched before he had any chance of disposing of anything that was there. With the same idea in his mind he asked him about his movements on the night of the murder. Berger stated that he had come in from Neuilly rather late and had walked to Jojo's Bar; he had found a lot of men there who had come in after the races. He got two or three drinks stood him, and Jordan, who'd had a good day, said he'd pay for his dinner. After he'd eaten he hung about for a bit, but it was very smoky and it made his head ache, so he went for a stroll on the boulevard. Then about eleven he went back to the bar and stayed there till it was time to catch the last Metro back to Neuilly.

" 'You were away just long enough to kill the Englishman in point of fact,' said the Commissaire in a joking sort of way.

"Berger burst out laughing.

" 'You're not going to accuse me of that?' he said.

" 'No, not that,' laughed the other.

" 'Believe me, Jordan's death is a loss to me. The fifty francs he lent me the day before he was murdered wasn't the first I'd had from him. I don't say it was very scrupulous, but when he'd had a few drinks it wasn't hard to get money out of him.'

" 'Still, he'd made a lot that day, and though he wasn't drunk when he left the bar, he was in a happy mood. You might have thought it worth while to make sure of a few thousand francs at one go rather than get it in fifties from time to time.'

"The Commissaire said this more to tease than because he thought there was anything in it. And he didn't think it a bad thing to let Berger suppose he was a possible object of suspicion. It would certainly not make him less disinclined to tell the culprit's name if he had an inkling of it. Berger took out the money in his pocket and put it on the table. It amounted to less than ten francs.

" 'If I'd robbed poor Jordan of his money you don't suppose I'd only have that in my pocket now.'

" 'My dear boy, I suppose nothing. I only pointed out that you had the time to kill Jordan and that money would have been useful to you.'

"Berger gave him his frank and disarming smile.

" 'Both those things, I admit,' he said.

" 'I will be perfectly open with you,' said the other. 'I don't think you murdered Jordan, but I'm fairly certain that if you don't know who did, you have at least a suspicion.'

"Berger denied this, and though the Commissaire pressed him, persisted in his denial. It was late by now and the Commissaire thought it would be better to resume the conversation next day, he thought also that a night in the cells would give Berger an opportunity to consider his position. Berger, who had been arrested twice before, knew that it was useless to protest.

"You know that the dope traffickers are up to every sort of trick to conceal their dope. They hide it in hollow walking-sticks, in the heels of shoes, in the lining of old clothes, in mattresses and pillows, in the frames of bedsteads, in every imaginable place, but the police know all their dodges, and you can bet your boots that if there'd been anything in the house at Neuilly they'd have found it. They found nothing. But when the Commissaire had been going through Lydia's bedroom he'd come across a vanity-case, and it struck him that it was an expensive one for a woman of that modest class to have. She had a watch on that looked as if it had cost quite a lot of money She said that her husband had given her both the watch and the vanity-case, and it occurred to the Commissaire that it might be interesting to find out how he had got the money to buy them. On getting back to his office he had inquiries made and in a very short while learnt that several women had reported that they had had bags stolen by a young man who had offered them lifts in a Citroën. One woman had left a description of a vanity-case which she had thus lost and it corresponded with that which the Commissaire had found in Lydia's possession; another stated that there had been in her bag a gold watch from such and such a maker. The same maker's name was on Lydia's. It was plain that the mysterious young man whom the police had never been able to lay their hands on was Robert Berger. That didn't seem to bring the solution of the Jordan murder any nearer, but it gave the Commissaire an additional weapon to induce Berger to spill the beans. He had him brought into his room and asked him to explain how he had come by the vanity-case and the watch. Berger said he'd bought one of them from a tart who wanted money and the other from a man he'd met in a bar. He could give the name of neither. They were casual persons whom he'd got into conversation with and had neither seen before nor since. The Commissaire then formally arrested him on a charge of theft, and telling him that he would be confronted next morning with the two women to whom he was convinced the articles belonged, tried to persuade him to save trouble by making a confession. But Berger stuck to his story and refused to answer any more questions till he had the assistance of a lawyer, which by French law, now that he was arrested, he was entitled to have at an examination. The Commissaire could do nothing but acquiesce, and that finished the proceedings for the night.

"On the following morning the two women in

question came to the Commissariat and immediately they were shown the objects recognized them. Berger was brought in and one of them at once identified him as the obliging young man who had given her a lift. The other was doubtful; it was night when she had accepted his offer to drive her home and she had not seen his face very well, but she thought she would recognize his voice. Berger was told to read out a couple of sentences from a paper and he had not read half a dozen words before the woman cried out that she was certain it was the same man. I may tell you that Berger had a peculiarly soft and caressing voice. The women were dismissed and Berger taken back to the cell. The vanity-case and the watch were on the table before him and the Commissaire looked at them idly. Suddenly his expression grew more intent."

Charley interrupted.

"Simon, how could you know that? You're romancing."

Simon laughed.

"I'm dramatizing a little. I'm telling you what I said in my first article. I had to make as good a story out of it as I could, you know."

"Go on then."

"Well, he sent for one of his men, and asked him if Berger had on a wrist-watch when he was arrested, and if he had, to bring it. Remember, all this came out at the trial afterwards. The cop got Berger's watch. It was an imitation gold thing, in a metal that I think's called aureum, and it had a round face. The press had given a lot of details about Jordan's murder; they'd said, for instance, that the knife with which the blow had been inflicted hadn't been found, and, incidentally, it never was; and they'd said that the police hadn't discovered any finger prints. You'd have expected to find some either on the leather note-case in which Jordan had kept his money or on the door handle; and of course they deduced from that that the murderer had worn gloves. But what they didn't say, because the police had taken care to keep it dark, was that when they had gone through Jordan's room with a fine comb they had found fragments of a broken watch-glass. It couldn't have belonged to Jordan's watch, and it needn't necessarily have belonged to the murderer's, but there was just a chance that somehow or other, in his nervousness or haste, by an accidental knock against a piece of furniture, the murderer had broken the glass of his watch. It wasn't a thing he would be likely to notice at such a moment. Not all the pieces had been found, but enough to show that the watch they had belonged to was small and oblong. The Commissaire had the pieces in an envelope, carefully wrapped up in tissue-paper, and he now laid them out before him. They would have exactly fitted Lydia's watch. It might be only a coincidence; there were in use thousands of watches of just that size and shape. Lydia's had a glass. But the Commissaire pondered. He turned over in his mind various possibilities. They seemed so far-fetched that he shrugged his shoulders. Of course during the period, three-quarters of an hour at least, that Berger claimed he'd been strolling along the boulevard, he would have had plenty of time to get to Jordan's apartment, a ten minutes' walk from Jojo's Bar, commit the murder, wash his hands, tidy himself up, and walk back again; but why should he have been wearing his wife's watch? He had one of his own. His own, of course, might have been out of order. The Commissaire nodded his head thoughtfully."

171

Charley giggled.

"Really, Simon."

"Shut up. He gave instructions that plain-clothes men should go to every watchmaker's within a radius of two miles round the house in Neuilly where the Bergers lived. They were to ask if within the last week any watchmaker had repaired a watch in imitation gold or had put a glass in a small lady's-watch with an oblong face. Within a few hours one of the men came back and said that a watchmaker, not more than a quarter of a mile from the Bergers' house, said that he had repaired a watch corresponding to the description and it had been called for, and at the same time the customer had brought another watch to have a glass put in. He had done it on the spot and she had come in for it half an hour later. He couldn't remember what the customer looked like, but he thought she had a Russian accent. The two watches were taken for the watchmaker to look at and he claimed that they were those he had repaired. The Commissaire beamed as he might have beamed if he had a great plate of bouilla-baisse set before him in the Old Port at Marseilles. He knew he'd got his man."

"What was the explanation?" asked Charley.

"Simple as A B C. Berger had broken his watch and borrowed the one he'd given to Lydia. She hardly ever went out and didn't need it. You must remember that in those days she was a quiet, modest, rather shy girl with few friends of her own, and I should say somewhat lethargic. At the trial two men swore that they'd noticed Berger wearing it. Jojo, who was a police informer, knew that Berger was a crook and wondered how he had got it. In a casual way he mentioned to Berger that he had a new watch on and Berger told him it was his wife's. Lydia went to the watchmaker's to get her husband's watch the morning after the murder, and very naturally, since she was there, had a new glass put in her own. It never occurred to her to mention it and Berger never knew that he had broken it."

"But you don't mean to say that he was convicted on that?"

"No. But it was enough to justify the Commissaire charging him with the murder. He thought, quite rightly as it turned out, that new evidence would be forthcoming. All through his interrogations Berger conducted himself with amazing adroitness and self-possession. He admitted everything that could be proved and no longer attempted to deny that it was he who had robbed all those women of their handbags, he admitted that even after his conviction he had gone on pinching cars whenever he wanted one; he said the ease with which it could be done was too much for him and the risk appealed to his adventurousness; but he denied absolutely that he'd had anything to do with the murder. He claimed that the fact of the pieces of glass fitting Lydia's watch proved nothing, and she swore black and blue that she'd broken the glass herself. The judge d'instruction in whose charge the case was of course eventually placed was puzzled because no trace could be found of the money Berger must have stolen, and actually it never was found. Another odd thing was that there was no trace of blood on the clothes that Berger was wearing on that particular night. The knife wasn't found either. It was proved that Berger had one, in the circles he moved in that was usual enough, but he swore that he'd lost it a month before. I told you that the detectives' work was pretty good. There'd been no finger-prints on the stolen cars

nor on the stolen handbags, which when he'd emptied
he'd apparently just thrown into the street and some
of which had eventually got into the hands of the police,
so it was pretty obvious that he had worn gloves. They
found a pair of leather gauntlets among his things, but
it was unlikely that he would have kept them on when
he went to see Jordan, and from the place in which the
body was found, which suggested that Jordan had been
changing a record when he was struck, it was plain that
Berger hadn't murdered him the moment Jordan let
him into the room. Besides, they were too large to go
in his pocket and if he had had them at the bar someone would have noticed them. Of course Berger's
photo had been published in all the papers, and in their
difficulty the police got the press to help them. They
asked anyone who could remember having sold about
such-and-such a date a pair of gloves, probably gray,
to a young man in a gray suit, to come forward. The
papers made rather a thing about it; they put his photo
in again with the caption: 'Did you sell him the gloves
he wore to kill Teddie Jordan?'

"You know, a thing that has always struck me is
people's fiendish eagerness to give anyone away. They
pretend it's public spirit, I don't believe a word of it;
I don't believe it's even, as a rule anyway, the desire
for notoriety; I believe it's just due to the baseness of
human nature that gets a kick out of injuring others.
You know, of course, that in England the Treasury and
the King's Proctor are supposed to have a wonderful
system of espionage to detect income-tax evasions, and
collusion and so forth in divorce cases. Well, there's
not a word of truth in it. They depend entirely on
anonymous letters. There are a whole mass of people
who can't wait if they have the chance of doing down

someone who's trying to get away with anything."

"It's a grim thought," said Charley, but added cheerfully: "I can only hope you're exaggerating."

"Well, anyhow, a woman from the glove department at the Trois Quartiers came forward and said she remembered selling a young man a pair of gray suède gloves on the day of the murder. She was a woman of about forty and she'd liked the look of him. He was particularly anxious that they should match his gray suit and he wanted them rather large so that he shouldn't have any difficulty in slipping into them. Berger was paraded with a dozen other young men and she picked him out at once, but, as his lawyer pointed out, that was easy since she had only just seen his picture in the paper. Then they got hold of one of Berger's crooked friends who said he'd met him on the night of the murder, not walking towards the boulevard, but in a direction that would have taken him to Jordan's apartment. He'd shaken hands with him and had noticed that he was wearing gloves. But that particular witness was a thorough scamp. He had a foul record, and Berger's counsel at the trial attacked him violently. Berger denied that he had seen him on that particular evening and his counsel tried to persuade the jury that it was a cooked-up story that the man had invented in order to ingratiate himself with the police. The damning thing was the trousers. There'd been a lot of stuff in the papers about Berger's smart clothes, the well-dressed gangster and all that sort of thing; you'd have thought, to read it, that he got his suits in Savile Row and his haberdashery at Charvet's. The prosecution was anxious to prove that he was in desperate need of money and they went round to all the shops that supplied things both to him and for the household to find out if there had been any pressure put to settle unpaid accounts. But it appeared that everything bought for the house was paid for on the nail and there were no outstanding debts. So far as clothes were concerned Berger, it turned out, had bought nothing since he lost his job but one gray suit. The detective who was interviewing the tailor asked when this had been paid for and the tailor turned up his books. He was an advertising tailor in a large way of business who made clothes to measure at a lowish price. It was then discovered that Berger had ordered an extra pair of trousers with the suit. The police had a list of every article in his wardrobe, and this pair of trousers didn't figure on it. They at once saw the importance of the fact and they made up their minds to keep it dark till the trial.

"It was a thrilling moment, believe me, when the prosecution introduced the subject. There could be no doubt that Berger had had two pairs of trousers to his new gray suit and that one of the pairs was missing. When he was asked about it he never even attempted to explain. He didn't seem flummoxed. He said he didn't know they were missing. He pointed out that he had had no opportunity of going over his wardrobe for some months, having been in prison awaiting trial, and when he was asked how he could possibly account for their disappearance suggested flippantly that perhaps one of the police officers who had searched the house was in need of a pair of new trousers and had sneaked them. But Madame Berger had her explanation pat, and I'm bound to say I thought it a very ingenious one. She said that Lydia had been ironing the trousers, as she always did after Robert had worn them, and the iron was too hot and she had burnt them. He was fussy about his clothes and it had been something of a

176

struggle to find the money to pay for the suit, they knew he would be angry with his wife, and Madame Berger, wishing to spare her his reproaches and seeing how scared she was, proposed that they shouldn't tell him; she would get rid of the trousers and Robert perhaps would never notice that they had disappeared. Asked what she had done with them she said that a tramp had come to the door, asking for money, and she had given him the trousers instead. The size of the burn was gone into. She claimed that it made the trousers unwearable, and when the public prosecutor pointed out that invisible mending would have repaired the damage, she answered that it would have cost more than the trousers were worth. Then he suggested that in their impoverished circumstances Berger might well have worn them in the house; it would surely have been better to risk his displeasure than to throw away a garment which might still be useful. Madame Berger said she never thought of that, she gave them to the tramp on an impulse, to get rid of them. The prosecutor put it to her that she had to get rid of them because they were blood-stained and that she hadn't given them to a tramp who had so conveniently presented himself, but had herself destroyed them. She hotly denied this. Then where was the tramp? He would read of the incident in the papers and knowing that a man's life was at stake would surely present himself. She turned to the press, throwing out her arms with a dramatic gesture.

" 'Let all these gentlemen,' she cried, 'spread it far and wide. Let them beseech him to come forward and save my son.'

"She was magnificent on the witness stand. The public prosecutor subjected her to a merciless examination; she fought like a fury. He took her through young

Berger's life and she admitted all his misdeeds, from the episode at the tennis club to his thefts from the broker who after his conviction had, out of charity, given him another chance. She took all the blame of them on herself. A French witness is allowed much greater latitude than is allowed to a witness in an English criminal trial, and with bitter self-reproach she confessed that his errors were due to the indulgence with which she had brought him up. He was an only child and she had spoilt him. Her husband had lost a leg in the war, while attending to the wounded under fire, and his ill health had made it necessary for her to give him unremitting attention to the detriment of her maternal duties. His untimely end had left the wretched boy without guidance. She appealed to the emotions of the jury by dwelling on the grief that had afflicted them both when death robbed their little family of its head. Then her son had been her only consolation. She described him as high-spirited, headstrong, easily led by bad companions, but deeply affectionate and, whatever else he was guilty of, incapable of murdering a man who had never shown him anything but kindness.

"But somehow she didn't create a favourable impression. She insisted on her own unimpeachable respectability in a way that grated on you. Even though she was defending the son she adored she missed no opportunity to remind the Court that she was the daughter of a staff officer. She was smartly dressed, in black, perhaps too smartly, she gave you the impression of a woman who was trying to live above her station; and she had a calculating expression on her hard, decided features; you couldn't believe that she'd have given a crust of bread, much less a pair of trousers, even though damaged, to a beggar."

"And Lydia?"

"Lydia was rather pathetic. She was very much in the family way. Her face was swollen with tears and her voice hardly rose above a whisper, so that you could only just hear what she said. No one believed her story that she had broken the glass of the watch herself, but the prosecutor wasn't hard on her as he'd been on her mother-in-law; she was too obviously the innocent victim of a cruel fate. Madame Berger and Robert had used her unmercifully for their own ends. The Court took it as natural enough that she should do everything in her power to save her husband. It was even rather touching when she told how kind and sweet he had always been to her. It was quite clear that she was madly in love with him. The look she gave him when she came on to the witness stand was very moving. Out of all that crowd of witnesses, policemen and detectives, jailors, bar-loungers, informers, crooks, mental experts—they called a couple of experts who had made a psychological examination of Berger and a pretty picture they painted of his character—out of all that crowd, I say, she was the only one who appeared to have any human feeling.

"They'd got Maître Lemoine, one of the best criminal lawyers at the French bar, to defend Berger; he was a very tall, thin man, with a long sallow face, immense black eyes and very black thick hair. He had the most eloquent hands I've ever seen. He was a striking figure in his black gown, with the white of his lawyer's bands under his chin. He had a deep, powerful voice. He reminded you, I hardly know why, of one of those mysterious figures in a Longhi picture. He was an actor as well as an orator. By a look he could express his opinion of a man's character and by a pause the im-

179

probability of his statements. I wish you could have seen the skill with which he treated the hostile witnesses, the suavity with which he inveigled them into contradicting themselves, the scorn with which he exposed their baseness, the ridicule with which he treated their pretensions. He could be winningly persuasive and brutally harsh. When the mental experts deposed that on repeated examinations of Berger in prison they had formed the opinion that he was vain, arrogant and mendacious, ruthless, devoid of moral sense, unscrupulous and insensible to remorse, he reasoned with them as though he were a trained psychologist. It was a delight to watch the working of his subtle brain. He spoke generally in an easy, conversational tone, but enriched by his lovely voice and with a beautiful choice of words; you felt that everything he said could have gone straight down in a book without alteration; but when he came to his final speech and used all the resources at his disposal the effect was stupendous. He insisted on the flimsiness of the evidence; he poured contempt on the credibility of the disreputable witnesses; he drew red herrings across the path; he contended that the prosecution hadn't made out a case upon which it was possible to convict. Now he was chatty and seemed to talk to the jury as man to man, now he worked up to a flight of impassioned pleading and his voice grew and grew in volume till it rang through the court-room like the pealing of thunder. Then a pause so dramatic that you felt your skin go all goosy. His peroration was magnificent. He told the jury that they must do their duty and decide according to their conscience, but he besought them to put out of their minds all the prejudice occasioned by the young man's admitted crimes, and his voice low

and tremulous with emotion—by God! it was effective
—he reminded them that the man the public prosecutor
asked them to sentence to death was the son of a widow,
herself the daughter of a soldier who had deserved well
of his country, and the son of an officer who had given
his life in its defence; he reminded them that he was
recently married, and had married for love, and his
young wife now bore in her womb the fruits of their
union. Could they let this innocent child be brought
into the world with the stigma that his father was a
convicted murderer? Claptrap? Of course it was claptrap, but if you'd been there and heard those thrilling,
grave accents you wouldn't have thought so. Gosh!
how people cried. I nearly did myself, only I saw the
tears coursing down Berger's cheeks and him wiping
his eyes with a handkerchief, and that seemed to me
so comic that I kept my head. But it was a fine effort,
and not all the huissiers in the world could have prevented the applause that burst from the crowd when
he sat down.

"The prosecuting counsel was a stout, rubicund
fellow of thirty-five, I should say, or forty, who looked
like a North Country farmer. He oozed self-satisfaction.
You felt that for him the case was a wonderful chance
to make a splash and so further his career. He was
verbose and confused, so that, if the presiding judge
hadn't come to his help now and then, the jury would
hardly have known what he was getting at. He was
cheaply melodramatic. On one occasion he turned to
Berger who had just made some remark aside to one
of the warders who sat in the dock with him, and said:

" 'You may smile now, but you won't smile when,
with your arms pinioned behind your back, you walk
in the cold gray light of dawn and see the guillotine

181

rear its horror before your eyes. No smile then will break on your lips, but your limbs will shake with terror, and remorse for your monstrous crime wring your heart.'

"Berger gave the warder an amused look, but so contemptuous of what the public prosecutor had said, that if he hadn't been eaten up with vanity he couldn't have failed to be disconcerted. It was grand to see the way Lemoine treated him. He paid him extravagant compliments, but charged with such corrosive irony that, for all his conceit, the public prosecutor couldn't help seeing he was made a fool of. Lemoine was so malicious, but with such perfect courtesy and with such a condescending urbanity, that you could see in the eyes of the presiding judge a twinkle of appreciation. I very much doubt if the prosecuting counsel advanced his career by his conduct of this case.

"The three judges sat in a row on the bench. They were rather impressive in their scarlet robes and black squarish caps. Two were middle-aged men and never opened their mouths. The presiding judge was a little old man, with the wrinkled face of a monkey, and a tired, flat voice, but he was very observant; he listened attentively, and when he spoke it was without severity, but with a passionless calm that was rather frightening. He had the exquisite reasonableness of a man who has no illusions about human nature, but having long since learnt that man is capable of any vileness accepts the fact as just as much a matter of course as that he has two arms and two legs. When the jury went out to consider their verdict we journalists scattered to have a chat, a drink or a cup of coffee. We all hoped they wouldn't be too long, because it was getting late and we wanted to get our stuff in. We had no doubt that they'd find Berger guilty. One of the odd circumstances I've noticed in the murder trials I've attended is how unlike the impression is you get about things in court to that which you get by reading about them in the paper. When you read the evidence you think that after all it's rather slight, and if you'd been on the jury you'd have given the accused the benefit of the doubt. But what you've left out of account is the general atmosphere, the feeling that you get; it puts an entirely different colour on the evidence. After about an hour we were told that the jury had arrived at a decision and we trooped in again. Berger was brought up from the cells and we all stood up as the three judges trailed in one after the other. The lights had been lit and it was rather sinister in that crowded court. There was a tremor of apprehension. Have you ever been to the Old Bailey?"

"No, in point of fact, I haven't," said Charley.

"I go often when I'm in London. It's a good place to learn about human nature. There's a difference in feeling between that and a French court that made a most peculiar impression on me. I don't pretend to understand it. At the Old Bailey you feel that a prisoner is confronted with the majesty of the law. It's something impersonal that he has to deal with, Justice in the abstract. An idea, in fact. It's awful in the literal sense of the word. But in that French court, during the two days I spent there, I was beset by a very different feeling, I didn't get the impression that it was permeated by a grandiose abstraction, I felt that the apparatus of law was an arrangement by which a bourgeois society protected its safety, its property, its privileges from the evil-doer who threatened them. I don't mean the trial wasn't fair or the verdict unjustified, what I mean is that you got the sensation of a society that was outraged because it feared, rather than of a principle that must be upheld. The prisoner was up against men who wanted to safeguard themselves, rather than, as with us, up against an idea that must prevail though the heavens fall. It was terrifying rather than awful. The verdict was guilty of murder with extenuating circumstances."

"What were the extenuating circumstances?"

"There were none, but French juries don't like to sentence a man to death, and by French law when there are extenuating circumstances capital punishment can't be inflicted. Berger got off with fifteen years' penal servitude."

Simon looked at his watch and got up.

"I must be going. I'll give you the stuff I wrote about the trial and you can read it at your leisure. And look, here's the article I wrote on crime as a form of sport. I showed it to your girl friend, but I don't think she liked it very much; anyhow, she returned it without a word of comment. As an exercise in sardonic humour it's not so dusty."

VII

SINCE he had no wish to read Simon's articles in Lydia's presence, Charley, on parting from his friend, went to the Dôme, ordered himself a cup of coffee, and settled himself down to their perusal. He was glad to read a connected account of the murder and the trial, for Lydia's various narratives had left him somewhat confused. She had told him this and that, not in the order in which it had occurred, but as her emotion dictated. Simon's three long articles were coherent, and though there were particulars which Charley had learnt from Lydia and of which he was ignorant, he had succeeded in constructing a graphic story which it was easy to follow. He wrote almost as he spoke, in a fluent journalistic style, but he had managed very effectively to present the background against which the events he described had been enacted. You got a sinister impression of a world, sordid, tumultuous, in which these gangsters, dope traffickers, bookies and race-course touts lived their dark and hazardous lives. Dregs of the population of a great city, living on their wits, suspicious of one another, ready to betray their best friend if it could be of advantage to themselves, open-handed, sociable, gaily cynical, even good-humoured, they seemed to enjoy that existence, with all its dangers and vicissitudes, which kept you up to the mark and made you feel that you really were living. Each man's hand was against his neighbour's, but the alertness which this forced upon you was exhilarating. It was a world in which a man would shoot another for a trifle, but was just as ready to take flowers and fruit, bought at no small sacrifice, to a third who was sick in hospital. The atmosphere with which Simon had not unskilfully encompassed his story filled Charley with a strange unease. The world he knew, the peaceful happy world of the surface, was like a pretty lake in which were reflected the dappled clouds and the willows that grew on its bank, where care-free boys paddled their canoes and the girls with them trailed their fingers in the soft water. It was terrifying to think that below, just below, dangerous weeds waved tentacles to ensnare you and all manner of strange, horrible things, poisonous snakes, fish with murderous jaws, waged an unceasing and hidden warfare. From a word here, a word there, Charley got the impression that Simon had peered fascinated into those secret depths, and he asked himself whether it was merely curiosity, or some horrible attraction, that led him to observe those crooks and blackguards with a cynical indulgence.

In this world Robert Berger had found himself wonderfully at home. Of a higher class and better educated than most of its inhabitants, he had enjoyed a certain prestige. His charm, his easy manner and his social position attracted his associates, but at the same time put them on their guard against him. They knew he was a crook, but curiously enough, because he was a garçon de bonne famille, a youth of respectable parentage, took it somewhat amiss that he should be. He worked chiefly alone, without confederates, and kept his own counsel. They had a notion that he despised them, but they were impressed when he had been to a concert and talked enthusiastically and, for all they could tell, with knowledge of the performance.

They did not realize that he felt himself wonderfully at ease in their company. In his mother's house, with his mother's friends, he felt lonely and oppressed; he was irritated by the inactivity of the respectable life. After his conviction on the charge of stealing a motor car he had said to Jojo in one of his rare moments of confidence:

"Now I needn't pretend any more. I wish my father were alive, he would have turned me out of the house and then I should be free to lead the only life I like. Evidently I can't leave my mother. I'm all she has."

"Crime doesn't pay," said Jojo.

"You seem to make a pretty good thing out of it," Robert laughed. "But it's not the money, it's the excitement and the power. It's like diving from a great height. The water looks terribly far away, but you make the plunge, and when you rise to the surface, gosh! you feel pleased with yourself."

Charley put the newspaper cuttings back in his pocket, and, his brow slightly frowning with the effort, tried to piece together what he now knew of Robert Berger in order to get some definite impression of the sort of man he really was. It was all very well to say he was a worthless scamp of whom society was well rid; that was true of course, but it was too simple and too sweeping a judgement to be satisfactory; the idea dawned in Charley's mind that perhaps men were more complicated than he had imagined, and if you just said that a man was this or that you couldn't get very far. There was Robert's passion for music, especially Russian music, which, so unfortunately for her, had brought Lydia and him together. Charley was very fond of music. He knew the delight it gave him, the pleasure, partly sensual, partly intellectual, when intoxicated by the loveliness that assailed his ears, he remained yet keenly appreciative of the subtlety with which the composer had worked out his idea. Looking into himself, as perhaps he had never looked before, to find out what exactly it was he felt when he listened to one of the greater symphonies, it seemed to him that it was a complex of emotions, excitement and at the same time peace, love for others and a desire to do something for them, a wish to be good and a delight in goodness, a pleasant languor and a funny detachment as though he were floating above the world and whatever happened there didn't very much matter; and perhaps if you had to combine all those feelings into one and give it a name, the name you'd give it was happiness. But what was it that Robert Berger got when he listened to music? Nothing like that, that was obvious. Or was it unjust to dismiss such emotions as music gave *him* as vile and worthless? Might it not be rather that in music he found release from the devil that possessed him, that devil which was stronger than himself so that he neither could be delivered, nor even wanted to be delivered, from the urge that drove him to crime because it was the expression of his warped nature, because by throwing himself into antagonism with the forces of law and order he realized his personality—might it not be that in music he found peace from that impelling force and for a while, resting in heavenly acquiescence, saw as though through a rift in the clouds a vision of love and goodness?

Charley knew what it was to be in love. He knew that it made you feel friendly to all men, he knew that you wanted to do everything in the world for the girl you loved, he knew that you couldn't bear the thought of hurting her and he knew that you couldn't help wondering what she saw in you, because of course she was wonderful, definitely, and if you were honest with yourself you were bound to confess that you couldn't hold a candle to her. And Charley supposed that if he felt like that everyone else must feel like that and therefore Robert Berger had too. There was no doubt that he loved Lydia with passion, but if love filled him with a sense of—Charley jibbed at the word that came to his mind, it made him almost blush with embarrassment to think of it—well, with a sense of holiness, it was strange that he could commit sordid and horrible crimes. There must be two men in him. Charley was perplexed, which can hardly be considered strange, for he was but twenty-three, and older, wiser men have failed to understand how a scoundrel can love as purely and disinterestedly as a saint. And was it possible for Lydia to love her husband even now with an all-forgiving devotion if he were entirely worthless?

"Human nature wants a bit of understanding," he muttered to himself.

Without knowing it, he had said a mouthful.

But when he came to consider the love that consumed Lydia, a love that was the cause of her every action, the inspiration of her every thought, so that it was like a symphonic accompaniment that gave depth and significance to the melodic line which was her life from day to day, he could only draw back in an almost horrified awe as he might have drawn back, terrified but fascinated, at the sight of a forest on fire or a river in flood. This was something with which his experience could not cope. By the side of this he knew that his own little love affairs had been but trivial flirtations, and the emotion which had from time to time brought charm and gaiety into his somewhat humdrum life no more than a boy's sentimentality. It was incomprehensible that in the body of that commonplace, drab little woman there should be room for a passion of such intensity. It was not only what she said that made you realize it, you felt it, intuitively as it were, in the aloofness which, for all the intimacy with which she treated you, kept you at a distance; you saw it in the depths of her transparent eyes, in the scorn of her lips when she didn't know you were looking at her, and you heard it in the undertones of her sing-song voice. It was not like any of the civilized feelings that Charley was familiar with, there was something wild and brutal in it, and notwithstanding her high-heeled shoes, her silk stockings, and her coat and skirt, Lydia did not seem a woman of to-day, but a savage with elemental instincts who still harboured in the darkest recesses of her soul the ape-like creature from which the human being is descended.

"By God! what have I let myself in for?" said Charley.

He turned to Simon's article. Simon had evidently taken pains over it, for the style was more elegant than that of his reports of the trial. It was an exercise in irony written with detachment, but beneath the detachment you felt the troubled curiosity with which he had considered the character of this man who was restrained neither by scruple nor by the fear of consequences. It was a clever little essay, but so callous that you could not read it without discomfort. Trying to make the most of his ingenious theme, Simon had forgotten that human beings, with feelings, were concerned; and if you smiled, for it was not lacking in a bitter wit, it was with malaise. It appeared that Simon had somehow gained admittance to the little house at Neuilly, and in order to give an impression of the environment in which Berger had lived, he described with acid humour the tasteless, stuffy and pretentious room into which he had been ushered. It was furnished with two drawing-room suites, one Louis Quinze and the other Empire. The Louis Quinze suite was in carved wood, gilt, and covered in blue silk with little pink flowers on it; the Empire suite was upholstered in light yellow satin. In the middle of the room was an elaborately-carved gilt table with a marble top. Both suites had evidently come from one of those shops in the Boulevard St. Antoine that manufacture period furniture wholesale, and had been then bought at auction when their first owners had wanted to get rid of them. With two sofas and all those chairs it was impossible to move without precaution and there was nowhere you could sit in comfort. On the walls were large oil paintings in heavy gold frames, which, it was obvious, had been bought at sale-rooms because they were going for nothing.

The prosecution had reconstructed the story of the murder with plausibility. It was evident that Jordan had taken a fancy to Robert Berger. The meals he had stood him, the winners he had given him and the money he had lent him, proved that. At last Berger had consented to come to his apartment, and so that their leaving the bar together should not attract attention they had arranged for one to go some minutes after the other. They met according to plan, and since the concierge was certain she had admitted that night no one who asked for Jordan, it was plain that they had entered the house together. Jordan lived on the ground floor. Berger, still wearing his smart new gloves, sat down and smoked a cigarette while Jordan busied himself getting the whiskey and soda and bringing in the cake from his tiny kitchen. He was the sort of man who always sat in his shirt-sleeves at home, and he took off his coat. He put on a record. It was a cheap, old-fashioned gramophone, without an automatic change, and it was while Jordan was putting on a new record that Berger, coming up behind him as though to see what it was, had stabbed him in the back. To claim, as the defence did, that he had not the strength to give a blow of such violence as the post-mortem indicated, was absurd. He was very wiry. Persons who had known him in his tennis days testified that he had been known for the power of his forehand drive. If he had never got into the first rank it was not due to an inadequate physique, but to some psychological failing that defeated his will to win.

Simon accepted the view of the prosecution. He thought they had got the facts pretty accurately, and that the reason they gave for Jordan's asking the young man to come to his apartment was correct, but he was convinced they were wrong in supposing that Berger had murdered him for the money he knew he had made during the day. For one thing, the purchase of the gloves showed that he had decided upon the deed before he knew that Jordan would be in possession that night of an unusually large sum. Though the money had never been found Simon was persuaded that he had taken it, but that was by the way; it was there for the taking and he was glad enough to get it, but to do so was not the motive of the murder. The police claimed that he had stolen between fifty and sixty cars; he had never even attempted to sell one of them;

he abandoned them sometimes after a few hours, at the most after a few days. He purloined them for the convenience of having one when he needed it, but much more to exercise his daring and resource. His robberies from women, by means of the simple trick he had devised, brought him little profit; they were practical jokes that appealed to his sense of humour. To carry them out required the charm which he loved to exert. It made him giggle to think of those women left speechless and gaping in an empty street while he sped on. The thing was, in short, a form of sport, and each time he had successfully brought it off he was filled with the self-satisfaction that he might have felt when by a clever lob or by a drop shot he won a point off an opponent at tennis. It gave him confidence. And it was the risk, the coolness that was needed, the power to make a quick decision if it looked as though discovery were inevitable, much more than the large profits, that had induced him to engage in the business of smuggling dope into France. It was like rock-climbing; you had to be sure of foot, you had to keep your head; your life depended on your nerve, your strength, your instinct; but when you had surmounted every difficulty and achieved your aim, how wonderful after that terrific strain was the feeling of deliverance and how intoxicating the sense of victory! Certainly for a man of his slender means he had got a good deal of money out of the broker who had employed him; but it had come in driblets and he had spent it on taking Lydia to night clubs and for excursions in the country, or with his friends at Jojo's Bar. Every penny had gone by the time he was caught; and it was only a chance that he was; the method he had conceived for robbing his employer was so adroit that he might very well have got away with it indefinitely. Here again it looked as though it were much more for the fun of the thing, than for profit, that he had committed a crime. He told his lawyer quite frankly that the broker was so confident of his own cleverness, he could not resist making a fool of him.

But by now, Simon went on, pursuing his idea, Robert Berger had exhausted the amusement he was capable of getting out of the smaller varieties of evil-doing. During one of the periods he spent in jail awaiting trial he had made friends with an old lag, and had listened to his stories with fascinated interest. The man was a cat burglar who specialized in jewellery and he made an exciting tale of some of his exploits. First there was the marking down of the prey, then the patient watching to discover her habits, the examination of the premises; you had to find out not only where the jewels were kept and how to get into the house, but also what were the chances of making a quick get-away if necessary; and after you had made sure of everything there was the long waiting for the suitable opportunity. Often months elapsed between the time when you made up your mind to go after the stuff and the time when at last you had a whack at it. That was what choked Berger off; he had the nerve, the agility and the presence of mind that were needed, but he would never have had the patience for the complicated business that must precede the burglary.

Simon likened Robert Berger to a man who has shot partridge and pheasant for years, and having ceased to find diversion in the exercise of his skill, craves for a sport in which there is an element of danger and so turns his mind to big game. No one could say when Berger began to be obsessed with the idea of murder, but it might be supposed that it took possession of him gradually. Like an artist heavy with the work demanding expression in his soul, who knows that he will not find peace till he has delivered himself of the burden, Berger felt that by killing he would fulfil himself. After that, having expressed his personality to its utmost, he would be at rest and then could settle down with Lydia to a life of humdrum respectability. His instincts would have been satisfied. He knew that it was a monstrous crime, he knew that he risked his neck, but it was the monstrousness of it that tempted him and the risk that made it worth the attempt.

Here Charley put the article down. He thought that Simon was really going too far. He could just fancy himself committing murder in a moment of ungovernable rage, but by no effort of imagination could he conceive of anyone doing such a thing—doing it not even for money, but for sport as Simon put it—because he was driven to it by an urge to destroy and so assert his own being. Did Simon really believe there was anything in his theory, or was it merely that he thought it would make an effective article? Charley, though with a slight frown on his handsome face, went on reading.

Perhaps, Simon continued, Robert Berger would have been satisfied merely to toy with the idea if circumstances had not offered him the predestined victim. He may often, when drinking with one of his boon companions, have considered the feasibility of killing him and put the notion aside because the difficulties were too great or detection too certain. But when chance threw him in contact with Teddie Jordan he must have felt that here was the very man he had been looking for. He was a foreigner, with a large acquaintance. but no close friends, who lived alone in a blind alley,

He was a crook; he was connected with the dope traffic; if he were found dead one day the police might well suppose that his murder was the result of a gangsters' quarrel. If they knew nothing of his sexual habits, they would be sure to find out about them after his death and likely enough to assume that he had been killed by some rough who wanted more money than he was prepared to give. Among the vast number of bullies, blackmailers, dope-peddlers and bad hats who might have done him in, the police would not know where to look, and in any case he was an undesirable alien and they would think he was just as well out of the way. They would make enquiries and if results were not soon obtained quietly shelve the case. Berger saw that Jordan had taken a fancy to him and he played him like an angler playing a trout. He made dates which he broke. He made half-promises which he did not keep. If Jordan, thinking he was being made a fool of, threatened to break away, he exercised his charm to induce him to have patience. Jordan thought it was he who pursued and the other who fled. Berger laughed in his sleeve. He tracked him as a hunter day after day tracks a shy and suspicious beast in the jungle, waiting for his opportunity, with the knowledge that, for all its instinctive caution, the brute will at last be delivered into his hands. And because Berger had no feeling of animosity for Jordan, neither liking him nor disliking him, he was able to devote himself without hindrance to the pleasure of the chase. When at length the deed was done and the little bookmaker lay dead at his feet, he felt neither fear nor remorse, but only a thrill so intense that he was transported.

Charley finished the essay. He shuddered. He did

not know whether it was Robert Berger's brutal treachery and callousness that more horrified him or the cool relish with which Simon described the workings of the murderer's depraved and tortuous mind. It was true that this description was the work of his own invention, but what fearful instinct was it in him that found delight in peering into such vile depths? Simon leaned over to look into Berger's soul, as one might lean over the edge of a fearful precipice, and you had the impression that what he saw filled him with envy. Charley did not know how he had got the impression (because there was nothing in those careful periods or in that half-flippant irony actually to suggest it) that while he wrote he asked himself whether there was in him, Simon Fenimore, the courage and the daring to do a deed so shocking, cruel and futile. Charley sighed.

"I've known Simon for nearly fifteen years. I thought I knew him inside out. I'm beginning to think I don't know the first thing about him."

But he smiled happily. There were his father and his mother and Patsy. They would be leaving the Terry-Masons next day, tired after those strenuous days of fun and laughter, but glad to get back to their bright, artistic and comfortable house.

"Thank God, they're decent, ordinary people. You know where you are with them."

He suddenly felt a wave of affection for them sweep over him.

But it was growing late; Lydia would be getting back and he did not want to keep her waiting, she would be lonely, poor thing, by herself in that sordid room; he stuffed the essay into his pocket with the other cuttings and walked back to the hotel. He need not have fashed himself. Lydia was not there. He took *Mansfield Park,* which with Blake's Poems was the only book he had brought with him, and began to read. It was a delight to move in the company of those well-mannered persons who after the lapse of more than a hundred years seemed as much alive as anyone you met to-day. There was a gracious ease in the ordered course of their lives, and the perturbations from which they suffered were not so serious as to distress you. It was true that Cinderella was an awful little prig and Prince Charming a monstrous pedant; it was true that you could not but wish that instead of setting her prim heart on such an owl she had accepted the proposals of the engaging and witty villain; but you accepted with indulgence Jane Austen's determination to reward good sense and punish levity. Nothing could lessen the delight of her gentle irony and caustic humour. It took Charley's mind off that story of depravity and crime in which he seemed to have got so strangely involved. He was removed from the dingy, cheerless room and in fancy saw himself sitting on a lawn, under a great cedar, on a pleasant summer evening; and from the fields beyond the garden came the scent of hay. But he began to feel hungry and looked at his watch. It was half-past eight. Lydia had not returned. Perhaps she had no intention of doing so? It wouldn't be very nice of her to leave him like that, without a word of explanation or farewell, and the possibility made him rather angry, but then he shrugged his shoulders.

"If she doesn't want to come back, let her stay away."

He didn't see why he should wait any longer, so he went out to dinner, leaving word at the porter's desk where he was going so that if she came she could join him. Charley wasn't quite sure if it amused, flattered or irritated him, that the staff should treat him with a sort of confidential familiarity as though they got a vicarious satisfaction out of the affair which, naturally enough, they were convinced he was having. The porter was smilingly benevolent and the young woman at the cashier's desk excited and curious. Charley chuckled at the thought of their shocked surprise if they had known how innocent were his relations with Lydia. He came back from his solitary dinner and she was not yet there. He went up to his room and went on reading, but now he had to make a certain effort to attend. If she didn't come back by twelve he made up his mind to give her up and go out on the loose. It was absurd to spend the best part of a week in Paris and not have a bit of fun. But soon after eleven she opened the door and entered, carrying a small and very shabby suitcase.

"Oh, I'm tired," she said. "I've brought a few things with me. I'll just have a wash and then we'll go out to dinner."

"Haven't you dined? I have."

"Have you?"

She seemed surprised.

"It's past eleven."

She laughed.

"How English you are! Must you always dine at the same hour?"

"I was hungry," he answered rather stiffly.

It seemed to him that she really might express some regret for having kept him waiting so long. It was plain, however, that nothing was farther from her thoughts.

"Oh, well, it doesn't matter, I don't want any dinner. What a day I've had! Alexey was drunk; he had a row with Paul this morning, because he didn't come home last night, and Paul knocked him down. Evgenia was crying, and she kept on saying: 'God has punished us for our sins. I have lived to see my son strike his father. What is going to happen to us all?' Alexey was crying too. 'It is the end of everything,' he said. 'Children no longer respect their parents. Oh, Russia, Russia!' "

Charley felt inclined to giggle, but he saw that Lydia was taking the scene in all seriousness.

"And did you cry too?"

"Naturally," she answered, with a certain coldness.

She had changed her dress and now wore one of black silk. It was plain enough but well cut. It suited her. It made her clear skin more delicate and deepened the colour of her blue eyes. She wore a black hat, rather saucy in shape, with a feather in it, and much more becoming than the old black felt. The smarter clothes had had an effect on her; she wore them more elegantly and carried herself with a graceful assurance. She no longer looked like a shop-girl, but like a young woman of some distinction, and prettier than Charley had ever seen her, but she gave you less than ever the impression that there was anything doing, as the phrase goes; if she had given before the effect of a respectable work-girl who knew how to take care of herself, she gave now that of a modish young woman perfectly capable of putting a too enterprising young man in his place.

"You've got a different frock on," said Charley, who was already beginning to get over his ill humour.

"Yes, it's the only nice one I've got. I thought it was too humiliating for you to have to be seen with such a little drab as I was looking. After all, the least a handsome young man in beautiful clothes can ask is that when he goes into a restaurant with a woman people shouldn't say: how can he go about with a slut who looks as though she were wearing the cast-off clothes of a maid of all work? I must at least try to be a credit to you."

Charley laughed. There was really something rather likeable about her.

"Well, we'd better go out and get you something to eat. I'll sit with you. If I know anything about your appetite you could eat a horse."

They started off in high spirits. He drank a whiskey and soda and smoked his pipe while Lydia ate a dozen oysters, a beefsteak and some fried potatoes. She told him at greater length of her visit to her Russian friends. She was greatly concerned at their situation. There was no money except the little the children earned. One of these days Paul would get sick of doing his share and would disappear into that equivocal night life of Paris, to end up, if he was lucky, when he had lost his youth and looks, as a waiter in a disreputable hotel. Alexey was growing more and more of a soak and even if by chance he got a job would never be able to hold it. Evgenia had no longer the courage to withstand the difficulties that beset her; she had lost heart. There was no hope for any of them.

"You see, it's twenty years since they left Russia. For a long time they thought there'd be a change there and they'd go back, but now they know there's no chance. It's been hard on people like that, the revolution; they've got nothing to do now, they and all their generation, but to die."

But it occurred to Lydia that Charley could not be much interested in people whom he had not even seen. She could not know that while she was talking to him about her friends he was telling himself uneasily that, if he guessed aright what was in Simon's mind, it was just such a fate that he was preparing for him, for his father, mother and sister, and for their friends. Lydia changed the subject.

"And what have you been doing with yourself this afternoon? Did you go and see any pictures?"

"No. I went to see Simon."

Lydia was looking at him with an expression of indulgent interest, but when he answered her question, she frowned.

"I don't like your friend Simon," she said. "What is it that you see in him?"

"I've known him since I was a kid. We were at school together and at Cambridge. He's been my friend always. Why don't you like him?"

"He's cold, calculating and inhuman."

"I think you're wrong there. No one knows better than I do that he's capable of great affection. He's a lonely creature. I think he hankers for a love that he can never arouse."

Lydia's eyes shone with mockery, but, as ever, there was in it a rueful note.

"You're very sentimental. How can anyone expect to arouse love who isn't prepared to give himself? In spite of all the years you've known him I wonder if you know him as well as I do. He comes a lot to the Sérail; he doesn't often go up with a girl, and then not from desire, but from curiosity. Madame makes him welcome, partly because he's a journalist and she likes to keep in with the press, and partly because he sometimes brings foreigners who drink a lot of champagne. He likes to talk to us and it never enters his head that we find him repulsive."

"Remember that if he knew that he wouldn't be

offended. He'd only be curious to know why. He has no vanity."

Lydia went on as though Charley had said nothing.

"He hardly looks upon us as human beings, he despises us and yet he seeks our company. He's at ease with us. I think he feels that our degradation is so great, he can be himself, whereas in the outside world he must always wear a mask. He's strangely insensitive. He thinks he can permit himself anything with us and he asks us questions that put us to shame and never sees how bitterly he wounds us."

Charley was silent. He knew well enough how Simon, with his insatiable curiosity, could cause people profound embarrassment and was only surprised and scornful when he found that they resented his inquiries. He was willing enough to display the nakedness of his soul and it never occurred to him that the reserves of others could be due, not to stupidity as he thought, but to modesty. Lydia continued:

"Yet he's capable of doing things that you'd never expect of him. One of our girls was suddenly taken ill. The doctor said she must be operated on at once, and Simon took her to a nursing home himself so that she shouldn't have to go to the hospital, and paid for the operation; and when she got better he paid her expenses to go away to a convalescent home. And he'd never even slept with her."

"I'm not surprised. He attaches no importance to money. Anyhow it shows you that he's capable of a disinterested action."

"Or do you think he wanted to examine in himself what the emotion of goodness exactly was?"

Charley laughed.

"It's obvious that you haven't got much use for poor Simon."

"He's talked to me a great deal. He wanted to find out all I could tell him about the Russian Revolution, and he wanted me to take him to see Alexey and Evgenia so that he could ask them. You know he reported Robert's trial. He tried to make me tell him all sorts of things that he wanted to know. He went to bed with me because he thought he could get me to tell him more. He wrote an article about it. All that pain, all that horror and disgrace, were no more to him than an occasion to string clever, flippant words together; and he gave it me to read to see how I would take it. I shall never forgive him that. Never."

Charley sighed. He knew that Simon, with his amazing insensitiveness to other people's feelings, had shown her that cruel essay with no intention of hurting, but from a perfectly honest desire to see how she reacted to it and to discover how far her intimate knowledge would confirm his fanciful theory.

"He's a strange creature," said Charley. "I daresay he has a lot of traits which one would rather he hadn't, but he has great qualities. There's one thing at all events that you can say about him: if he doesn't spare others, he doesn't spare himself. After not seeing him for two years, and he's changed a lot in that time, I can't help finding his personality rather impressive."

"Frightening, I should have said."

Charley moved uneasily on his plush seat, for that also, somewhat to his dismay, was what he had found it.

"He lives an extraordinary life, you know. He works sixteen hours a day. The squalor and discomfort of his surroundings are indescribable. He's trained himself to eat only one meal a day."

"What is the object of that?"

"He wants to strengthen and deepen his character. He wants to make himself independent of circumstances. He wants to prepare himself for the role he expects one day to be called upon to play."

"And has he told you what that role is?"

"Not precisely."

"Have you ever heard of Dzerjinsky?"

"No."

"Simon has talked to me about him a great deal. Alexey was a lawyer in the old days, a clever one with liberal principles, and he defended Dzerjinsky at one of his trials. That didn't prevent Dzerjinsky from having Alexey arrested as a counter revolutionary and sending him for three years to Alexandrovsk. That was one of the reasons why Simon wanted me so much to take him to see Alexey. And when I wouldn't, because I couldn't bear that he should see to what depths that poor, broken-down man had sunk, he charged me with questions to put to him."

"But who was Dzerjinsky?" asked Charley.

"He was the head of the Cheka. He was the real master of Russia. He had an unlimited power over the life and death of the whole population. He was monstrously cruel; he imprisoned, tortured and killed thousands upon thousands of people. At first I thought it strange that Simon should be so interested in that abominable man, he seemed to be fascinated by him, and then I guessed the reason. That is the role he means to play when the revolution he's working for takes place. He knows that the man who is master of the police is master of the country."

Charley's eyes twinkled.

"You make my flesh creep, dear. But you know,

England isn't like Russia; I think Simon will have to wait a hell of a long time before he's dictator of England."

But this was a matter upon which Lydia could brook no flippancy. She gave him a dark look.

"He's prepared to wait. Didn't Lenin wait? Do you still think the English are made of different clay from other men? Do you think the proletariat, which is growing increasingly conscious of its power, is going to leave the class you belong to indefinitely in possession of its privileges? Do you think that a war, whether it results in your defeat or your victory, is going to result in anything but a great social upheaval?"

Charley was not interested in politics. Though, like his father, of liberal views, with mildly socialistic tendencies so long as they were not carried beyond the limits of prudence, by which, though he didn't know it, he meant so long as they didn't interfere with his comfort and his income, he was quite prepared to leave the affairs of the country to those whose business it was to deal with them; but he could not let these provocative questions of Lydia's go without an answer.

"You talk as though we did nothing for the working classes. You don't seem to know that in the last fifty years their condition has changed out of all recognition. They work fewer hours than they did and get higher wages for what they do. They have better houses to live in. Why, on our own estate we're doing away with slums as quickly as it's economically possible. We've given them old age pensions and we provide them with enough to live on when they're out of work. They get free schooling, free hospitals, and now we're beginning to give them holidays with pay. I really don't think the British working man has much to complain of."

"You must remember that the views of a benefactor and the views of a beneficiary on the value of a benefaction are apt to differ. Do you really expect the working man to be grateful to you for the advantages he's extracted from you at the point of a pistol? Do you think he doesn't know that he owes the favours you've conferred on him to your fear rather than to your generosity?"

Charley was not going to let himself be drawn into a political discussion if he could help it, but there was one more thing he couldn't refrain from saying.

"I shouldn't have thought that the condition in which you and your Russian friends now find yourselves would lead you to believe that mob-rule was a great success."

"That is the bitterest part of our tragedy. However much we may deny it, we know in our hearts that whatever has happened to us, we've deserved it."

Lydia said this with a tragic intensity that somewhat disconcerted Charley. She was a difficult woman; she could take nothing lightly. She was the sort of woman who couldn't even ask you to pass the salt without giving you the impression that it was no laughing matter. Charley sighed; he supposed he must make allowances, for she had had a rotten deal, poor thing; but was the future really so black?

"Tell me about Dzerjinsky," he said, stumbling a little over the pronunciation of the difficult name.

"I can only tell you what Alexey has told me. He says the most remarkable thing about him was the power of his eyes; he had a curious gift, he was able to fix them upon you for an immensely long time, and the glassy stare of them, with their dilated pupils, was simply terrifying. He was extremely thin, he'd con-tracted tuberculosis in prison, and he was tall; not bad-looking, with good features. He was absolutely single-minded, that was the secret of his power, he had a cold, arid temperament; I don't suppose he'd ever given himself up with a whole heart to a moment's pleasure. The only thing he cared about was his work; he worked day and night. At the height of his career he lived in one small room with nothing in it but a desk and an old screen, and behind the screen a narrow iron bed. They say that in the year of famine, when they brought him decent food instead of horseflesh, he sent it away, demanding the same rations as were given to the other workers in the Cheka. He lived for the Cheka and nothing else. There was no humanity in him, neither pity nor love, only fanaticism and hatred. He was terrible and implacable."

Charley shuddered a little. He could not but see why Lydia had told him about the terrorist, and in truth it was startling to note how close the resemblance was between the sinister man she had described and the man he had so surprisingly discovered that Simon was become. There was the same asceticism, the same indifference to the pleasant things of life, the same power of work, and perhaps the same ruthlessness. Charley smiled his good-natured smile.

"I daresay Simon has his faults like the rest of us. One has to be tolerant with him because he hasn't had a very happy or a very easy life. I think perhaps he craves for affection, and there's something that people find repellent in his personality which prevents him from getting it. He's frightfully sensitive and things which wouldn't affect ordinary people wound him to the quick. But at heart I think he's kind and generous."

"You're deceived in him. You think he has your own good nature and unselfish consideration. I tell you, he's dangerous. Dzerjinsky was the narrow idealist who for the sake of his ideal could bring destruction upon his country without a qualm. Simon isn't even that. He has no heart, no conscience, no scruple, and if the occasion arises he will sacrifice you who are his dearest friend without hesitation and without remorse "

VIII

THEY woke next day at what was for them an early hour. They had breakfast in bed, each with his tray, and after breakfast, while Charley, smoking his pipe, read the *Mail*, Lydia, a cigarette between her lips, did her hands. You would have thought, to see them, each engaged on his respective occupation, that they were a young married couple whose first passion had dwindled into an easy friendship. Lydia painted her nails and spread out her fingers on the sheet to let them dry. She gave Charley a mischievous glance.

"Would you like to go to the Louvre this morning? You came to Paris to see pictures, didn't you?"

"I suppose I did."

"Well, let's get up, then, and go."

When the maid who brought them their coffee drew the curtains the day that filtered into the room from the courtyard had looked as gray and bleak as on the mornings that had gone before; and they were surprised, on stepping into the street, to see that the weather had suddenly changed. It was cold still, but the sun was bright and the clouds, high up in the heavens, were white and shining. The air had a frosty bite that made your blood tingle.

"Let's walk," said Lydia.

In that gay, quivering light the Rue de Rennes lost its dinginess, and the gray, shabby houses no longer wore the down-at-heel, despondent air they usually do, but had a mellow friendliness as though, like old women in reduced circumstances, they felt less forlorn now that the unexpected sunshine smiled on them as familiarly as on the grand new buildings on the other side of the river. When they crossed the Place St. Germain-des-Prés and there was a confusion of buses and trams, recklessly-speeding taxis, lorries and private cars, Lydia took Charley's arm; and like lovers, or a grocer·and his wife taking a walk of a Sunday afternoon, they sauntered arm in arm, stopping now and then to look into the window of a picture-dealer, down the narrow Rue de Seine. Then they came on to the quay. Here the Paris day burst upon them in all its winter beauty and Charley gave a little exclamation of delight.

"You like this?" smiled Lydia.

"It's a picture by Raffaelli." He remembered a line in a poem that he had read at Tours: "Le vierge, le vivace et le bel aujourd'hui."

The air had a sparkle so that you felt you could take it up in your hands and let it run through your fingers like the water of a fountain. To Charley's eyes, accustomed to the misty distances and soft haze of London, it seemed amazingly transparent. It outlined the buildings, the bridge, the parapet by the side of the river, with an elegant distinctness, but the lines, as though drawn by a sensitive hand, were tender and gracious. Tender too was the colour, the colour of sky and cloud, the colour of stone; they were the colours of the eighteenth-century pastelists; and the leafless trees, their slim branches a faint mauve against the blue, repeated with exquisite variety a pattern of delicate intricacy. Because he had seen pictures of just that scene Charley was able to take it in, without any sense of surprise, but with a loving, understanding recognition; its beauty did not shatter him by its strangeness, nor perplex him by its unexpectedness, but filled him with a sense of familiar joy such as a countryman might feel when after an absence of years he sees once more the dear, straggling street of his native village.

"Isn't it lovely to be alive?" he cried.

"It's lovely to be as young and enthusiastic as you are," said Lydia, giving his arm a little squeeze, and if she choked down a sob he did not notice it.

Charley knew the Louvre well, for every time his parents spent a few days in Paris (to let Venetia get her clothes from the little dressmaker who was just as good as those expensive places in the Rue Royale and the Rue Cambon) they made a point of taking their children there. Leslie Mason made no bones at confessing that he preferred new pictures to old.

"But after all, it's part of a gentleman's education to have done the great galleries of Europe, and when people talk about Rembrandt and Titian and so on, you look a bit of a fool if you can't put your word in. And I don't mind telling you that you couldn't have a better guide than your mother. She's very artistic, and she knows what's what, and she won't waste your time over a lot of tripe."

"I don't claim that your grandfather was a great artist," said Mrs. Mason, with the modest self-assurance of someone who is without conceit aware that he knows his subject, "but he knew what was good. All I know about art he taught me."

"Of course you had a flair," said her husband.

Mrs. Mason considered this for a moment.

"Yes, I suppose you're right, Leslie. I had a flair."

What made it easier to do the Louvre with expedition and spiritual profit was that in those days they had not rearranged it, and the Salon Carré contained most of the

212

pictures which Mrs. Mason thought worthy of her children's attention. When they entered that room they walked straight to Leonardo's Gioconda.

"I always think one ought to look at that first," she said. "It puts you in the right mood for the Louvre."

The four of them stood in front of the picture and with reverence gazed at the insipid smile of that prim and sex-starved young woman. After a decent interval for meditation Mrs. Mason turned to her husband and her two children. There were tears in her eyes.

"Words fail me to express what that picture always makes me feel," she said, with a sigh. "Leonardo was a Great Artist. I think everybody's bound to acknowledge that."

"I don't mind admitting that I'm a bit of a philistine when it comes to old masters," said Leslie, "but that's got a je ne sais quoi that gets you, there's no denying that. Can you remember that bit of Pater's, Venetia? He hit the nail on the head and no mistake."

Mrs. Mason, a faint, enigmatic smile on her lips, in a low but thrilling voice repeated the celebrated lines that two generations ago wrought such havoc on the aesthetic young.

"Hers is the head upon which all the ends of the world are come, and the eyelids are a little weary. It is a beauty wrought out from within upon the flesh, the deposit, little cell by cell, of strange thoughts and fantastic reveries and exquisite passions."

They listened to her in awed silence. She broke off, and in her natural voice said brightly:

"Now let's go and look at the Raphael."

But it was impossible to avoid seeing the two vast canvases of Paolo Veronese that faced one another on opposite walls.

213

"It's worth while giving them a glance," she said. "Your grandfather had a very high opinion of them. Of course Veronese was neither subtle nor profound. He had no soul. But he certainly had a gift of composition, and you must remember that there's no one now who could arrange so great a number of figures in a harmonious, and yet natural, design. You must admire them if for no other reason because of their vitality and for the sheer physical vigour Veronese must have had to paint such enormous pictures. But I think there's more in them than that. They do give you an impression of the abundant, multicoloured life of the period and of the pleasure-loving, pagan spirit which was characteristic of patrician Venice in the heyday of its glory."

"I've often tried to count the number of figures in the Marriage of Cana," said Leslie Mason, "but every time I make it different."

The four of them began to count, but none of the results they reached agreed. Presently they strolled into the Grande Galerie.

"Now here is L'Homme au Gant," said Mrs. Mason. "I'm not sorry you looked at the Veroneses first, because they do bring out very clearly the peculiar merit of Titian. You remember what I said about Veronese having no soul; well, you've only got to look at L'Homme au Gant to see that soul is just what Titian had."

"He was a remarkable old buffer," said Leslie Mason. "He lived to the age of ninety-nine and then it needed the plague to kill him."

Mrs. Mason smiled slightly.

"I have no hesitation," she continued, "in saying that I consider this one of the finest portraits that's ever been painted. Of course one can't compare it with a portrait by Cézanne or even by Manet."

"We mustn't forget to show them the Manet, Venetia."

"No, we won't do that. We'll come to that presently. But what I mean to say is that you must accept the idiom of the time at which it was painted, and bearing that in mind I don't think anyone can deny that it's a masterpiece. Of course just as a piece of painting it's beyond praise, but it's got a distinction and an imaginative quality which are very unique. Don't you think so, Leslie?"

"Definitely."

"When I was a girl I used to spend hours looking at it. It's a picture that makes you dream. Personally I think it's a finer portrait than Velasquez's Pope, the one in Rome, you know, just because it's more suggestive. Velasquez was a very great painter, I admit that, and he had an enormous influence on Manet, but what I miss in him is exactly what Titian had— Soul."

Leslie Mason looked at his watch.

"We mustn't waste too much time here, Venetia," he said, "or we shall be late for lunch."

"All right. We'll just go and look at the Ingres and the Manet."

They walked on, glancing right and left at the pictures that lined the walls, but there was nothing that Mrs. Mason thought worth lingering over.

"It's no good burdening their minds with a lot of impressions that'll only confuse them," she told her husband. "It's much better that they should concentrate on what's really important."

"Definitely," he answered.

They entered the Salle des États, but at the threshold Mrs. Mason stopped.

"We won't bother about the Poussins to-day," she said. "You have to come to the Louvre to see them, and there's no doubt that he was a Great Artist. But he was more of a painter's painter than a layman's, and I think you're a little young to appreciate him. One day when you're both of you a bit older we'll come and have a good go at him. I mean you have to be rather sophisticated to thoroughly understand him. The room that we're coming to now is nineteenth century. But I don't think we need bother about Delacroix either. He was a painter's painter too, and I wouldn't expect you to see in him what I do; you must take my word for it that he was a very considerable artist. He was no mean colourist and he had a strong romantic feeling. And you certainly needn't trouble your heads with the Barbizon School. In my young days they were very much admired, but that was before we understood the Impressionists even, and of course we hadn't so much as heard of Cézanne or Matisse; they don't amount to anything and they can be safely ignored. I want you to look first at the Odalisque of Ingres and then at the Olympia of Manet. They're wonderfully placed, opposite one another, so that you can look at both of them at the same time, compare them and draw your own conclusions."

Having said this Mrs. Mason advanced into the room with her husband by her side, while Charley and Patsy followed together a step or two behind. But her eyes falling on Millet's The Gleaners, she paused.

"I'd just like you to look at this for a minute. I don't want you to admire it, but I want you to give it a glance because at one time it was thought very highly of. I'm ashamed to say that when I was a girl it used to bring tears to my eyes. I thought it a very beautiful and moving picture. But when I look at it now I simply can't think what I ever saw in it. It just shows how one's opinions change as one grows older."

"It shows also how even the youngest of us may err," said Leslie, with a shrewd smile, as though he had just invented the phrase.

They turned away and presently Venetia reached the exact spot where she thought the two pictures which she particularly wanted her offspring to admire could be seen to best advantage. She stopped with the triumphant air with which a conjurer extracts a rabbit from a hat and cried:

"There!"

They stood in a row for some minutes and Mrs. Mason gazed at the two nudes with rapture. Then she turned to the children.

"Now let's go and examine them close at hand."

They stood in front of the Odalisque.

"It's no good, Venetia," said Leslie. "You may say I'm a philistine, but I don't like the colour. The pink of that body is just the pink of that face cream you used to put on at night till I made you stop it."

"You needn't reveal the secrets of the alcove to these innocent children," said Venetia with a prim and at the same time roguish smile. "But I would never claim for a moment that Ingres was a great colourist; all the same I do think that blue is a very sweet colour and I've often thought I'd like an evening dress just like it. D'you think it would be too young, Patsy?"

"No, darling. Not a bit."

"But that's neither here nor there. Ingres was

probably the greatest draughtsman who ever lived. I don't know how anyone can look at those firm and lovely lines and not feel he's in the presence of one of the great manifestations of the human spirit. I remember my father telling me that once he came here with one of his fellow-students from Julian's who'd never seen it, and when his eyes fell on it he was so overcome with its beauty of line that he actually fainted."

"I think it's much more likely that it was long past the hour at which reasonable people have lunch and that he fainted with hunger."

"Isn't your father awful?" smiled Mrs. Mason. "Well, let's just have five minutes more for the Olympia, Leslie, and then I'm ready to go."

They marched up to Manet's great picture.

"When you come to a masterpiece like this," said Mrs. Mason, "you can do nothing but keep your mouth shut and admire. The rest, as Hamlet said, is silence. No one, not even Renoir, not even El Greco, has ever painted flesh like that. Look at that right breast. It's a miracle of loveliness. One is simply left gasping. Even my poor father, who couldn't bear the moderns, was forced to admit that the painting of that breast was pretty good. Pretty good? I ask you. Now I suppose you see a black line all round the figure. You do, Charley, don't you?"

Charley acknowledged that he did.

"And you, Patsy?"

"Yes."

"Well, I don't," she cried triumphantly. "I used to see it, I know it's there, but I give you my word, I don't see it any more."

After that they went to lunch at one of the little

places Mr. and Mrs. Mason had discovered where no English ever went. It was just as good as the fashionable restaurants foreigners went to and half the price. It was fairly full and, oddly enough, there were English people at the table on the right of theirs and Americans on the left. Opposite sat two tall blond Swedes and a little way off some Japanese. In fact you heard almost every language but French. Leslie gave the company a sweeping glance of disapproval.

"It looks to me, Venetia, as though this place is getting spoilt."

The four of them were given huge menus written in violet ink and they looked at them in some perplexity. Leslie rubbed his hands cheerfully.

"Now what are we going to start on? I suppose in France we'd better do as the French do, so what do you all say to snails to begin with and frogs to follow?"

"Don't be disgusting, daddy," said Patsy.

"You're merely showing your ignorance when you say that, my child. They're a great delicacy. I don't see them on the bill of fare." He could never quite remember whether in French grenouille was a frog and crapaud a toad or the other way about; he looked up at the head waiter who was standing beside him and in his sturdy British accent said: "Garçong, est-ce-quer vous avez des crapauds?"

The head waiter didn't much like being addressed as garçong, but he gravely answered that it was not the season.

"How sickening," cried Leslie. "Well, what about snails? Escargots?"

"Daddy, I shall be sick if you eat snails."

"He's only teasing you, darling," said Mrs. Mason.

"I think we'd better have a nice omelette. You can always be sure of an omelette in France."

"That's true," said Leslie. "No matter where you go in France you can be sure of getting a good omelette. Very well. Garçong, une omelette pour quatre."

Then, for the sake of the children, they ordered rosbif à l'anglaise. The young people had vanilla ice cream after that while their parents had camembert. They often had it in England, but they agreed that somehow or other it tasted quite different in France. They ended up with an infusion of chicory, and as she sipped it with relish Mrs. Mason said:

"You have to come to France to know what coffee really tastes like."

Through his long-standing acquaintance with the famous gallery and the useful information he had acquired from his mother, Charley, with Lydia by his side, entered the Salon Carré now with something of the confidence of a good tennis-player stepping on to the court. He was eager to show Lydia his favourite pictures and ready to explain to her exactly what was admirable in them. It was, however, something of a surprise to discover that the room had been rearranged and the Gioconda, to which he would naturally have taken her first, was nowhere to be seen. They spent but ten minutes there. When Charley went with his parents it took them an hour to do that room and even then, his mother said, they hadn't exhausted its treasures. But L'Homme au Gant was in its old place and he gently led her up to it. They looked at it for a while.

"Stunning, isn't it?" he said then, giving her arm an affectionate pressure.

"Yes, it's all right. What business is it of yours?"

Charley turned his head sharply. No one had ever

asked him a question like that about a picture before.

"What on earth d'you mean? It's one of the great portraits of the world. Titian, you know."

"I daresay. But what's it got to do with you?"

Charley didn't quite know what to say.

"Well, it's a very fine picture and it's beautifully painted. Of course it doesn't tell a story if that's what you mean."

"No, I don't," she smiled.

"I don't suppose it's got anything to do with me really."

"Then why should you bother about it?"

Lydia moved on and Charley followed her. She gave other pictures an indifferent glance. Charley was troubled by what she had said and he puzzled his brains to discover what could be at the back of her mind. She gave him an amused smile.

"Come," she said. "I'll show you some pictures."

She took his arm and they walked on. Suddenly he caught sight of the Gioconda.

"There she is," he cried. "I must stop and have a good look at that. I make a point of it when I come to the Louvre."

"Why?"

"Hang it all, it's Leonardo's most celebrated picture. It's one of the most important pictures in the world."

"Important to you?"

Charley was beginning to find her a trifle irritating; he couldn't make out what she was getting at; but he was a good-humoured youth, and he wasn't going to lose his temper.

"A picture may be important even if it isn't very important to me."

"But it's only you who count. So far as you're

concerned the only meaning a picture has is the meaning it has for you."

"That seems an awfully conceited way of looking at it."

"Does that picture say anything to you really?"

"Of course it does. It says all sorts of things, but I don't suppose I could put them any better than Pater did. Unfortunately I haven't got my mother's memory. She can repeat the whole passage by heart."

But even as he spoke he recognized that his answer was lame. He was beginning to have a vague inkling of what Lydia meant, and then the uneasy feeling came to him that there was something in art that he'd never been told about. But he fortunately remembered what his mother had said about Manet's Olympia.

"In point of fact I don't know why you should say anything about a picture at all. You either like it or you don't."

"And you really like that one?" she asked in a tone of mild interrogation.

"Very much."

"Why?"

He thought for a moment.

"Well, you see, I've known it practically all my life."

"That's why you like your friend Simon, isn't it?" she smiled.

He felt it was an unfair retort.

"All right. You take me and show me the pictures you like."

The position was reversed. It was not he, as he had expected, who was leading the way and with such information as would add interest to the respective canvases, sympathetically drawing her attention to the great masterpieces he had always cared for; but it was

222

she who was conducting him. Very well. He was quite ready to put himself in her hands and see what it was all about.

"Of course," he said to himself, "she's Russian. One has to make allowances for that."

They trudged past acres of canvas, through one room after another, for Lydia had some difficulty in finding her way; but finally she stopped him in front of a small picture that you might easily have missed if you had not been looking for it.

"Chardin," he said. "Yes, I've seen that before."

"But have you ever looked at it?"

"Oh, yes. Chardin wasn't half a bad painter in his way. My mother thinks a lot of him. I've always rather liked his still lifes myself."

"Is that all it means to you? It breaks my heart."

"That?" cried Charley with astonishment. "A loaf of bread and a flagon of wine? Of course it's very well painted."

"Yes, you're right; it's very well painted; it's painted with pity and love. It's not only a loaf of bread and a flagon of wine; it's the bread of life and the blood of Christ, but not held back from those who starve and thirst for them and doled out by priests on stated occasions; it's the daily fare of suffering men and women. It's so humble, so natural, so friendly; it's the bread and wine of the poor who ask no more than that they should be left in peace, allowed to work and eat their simple food in freedom. It's the cry of the despised and rejected. It tells you that whatever their sins men at heart are good. That loaf of bread and that flagon of wine are symbols of the joys and sorrows of the meek and lowly. They ask for your mercy and your affection; they tell you that they're of the same flesh and blood as you. They tell you that life is short and hard and the grave is cold and lonely. It's not only a loaf of bread and a flagon of wine; it's the mystery of man's lot on earth, his craving for a little friendship and a little love, the humility of his resignation when he sees that even they must be denied him."

Lydia's voice was tremulous and now the tears flowed from her eyes. She brushed them away impatiently.

"And isn't it wonderful that with those simple objects, with his painter's exquisite sensibility, moved by the charity in his heart, that funny, dear old man should have made something so beautiful that it breaks you? It was as though, unconsciously perhaps, hardly knowing what he was doing, he wanted to show you that if you only have enough love, if you only have enough sympathy, out of pain and distress and unkindness, out of all the evil of the world, you can create beauty."

She was silent and for long stood looking at the little picture. Charley looked at it too, but with perplexity. It was a very good picture; he hadn't really given it more than a glance before, and he was glad Lydia had drawn his attention to it; in some odd way it was rather moving; but of course he could never have seen in it all she saw. Strange, unstable woman! It was rather embarrassing that she should cry in a public gallery; they did put you in an awkward position, these Russians; but who would have thought a picture could affect anyone like that? He remembered his mother's story of how a student friend of his grandfather's had fainted when he first saw the Odalisque of Ingres; but that was away back in the nineteenth century, they were very romantic and emotional in those days. Lydia

turned to him with a sunny smile on her lips. It disconcerted him to see with what suddenness she could go from tears to laughter.

"Shall we go now?" she said.

"But don't you want to see any more pictures?"

"Why? I've seen one. I feel happy and peaceful. What could I get if I saw another?"

"Oh, all right."

It seemed a very odd way of doing a picture gallery. After all, they hadn't looked at the Watteaus or the Fragonards. His mother was bound to ask him if he'd seen the Embarkation for Cythera. Someone had told her they'd cleaned it and she'd want to know how the colours had come out.

They did a little shopping and then lunched at a restaurant on the quay on the other side of the river and Lydia, as usual, ate with a very good appetite. She liked the crowd that surrounded them and the traffic that passed noisily in the roadway. She was in a good humour. It was as though the violent emotion from which she had suffered had rinsed her spirit clean, and she talked of trivial things with a pleasant cheerfulness. But Charley was thoughtful. He did not find it so easy to dismiss the disquietude that affected him. She did not usually notice his moods, but the trouble of his mind was so clearly reflected on his face that at last she could not but be struck by it.

"Why are you so silent?" she asked him, with a kindly, sympathetic smile.

"I was thinking. You see, I've been interested in art all my life. My parents are very artistic, I mean some people might even say they were rather highbrow, and they were always keen on my sister and me having a real appreciation of art; and I think we have. It rather worries me to think that with all the pains I've taken, and the advantages I've had, I don't seem really to know so much about it as you do."

"But I know nothing about art," she laughed.

"But you do seem to feel about it very strongly, and I suppose art is really a matter of feeling. It's not as though I didn't like pictures. I get an enormous kick out of them."

"You mustn't be worried. It's very natural that you should look at pictures differently from me. You're young and healthy, happy and prosperous. You're not stupid. They're a pleasure to you among a lot of other pleasures. It gives you a feeling of warmth and satisfaction to look at them. To walk through a gallery is a very agreeable way of passing an idle hour. What more can you want? But you see, I've always been poor, often hungry, and sometimes terribly lonely. They've been riches to me, food and drink and company. When I was working and my employer had nagged me to distraction I used to slip into the Louvre at the luncheon hour and her scolding didn't matter any more. And when my mother died and I had nobody left, it comforted me. During those long months when Robert was in prison before the trial and I was pregnant, I think I should have gone mad and killed myself if it hadn't been that I could go there, where nobody knew me and nobody stared at me, and be alone with my friends. It was rest and peace. It gave me courage. It wasn't so much the great well-known masterpieces that helped me, it was the smaller, shyer pictures that no one noticed, and I felt they were pleased that I looked at them. I felt that nothing really mattered so very much, because everything passed. Patience! Patience! That's what I learnt there. And I felt that above all the horror and misery and cruelty of the world, there was something that helped you to bear it, something that was greater and more important than all that, the spirit of man and the beauty he created. Is it really strange that that little picture I showed you this morning should mean so much to me?"

To make the most of the fine weather they walked up the busy Boulevard St. Michel and when they got to the top turned into the gardens of the Luxembourg. They sat down and, talking little, idly watched the nurses, no longer, alas, wearing the long satin streamers of a generation ago, trundling prams, the old ladies in black who walked with sober gait in charge of little children, and the elderly gentlemen, with thick scarves up to their noses, who paced up and down immersed in thought; with friendly hearts they looked at the long-legged boys and girls who ran about playing games, and when a pair of young students passed wondered what it was they so earnestly discussed. It seemed not a public park, but a private garden for the people on the left bank, and the scene had a moving intimacy. But the chilly rays of the waning sun gave it withal a certain melancholy, for within the iron grille that separated it from the bustle of the great city, the garden had a singular air of unreality, and you had a feeling that those old people who trod the gravel paths those children whose cries made a cheerful hubbub, were ghosts taking phantom walks or playing phantom games, who at dusk would dissolve, like the smoke of a cigarette, into the oncoming darkness. It was growing very cold, and Charley and Lydia wandered back, silent friendly companions, to the hotel.

When they got to their room Lydia took out of her suit-case a thin sheaf of piano pieces.

"I brought some of the things Robert used to play. I play so badly and we haven't got a piano at Alexey's. D'you think you could play them?"

Charley looked at the music. It was Russian. Some of the pieces were familiar to him.

"I think so," he said.

"There's a piano downstairs and there'll be nobody in the salon now. Let's go down."

The piano badly wanted tuning. It was an upright. The keyboard was yellow with age and because it was seldom played on the notes were stiff. There was a long music stool and Lydia sat down by Charley's side. He put on the rack a piece by Scriabin that he knew and after a few resounding chords to try the instrument began to play. Lydia followed the score and turned the pages for him. Charley had had as good masters as could be found in London, and he had worked hard. He had played at concerts at school and afterwards at Cambridge, so that he had acquired confidence. He had a light, pleasant touch. He enjoyed playing.

"There," he said when he came to the end of the piece.

He was not displeased with himself. He knew that he had played it according to the composer's intention and with the clear, neat straightforwardness that he liked in piano-playing.

"Play something else," said Lydia.

She chose a piece. It was an arrangement for the piano of folk songs and folk dances by a composer of whom Charley had never heard. It startled him to see the name of Robert Berger written in a firm, bold hand on the cover. Lydia stared at it in silence and then turned the page. He looked at the music he was about to play and wondered what Lydia was thinking now.

She must have sat by Robert's side just as she was sitting by his. Why did she want to torture herself by making him play those pieces that must recall to her bitter memories of her short happiness and the misery that followed it?

"Well, begin."

He played well at sight and the music was not difficult. He thought he acquitted himself of his task without discredit. Having struck the last chord he waited for a word of praise.

"You played it very nicely," said Lydia, "but where does Russia come in?"

"What exactly d'you mean by that?" he asked, somewhat affronted.

"You play it as if it was about a Sunday afternoon in London with people in their best clothes walking around those great empty squares and wishing it was time for tea. But that's not what it is at all. It's the old, old song of peasants who lament the shortness and the hardness of their life, it's the wide fields of golden corn and the labour of gathering in the harvest, it's the great forest of beech-trees, and the nostalgia of the workers for an age when peace and plenty reigned on the earth, and it's the wild dance that for a brief period brings them forgetfulness of their lot."

"Well, you play it better."

"I can't play," she answered, but she edged him along the bench and took his seat.

He listened. She played badly, but for all that got something out of the music that he hadn't seen in it. She managed, though at a price, to bring out the tumult of its emotion and the bitterness of its melancholy; and she infused the dance rhythms with a barbaric vitality that stirred the blood. But Charley was put out.

"I must confess I don't see why you should think you get the Russian atmosphere better by playing false notes and keeping your foot firmly on the loud pedal," he said acidly, when she finished.

She burst out laughing and flinging both her arms round his neck kissed him on the cheeks.

"You are a sweet," she cried.

"It's very nice of you to say so," he answered coldly, disengaging himself.

"Have I offended you?"

"Not at all."

She shook her head and smiled at him with soft tenderness.

"You play very well and your technique is excellent, but it's no good thinking you can play Russian music; you can't. Play me some Schumann. I'm sure you can."

"No, I'm not going to play any more."

"If you're angry with me, why don't you hit me?"

Charley couldn't help chuckling.

"You fool. It never occurred to me. Besides, I'm not angry."

"You're so big and strong and handsome, I forget that you're only a young boy." She sighed. "And you're so unprepared for life. Sometimes when I look at you I get such a pang."

"Now don't get all Russian and emotional."

"Be nice to me and play some Schumann."

When Lydia liked she could be very persuasive. With a diffident smile Charley resumed his seat. Schumann, in point of fact, was the composer he liked best and he knew a great deal by heart. He played to her for an hour, and whenever he wanted to stop she urged him to go on. The young woman at the cashier's desk was curious to see who was playing the piano and peeped in. When she went back to her counter she murmured to the porter with an arch and meaning smile:

"The turtle doves are having a good time."

When at last Charley stopped, Lydia gave a little sigh of contentment.

"I knew that was the music to suit you. It's like you, healthy and comfortable and wholesome. There's fresh air in it and sunshine and the delicious scent of pine-trees. It's done me good to listen to it and it's done me good to be with you. Your mother must love you very much."

"Oh, come off it."

"Why are you so good to me? I'm tiresome, dull and exasperating. You don't even like me very much, do you?"

Charley considered this for a moment.

"Well, I don't very much, to tell you the truth."

She laughed.

"Then why do you bother about me? Why don't you just turn me out into the street?"

"I can't imagine."

"Shall I tell you? Goodness. Just pure, simple, stupid goodness."

"Go to hell."

They dined in the Quarter. It had not escaped Charley's notice that Lydia took no interest in him as an individual. She accepted him as you might accept a person with whom you find yourself on a ship for a few days and so forced to a certain intimacy, but it does not matter to you where he came from and what sort of a man he is; he emerged from non-existence when he stepped on board and will return to it when, on reaching port, you part company with him. Charley was modest enough not to be piqued by this, for he could not but realize that her own troubles and perplexities were so great that they must absorb her attention; and he was not a little surprised now when she led him to talk about himself. He told her of his artistic inclinations and of the wish he had so long harboured to be an artist, and she approved his common sense which in the end had persuaded him to prefer the assured life of a business man. He had never seen her more cheerful and more human. Knowing English domestic life only through Dickens, Thackeray and H. G. Wells, she was curious to hear how existence was pursued in those prosperous, sober houses in Bayswater that she knew but from their outside. She asked him about his home and his family. These were subjects on which he was always glad to talk. He spoke of his father and mother with a faintly mocking irony which Lydia saw well enough he assumed only to conceal the loving admiration with which he regarded them. Without knowing it he drew a very pleasant picture of an affectionate, happy family who lived unpretentiously in circumstances of moderate affluence at peace with themselves and the world and undisturbed by any fear that anything might happen to affect their security. The life he described lacked neither grace nor dignity; it was healthy and normal, and through its intellectual interests not entirely material; the persons who led it were simple and honest, neither ambitious nor envious, prepared to do their duty by the state and by their neighbours according to their lights; and there was in them neither harm nor malice. If Lydia saw how much of their good nature, their kindliness, their not unpleasing self-complacency depended on the long-established and well-ordered prosperity of the country that had given them birth; if she had an inkling that, like children building castles on the sea sand, they might at any moment be swept away by a tidal wave, she allowed no sign of it to appear on her face.

"How lucky you English are," she said.

But Charley was a trifle surprised at the impression his own words made on him. In the course of his recital he had for the first time seen himself from the standpoint of an observer. Until now, like an actor who says his lines, but never having seen the play from the front, has but a vague idea of what it is all about, he had played his part without asking himself whether it had any meaning. It would be too much to say that it made him uneasy, it slightly perplexed him, to realize that while they were all, his father, his mother, his sister, himself, busy from morning till night, so that the days were not long enough for what they wanted to do; yet when you came to look upon the life they led from one year's end to another it gave you an uncomfortable feeling that they, none of them, did anything at all. It was like one of those comedies where the sets are good and the clothes pretty, where the dialogue is clever and the acting competent, so that you pass an agreeable evening, but a week later cannot remember a thing about it.

When they had finished dinner they took a taxi to a cinema on the other side of the river. It was a film of the Marx brothers and they rocked with laughter at the extravagant humour of the marvellous clowns; but they laughed not only at Groucho's wise-cracks and at Harpo's comic quandaries, they laughed at one another's laughter. The picture finished at midnight, but Charley was too excited to go quietly to bed and he asked Lydia if she would come with him to some place where they could dance.

"Where would you like to go?" asked Lydia. "Montmartre?"

"Wherever you like as long as it's gay." And then, remembering his parents' constant, but seldom achieved, desire when they came to Paris: "Where there aren't a lot of English people."

Lydia gave him the slightly mischievous smile that he had seen on her lips once or twice before. It surprised him, but at the same time was sympathetic to him. It surprised him because it went so strangely with what he thought he knew of her character; and it was sympathetic to him because it suggested that, for all her tragic history, there was in her a vein of high spirits and of a rather pleasing, teasing malice.

"I'll take you somewhere. It won't be gay, but it may be interesting. There's a Russian woman who sings there."

They drove a long way, and when they stopped Charley saw that they were on the quay. The twin towers of Notre-Dame were distinct against the frosty, starry night. They walked a few steps up a dark street and then went through a narrow door; they descended a flight of stairs and Charley, to his astonishment, found himself in a large cellar with stone walls; from these jutted out wooden tables large enough to accommodate ten or twelve persons, and there were wooden benches on each side of them. The heat was stifling and the air gray with smoke. In the space left by the tables a dense throng was dancing to a melancholy tune. A slatternly waiter in shirt-sleeves found them two places and took their order. People sitting here and there looked at them curiously and whispered to one another; and indeed Charley in his well-cut English blue serge, Lydia in her black silk and her smart hat with the feather in it, contrasted violently with the rest of the company. The men wore neither collars nor ties, and they danced with their caps on, the end of a cigarette stuck to their lips. The women were bare-headed and extravagantly painted.

"They look pretty tough," said Charley.

"They are. Most of them have been in jug and those that haven't should be. If there's a row and they start throwing glasses or pulling knives, just stand against the wall and don't move."

"I don't think they much like the look of us," said Charley. "We seem to be attracting a good deal of attention."

"They think we're sight-seers and that always puts their backs up. But it'll be all right. I know the patron."

When the waiter brought the two beers they had ordered Lydia asked him to get the landlord along. In a moment he came, a big fellow with the naked look of a fat priest, and immediately recognized Lydia. He gave Charley a shrewd, suspicious stare, but when Lydia introduced him as a friend of hers, shook hands with him warmly and said he was glad to see him. He sat down and for a few minutes talked with Lydia in an undertone. Charley noticed that their neighbours watched the scene and he caught one man giving another a wink. They were evidently satisfied that it was all right. The dance came to an end and the other occupants of the table at which they sat came back. They gave the strangers hostile looks, but the patron explained that they were friends, whereupon one of the party, a sinister-looking chap, with the scar of a razor wound on his face, insisted on offering them a glass of wine. Soon they were all talking merrily together. They were plainly eager to make the young Englishman at home, and a man sitting by his side explained to him that though the company looked a bit rough they were all good fellows with their hearts in the right place. He was a little drunk. Charley, having got over his first uneasiness, began to enjoy himself.

Presently the saxophone player got up and advanced his chair. The Russian singer of whom Lydia had spoken came forward with a guitar in her hand and sat down. There was a burst of applause.

"C'est La Marishka," said Charley's drunken friend, "there's no one like her. She was the mistress of one of the commissars, but Stalin had him shot, and if she hadn't managed to get out of Russia he'd have shot her too."

A woman on the other side of the table overheard him.

"What nonsense you're telling him, Loulou," she cried. "La Marishka was the mistress of a grand duke before the revolution, everyone knows that, and she had diamonds worth millions, but the Bolsheviks took everything from her. She escaped disguised as a peasant."

La Marishka was a woman of forty, haggard and sombre, with gaunt, masculine features, a brown skin, and enormous, blazing eyes under black, heavy, arching brows. In a raucous voice, at the top of her lungs, she sang a wild, joyless song, and though Charley could not understand the Russian words a cold feeling ran down his spine. She was loudly applauded. Then she sang a sentimental ballad in French, the lament of a girl for her lover who was to be executed next morning, which roused her audience to frenzy. She finished, for the time being, with another Russian song, lively this time, and her face lost its tragic cast; it took on a look of rude and brutal gaiety, and her voice, deep and harsh, acquired a rollicking quality; your blood was stirred and you could not but exult, but at the same time you were moved, for below the bacchanalian merriment was the desolation of futile tears. Charley looked at Lydia and caught her mocking glance. He smiled good-naturedly. That grim woman got something out of the music which he was conscious now was beyond his reach. Another burst of applause greeted the end of the number, but La Marishka, as though she did not hear it, without a sign of acknowledgement, rose from her chair and came over to Lydia. The two women began to talk in Russian. Lydia turned to Charley.

"She'll have a glass of champagne if you'll offer it to her."

"Of course."

He signalled to a waiter and ordered a bottle; then, with a glance at the half-dozen people sitting at the table, changed his order.

"Two bottles and some glasses. Perhaps these gentlemen and ladies will allow me to offer them a glass too."

There was a murmur of polite acceptance. The wine was brought and Charley filled a number of glasses and passed them down the table. There was a great deal of health-drinking and clinking of glasses together.

"Vive l'Entente Cordiale."

"A nos alliés."

They all got very friendly and merry. Charley was having a grand time. But he had come to dance, and when the orchestra began once more to play he pulled Lydia to her feet. The floor was soon crowded and he noticed that a lot of curious eyes were fixed upon her; he guessed that it had spread through the company who she was; it made her to those bullies and their women, somewhat to Charley's embarrassment, an object of interest, but she did not seem even to be aware that anyone looked at her.

Presently the patron touched her on the shoulder.

"I have a word to say to you," he muttered.

Lydia released herself from Charley's arms and going to one side with the fat landlord listened to what he said. Charley could see that she was startled. He was evidently trying to point someone out to her, for Charley saw her craning her neck; but with the thick mass of dancers in the way she could see nothing, and in a moment she followed the patron to the other end of the long cellar. She seemed to have forgotten Charley. Somewhat piqued, he went back to his table. Two couples were sitting there comfortably enjoying his champagne, and they greeted him heartily. They were all very familiar now and they asked him what he had done with his little friend. He told them what had happened. One of the men was a short thick-set fellow with a red face and a magnificent moustache. His shirt open at the neck showed his hairy chest, and his arms, for he had taken off his coat in that stifling heat and turned up his shirt-sleeves, were profusely tattooed. He was with a girl who might have been twenty years younger than he. She had very sleek black hair, parted in the middle, with a bun on her neck, a face dead-white with powder, scarlet lips and eyes heavy with mascara. The man nudged her with his elbow.

"Now then, why don't you dance with the Englishman? You've drunk his bubbly, haven't you?"

"I don't mind," she said.

She danced clingingly. She smelt strongly of scent, but not so strongly as to disguise the fact that she had eaten at dinner a dish highly flavoured with garlic. She smiled alluringly at Charley.

"He must be rotten with vice, this pretty little Englishman," she gurgled, with a squirm of a lithe body in her black, but dusty, velvet gown.

"Why do you say that?" he smiled.

"To be with the wife of Berger, what's that if it isn't vice?"

"She's my sister," said Charley gaily.

She thought this such a good joke that when the band stopped and they went back to the table she repeated it to the assembled company. They all thought it very funny, and the thick-set man with the hairy chest slapped him on the back.

"Farceur, va!"

Charley was not displeased to be looked upon as a humorist. It was nice to be a success. He realized that as the lover of a notorious murderer's wife he was something of a personage there. They urged him to come again.

"But come alone next time," said the girl he had just danced with.

"We'll find you a girl. What d'you want to get mixed up with one of the Russians for? The wine of the country, that's what you want."

Charley ordered another bottle of champagne. He was far from tight, but he was merry. He was seeing life with a vengeance. When Lydia came back he was talking and laughing with his new friends as if he had known them all his life. He danced the next dance with her. He noticed that she was not keeping step with him and he gave her a little shake.

"You're not attending."

She laughed.

"I'm sorry. I'm tired. Let's go."

"Has something happened to upset you?"

239

"No. It's getting very late and the heat's awful."

Having warmly shaken hands with their new friends, they left and got into a taxi. Lydia sank back exhausted. He was feeling happy and affectionate and he took her hand and held it. They drove in silence.

They went to bed, and in a few minutes Charley became aware from her regular breathing that Lydia had fallen asleep. But he was too excited to sleep. The evening had amused him and he was keenly alert. He thought it all over for a while and chuckled at the grand story he would make of it when he got home. He turned on the light to read. But he could not give his attention to the poems of Blake just then. Disordered notions flitted across his mind. He switched off the light and presently fell into a light doze, but in a little while awoke. He was tingling with desire. He heard the quiet breathing of the sleeping woman in the bed by his side and a peculiar sensation stirred his heart. Except on that first evening at the Sérail no feeling for Lydia had touched him except pity and kindliness. Sexually she did not in the least attract him. After seeing her for several days all day long he did not even think her pretty; he did not like the squareness of her face, her high cheek-bones, and the way her pale eyes were set flat in their orbits; sometimes, indeed, he thought her really plain. Notwithstanding the life she had adopted—for what strange, unnatural reason—she gave him a sense of such deadly respectability that it choked him off. And then her indifference to sexual congress was chilling. She looked with contempt and loathing on the men who for money sought their pleasure of her. The passionate love she bore for Robert gave her an aloofness from all human affections that killed desire. But besides all that Charley didn't think he liked her very much for herself; she was sometimes sullen, almost always indifferent; she took whatever he did for her as her right; it was all very well to say that she asked for nothing, it would have been graceful if she had shown, not gratitude, but a glimmering recognition of the fact that he was trying to do his best for her. Charley had an uneasy fear that she was making a mug of him; if what Simon said was true and she was making money at the brothel in order to help Robert to escape, she was nothing but a callous liar; he flushed hotly when it occurred to him that she was laughing behind his back at his simplicity. No, he didn't admire her, and the more he thought of her the less he thought he liked her. And yet at that moment he was so breathless with desire of her that he felt he would choke. He thought of her not as he saw her every day, rather drab, like a teacher at a Sunday school, but as he had first seen her in those baggy Turkish trousers and the blue turban spangled with little stars, her cheeks painted and her lashes black with mascara; he thought of her slender waist, her clear, soft, honey-coloured skin, and her small firm breasts with their rosy nipples. He tossed on his bed. His desire now was uncontrollable. It was anguish. After all, it wasn't fair; he was young and strong and normal; why shouldn't he have a bit of fun when he had the chance? She was there for that, she'd said so herself. What did it matter if she thought him a dirty swine? He'd done pretty well by her, he deserved something in return. The faint sound of her quiet breathing was strangely exciting and it quickened his own. He thought of the feel of her soft lips when he pressed his mouth to hers and the feel of her little breasts when he took them in his hands; he thought of the feel of her lissom body in his arms and the feel of his long legs lying against hers. He put on the light, thinking it might wake her, and got out of bed. He leaned over her. She lay on her back, her hands crossed over her breast like a stone figure on a tomb; tears were running out of her closed eyes and her mouth was distorted with grief. She was crying in her sleep. She looked like a child, lying there, and her face had a child's look of hopeless misery, for a child does not know that sorrow, like all other things, will pass. Charley gave a gasp. The unhappiness of that sleeping woman was intolerable to see, and all his passion, all his desire, were extinguished by the pity that overcame him. She had been gay during the day, easy to talk to and companionable, and it had seemed to him that she was free, at least for a while, from the pain that, he was conscious, lurked always in the depths of her being; but in sleep it had returned to her and he knew only too well what unhappy dreams distraught her. He gave a deep sigh.

But he felt more disinclined for sleep than ever, and he could not bear the thought of getting into bed again. He turned the shade down so that the light should not disturb Lydia, and going to the table filled his pipe and lit it. He drew the heavy curtain that was over the window and sitting down looked out into the court. It was in darkness but for one lighted window, and this had a sinister look. He wondered whether someone lay ill in that room or, simply sleepless like himself, brooded over the perplexity of life. Or perhaps some man had brought a woman in, and their lust appeased, they lay contented in one another's arms. Charley smoked. He felt dull and flat. He did not think of anything in particular. At last he went back to bed and fell asleep.

IX

CHARLEY was awakened by the maid bringing in the morning coffee. For a moment he forgot the events of the previous night.

"Oh, I was sleeping so soundly," he said, rubbing his eyes.

"I'm sorry, but it's half-past ten and I have an engagement at eleven-thirty."

"It doesn't matter. It's my last day in Paris and it would be silly to waste it in sleep."

The maid had brought the two breakfasts on one tray and Lydia told her to give it to Charley. She put on a dressing-gown and sat down at the end of his bed, leaning against the foot. She poured out a cup of coffee, cut a roll in two and buttered it for him.

"I've been watching you sleep," she said. "It's nice; you sleep like an animal or a child, so deep, so quiet, it rests one just to look at you."

Then he remembered.

"I'm afraid you didn't have a very good night."

"Oh, yes, I did. I slept like a top. I was tired out, you know. That's one of the things I'm most grateful to you for, I've had such wonderful nights. I dream terribly. But since I've been here I haven't dreamt once; I've slept quite peacefully. And I who thought I should never sleep like that again."

He knew that she had been dreaming that night and he knew what her dreams were about. She had forgotten them. He forbore to look at her. It gave him a grim, horrible, and rather uncanny sensation to think that a vivid, lacerating life could go on when one was sunk in unconsciousness, a life so real that it could cause tears to stream down the face and twist the mouth in woe, and yet when the sleeper woke left no recollection behind. An uncomfortable thought crossed his mind. He could not quite make it explicit, but had he been able to, he would perhaps have asked himself:

"Who are we really? What do we know about ourselves? And that other life of ours, is that less real than this one?"

It was all very strange and complicated. It looked as though nothing were quite so simple as it seemed; it looked as though the people we thought we knew best carried secrets that they didn't even know themselves. Charley had a sudden inkling that human beings were infinitely mysterious. The fact was that you knew nothing about anybody.

"What's this engagement you've got?" he asked, more for the sake of saying something than because he wanted to know.

Lydia lit a cigarette before she answered.

"Marcel, the fat man who runs the place we were at last night, introduced me to two men there and I've made an appointment to meet them at the Palette this morning. We couldn't talk in all that crowd."

"Oh!"

He was too discreet to ask who they were.

"Marcel's in touch with Cayenne and St. Laurent. He often gets news. That's why I wanted to go there. They landed at St. Nazaire last week."

"Who? The two men? Are they escaped convicts?"

"No. They've served their sentence. They got their passage paid by the Salvation Army. They knew Robert." She hesitated a moment. "If you want to, you

244

can come with me. They've got no money. They'd be grateful if you gave them a little."

"All right. Yes, I'd like to come."

"They seem very decent fellows. One of them doesn't look more than thirty now. Marcel told me he was a cook and he was sent out for killing another man in the kitchen of the restaurant where he worked. I don't know what the other had done. You'd better go and have your bath." She went over to the dressing-table and looked at herself in the glass. "Funny, I wonder why my eyelids are swollen. To look at me you'd think I'd been crying, and you know I haven't, don't you?"

"Perhaps it was that smoky atmosphere last night. By George! you could have cut it with a knife."

"I'll ring down for some ice. They'll be all right after we've been out in the air for five minutes."

The Palette was empty when they got there. Late breakfasters had had their coffee and gone, and it was too early for anyone to have come in for an apéritif before luncheon. They sat in a corner, near the window, so that they could look out into the street. They waited for several minutes.

"There they are," said Lydia.

Charley looked out and saw two men walking past. They glanced in, hesitated a moment and strolled on, then came back; Lydia gave them a smile, but they took no notice of her; they stood still, looking up and down the street, and then doubtfully at the café. It looked as though they couldn't make up their minds to enter. Their manner was timid and furtive. They said a few words to one another and the younger of the two gave a hasty anxious glance behind him. The other seemed on a sudden to force himself to a decision and

walked towards the door. His friend followed quickly.
Lydia gave them a wave and a smile when they came
in. They still took no notice. They looked round
stealthily, as though to assure themselves that they
were safe, and then, the first with averted eyes, the
other fixing the ground, came up. Lydia shook hands
with them and introduced Charley. They evidently
had expected her to be alone and his presence disconcerted them. They gave him a look of suspicion.
Lydia explained that he was an Englishman, a friend
who was spending a few days in Paris. Charley, a
smile on his lips which he sought to make cordial,
stretched out his hand; they took it, one after the other,
and gave it a limp pressure. They seemed to have
nothing to say. Lydia bade them sit down and asked
them what they would have.

"A cup of coffee."

"You'll have something to eat?"

The elder one gave the other a faint smile.

"A cake, if there is one. The boy has a sweet tooth,
and over there, from where we come, there wasn't
much in that line."

The man who spoke was a little under the middle
height. He might have been forty. The other was two
or three inches taller and perhaps ten years younger.
Both were very thin. They both wore collars and ties
and thick suits, one of a gray-and-white check and the
other dark green, but the suits were ill-cut and sat
loosely on them. They did not look at ease in them.
The elder one, sturdy though short, had a well-knit
figure; his sallow, colourless face was much lined. He
had an air of determination. The other's face was as
sallow and colourless, but his skin, drawn tightly over
the bones, was smooth and unlined; he looked very

ill. There was another trait they shared; the eyes of both seemed preternaturally large, and when they turned them on you they did not appear to look at you, but beyond, with a demented stare, as though they were gazing at something that filled them with horror. It was very painful. At first they were shy, and since Charley was shy too, though he tried to show his friendliness by offering them cigarettes, while Lydia, seeming to find no need for words, contented herself with looking at them, they sat in silence. But she looked at them with such tender concern that the silence was not embarrassing. The waiter brought them coffee and a dish of cakes. The elder man toyed with one of them, but the other ate greedily, and as he ate he gave his friend now and then little touching looks of surprised delight.

"The first thing we did when we got out by ourselves in Paris was to go to a confectioner's, and the boy ate six chocolate éclairs one after the other. But he paid for it."

"Yes," said the other seriously. "When we got out into the street I was sick. You see, my stomach wasn't used to it. But it was worth it."

"Did you eat very badly over there?"

The elder man shrugged his shoulders.

"Beef three hundred and sixty-five days of the year. One doesn't notice it after a time. And then, if you behave yourself you get cheese and a little wine. And it's better to behave yourself. Of course it's worse when you've done your sentence and you're freed. When you're in prison you get board and lodging, but when you're free you have to shift for yourself."

"My friend doesn't know," said Lydia. "Explain to him. They don't have the same system in England."

"It's like this. You're sentenced to a term of imprisonment, eight, ten, fifteen, twenty years, and when you've done it you're a libéré. You have to stay in the colony the same number of years that you were sentenced to. It's hard to get work. The libérés have a bad name and people won't employ them. It's true that you can get a plot of land and cultivate it, but it's not everyone who can do that. After being in prison for years, taking orders from the warders and half the time doing nothing, you've lost your initiative; and then there's malaria and hook-worm; you've lost your energy. Most of them get work only when a ship comes in to harbour and they can earn a little by unloading the cargo. There's nothing much for the libéré but to sleep in the market, drink rafia when he gets the chance, and starve. I was lucky. You see, I'm an electrician by trade, and a good one; I know my job as well as anyone, so they needed me. I didn't do so badly."

"How long was your sentence?" asked Lydia.

"Only eight years."

"And what did you do?"

He slightly shrugged his shoulders and gave Lydia a deprecating smile.

"Folly of youth. One's young, one gets into bad company, one drinks too much and then one day something happens and one has to pay for it all one's life. I was twenty-four when I went out and I'm forty now. I've spent my best years in that hell."

"He could have got away before," said the other, "but he wouldn't."

"You mean you could have escaped?" said Lydia.

Charley gave her a quick, searching glance but her face told him nothing.

"Escape? No, that's a mug's game. One can always

248

escape, but there are few who get away. Where can you go? Into the bush? Fever, wild animals, starvation, and the natives who'll take you for the sake of the reward. A good many try it. You see, they get so fed up with the monotony, the food, the orders, the sight of all the rest of the prisoners, they think anything's better, but they can't stick it out; if they don't die of illness or starvation, they're captured or give themselves up; and then it's two years' solitary confinement, or more, and you have to be a hefty chap if that doesn't break you. It was easier in the old days when the Dutch were building their railway, you could get across the river and they'd put you to work on it, but now they've finished the railway and they don't want labour any more. They catch you and send you back. But even that had its risks. There was a customs official who used to promise to take you over the river for a certain sum, he had a regular tariff, you'd arrange to meet him at a place in the jungle at night, and when you kept the appointment he just shot you dead and emptied your pockets. They say he did away with more than thirty fellows before he was caught. Some of them get away by sea. Half a dozen club together and get a libéré to buy a rickety boat for them. It's a hard journey, without a compass or anything, and one never knows when a storm will spring up; it's more by luck than good management if they get anywhere. And where can they go? They won't have them in Venezuela any longer and if they land there they're just put in prison and sent back. If they land in Trinidad the authorities keep them for a week, stock them up with provisions, even give them a boat if theirs isn't seaworthy, and then send them off, out into the sea with no place to go to. No, it's silly to try to escape."

"But men do," said Lydia. "There was that doctor, what was his name? They say he's practising somewhere in South America and doing well."

"Yes, if you've got money you can get away sometimes, not if you're on the islands, but if you're at Cayenne or St. Laurent. You can get the skipper of a Brazilian schooner to pick you up at sea, and if he's honest he'll land you somewhere down the coast and you're pretty safe. If he isn't, he takes your money and chucks you overboard. But he'll want twelve thousand francs now, and that means double because the libéré who gets the money in for you takes half as his commission. And then you can't land in Brazil without a penny in your pocket. You've got to have at least thirty thousand francs, and who's got that?"

Lydia asked a question and once more Charley gave her an inquiring look.

"But how can you be sure that the libéré will hand over the money that's sent him?" she said.

"You can't. Sometimes he doesn't, but then he ends with a knife in his back, and he knows very well the authorities aren't going to bother very much if a damned libéré is found dead one morning."

"Your friend said just now you could have got away sooner, but didn't. What did he mean by that?"

The little man gave his shoulders a deprecating shrug.

"I made myself useful. The commandant was a decent chap and he knew I was a good worker and honest. They soon found out they could leave me in a house by myself when they wanted a job done and I wouldn't touch a thing. He got me permission to go back to France when I still had two more years to go of my time as a libéré." He gave his friend a touching smile. "But I didn't like to leave that young scamp.

I knew that without me to look after him he'd get into trouble."

"It's true," said the other. "I owe everything to him."

"He was only a kid when he came out. He had the next bed to mine. He put up a pretty good show in the daytime, but at night he'd cry for his mother. I felt sorry for him. I don't know how it happened, I got an affection for him; he was lost among all those men, poor little chap, and I had to look after him. Some of them were inclined to be nasty to him, one Algerian was always bothering, but I settled his hash and after that they left the boy in peace."

"How did you do that?"

The little man gave a grin so cheerful and roguish that it made him look on a sudden ten years younger.

"Well, you know, in that life a man can only make himself respected if he knows how to use his knife. I ripped him up the belly."

Charley gave a gasp. The man made the statement so naturally that one could hardly believe one had heard right.

"You see, one's shut up in the dormitory from nine till five and the warders don't come in. To tell you the truth, it would be as much as their lives were worth. If in the morning a man's found with a hole in his gizzard, the authorities ask no questions so as they won't be told no lies. So you see, I felt a kind of responsibility for the boy. I had to teach him everything. I've got a good brain and I soon discovered that out there if you want to make it easy for yourself the only thing is to do what you're told and give no trouble. It's not justice that reigns on the earth, it's force, and they've got the force, the authorities; one of these days perhaps we shall have it, we the working men, and then we shall get a bit of our own back on the bourgeois, but till then we've got to obey. That's what I taught him, and I taught him my job too, and now he's almost as good an electrician as I am."

"The only thing now is to find work," said the other. "Work together."

"We've gone through so much together we can't be parted now. You see, he's all I've got. I've got no mother, no wife, no kids. I had, but my mother's dead, and I lost my wife and my kids when I had my trouble. Women are bitches. It's hard for a chap to live without any affection in his life."

"And I, who have I got? It's for life, us two."

There was something very affecting in the friendship that bound those two hapless men together. It gave Charley a sense of exaltation that somewhat embarrassed him; he would have liked to tell them that he thought it brave and beautiful, but he knew he could never bring himself to say anything so unusual. But Lydia had none of his shyness.

"I don't think there are many men who would have stayed in that hell for two long years when they could get away, for the sake of a friend."

The man chuckled.

"You see, over there time is just the opposite of money; there a little money is a great deal and a lot of time is nothing very much. While six sous is a sum that you hoard as if it was a fortune, two years is a period that's hardly worth talking about."

Lydia sighed deeply. It was plain of what she was thinking.

"Berger isn't there for so long, is he?"

"Fifteen years."

There was a silence. One could see that Lydia was making a great effort to control her emotion, but when she spoke there was a break in her voice.

"Did you see him?"

"Yes. I talked to him. We were in hospital together. I went in to have my appendix out, I didn't want to get back to France and have trouble with it here. He'd been working on the road they're making from St. Laurent to Cayenne and he got a bad go of malaria."

"I didn't know. I've had one letter from him, but he said nothing about it."

"Out there everyone has malaria sooner or later. It's not worth making a song and dance about. He's lucky to have got it so soon. The chief medical officer took a fancy to him, he's an educated man, Berger, and there aren't many of them. They were going to apply to get him transferred to the hospital service when he recovered. He'll be all right there."

"Marcel told me last night that he'd given you a message for me."

"Yes, he gave me an address." He took a bundle of papers out of his pocket and gave Lydia a scrap on which something was written. "If you can send any money, send it there. But remember that he'll only get half what you send."

Lydia took the bit of paper, looked at it, and put it in her bag.

"Anything else?"

"Yes. He said you weren't to worry. He said it wasn't so bad as it might be, and he was finding his feet and he'd make out all right. And that's true, you know. He's no fool. He won't make many mistakes. He's a chap who'll make the best of a bad job. You'll see, he'll be happy enough."

"How can he be happy?"

"It's funny what one can get used to. He's a bit of a wag, isn't he? He used to make us laugh at some of the things he said. He's a rare one for seeing the funny side of things, there's no mistake about that."

Lydia was very pale. She looked down in silence. The elder man turned to his friend.

"What was that funny thing I told you he'd said about that cove in the hospital who cut his blasted throat?"

"Oh, I remember. Now what was it? It's clean gone out of my mind, but I know it made me laugh my head off."

A long silence fell. There seemed nothing more to say. Lydia was pensive; and the two men sat limp on their chairs, their eyes vacant, like the mechanical dolls they sell on the Boulevard Montparnasse which gyrate, rocking, round and round and then on a sudden stop dead. Lydia sighed.

"I think that's about all," she said. "Thank you for coming. I hope you'll get the job you're looking for."

"The Salvation Army are doing what they can for us. I expect something will turn up."

Charley fished his note-case out of his pocket.

"I don't suppose you're very flush. I'd like to give you something to help you along till you find work."

"It would be useful," the man smiled pleasantly. "The Army doesn't do much but give one board and lodging."

Charley handed them five hundred francs.

"Give it to the kid to take care of. He's got the saving disposition of the peasant he is, he sweats blood when he has to spend money, and he can make five francs go farther than any old woman in the world."

They went out of the café, the four of them, and shook hands. During the hour they had spent together the two men had lost their shyness, but when they got out into the street it seized them again. They seemed to shrink as though they desired to make themselves as inconspicuous as possible, and looked furtively to right and left as if afraid that someone would pounce upon them. They walked off side by side, with bent heads, and after another quick glance backward slunk round the nearest corner.

"I suppose it's only prejudice on my part," said Charley, "but I'm bound to say that I didn't feel very much at my ease in that company."

Lydia made no reply. They walked along the boulevard in silence; they lunched in silence. Lydia was immersed in thought the nature of which he could guess and he felt that any attempt on his part at small talk would be unwelcome. Besides, he had thoughts of his own to occupy him. The conversation they had had with the two convicts, the questions Lydia asked, had revived the suspicion which Simon had sown in his mind and which, though he had tried to put it aside, had since then lurked in his consciousness like the musty smell of a long closed room which no opening of windows can quite dispel. It worried him, not so much because he minded being made a fool of, as because he did not want to think that Lydia was a liar and a hypocrite.

"I'm going along to see Simon," he said when they had finished luncheon. "I came over largely to see him and I've hardly had a glimpse of him. I ought at least to go and say good-bye."

"Yes, I suppose you ought."

He also wanted to return to Simon the newspaper

cuttings and the article which he had lent him. He had them in his pocket.

"If you want to spend the afternoon with your Russian friends, I'll drive you there first if you like."

"No, I'll go back to the hotel."

"I don't suppose I shall be back till late. You know what Simon is when he gets talking. Won't you be bored by yourself?"

"I'm not used to so much consideration," she smiled. "No, I shan't be bored. It's not often I have the chance to be alone. To sit in a room by oneself and to know that no one can come in—why, I can't imagine a greater luxury."

They parted and Charley walked to Simon's. He knew that at that hour he stood a good chance of finding him in. Simon opened the door on his ring. He was in pyjamas and a dressing-gown.

"Hulloa! I thought you might breeze along. I didn't have to go out this morning, so I didn't dress!"

He hadn't shaved and he looked as though he hadn't washed either. His long straight hair was in disorder. By the bleak light that came through the north window his restless, angry eyes looked coal-black in his white thin face and there were dark shadows beneath them.

"Sit down," he continued. "I've got a good fire to-day and the studio's warm."

It was, but it was as forlorn, cheerless and unswept as before.

"Is the love affair still going strong?"

"I've just left Lydia."

"You're going back to London to-morrow, aren't you? Don't let her sting you too much. There's no reason why you should help to get her rotten husband out of jug."

Charley took the cuttings from his pocket

"By your article I judged that you had a certain amount of sympathy for him."

"Sympathy, no. I found him interesting just because he was such an unmitigated, cold-blooded, unscrupulous cad. I admired his nerve. In other circumstances he might have been a useful instrument. In a revolution a man like that who'll stick at nothing, who has courage and no scruples, may be invaluable."

"I shouldn't have thought a very reliable instrument."

"Wasn't it Danton who said that in a revolution it's the scum of society, the rogues and criminals, who rise to the surface? It's natural. They're needed for certain work and when they've served their purpose they can be disposed of."

"You seem to have it all cut and dried, old boy," said Charley, with a cheerful grin.

Simon impatiently shrugged his bony shoulders.

"I've studied the French Revolution and the Commune. The Russians did too and they learnt a lot from them, but we've got the advantage now that we can profit by the lessons we've learnt from subsequent events. They made a bad mess of things in Hungary, but they made a pretty good job of it in Russia and they didn't do so badly either in Italy or in Germany. If we've got any sense we ought to be able to emulate their success, but avoid their mistakes. Bela Kun's revolution failed because people were hungry. The rise of the proletariat has made it comparatively simple to make a revolution, but the proletariat must be fed. Organization is needed to see that means of transport are adequate and food supplies abundant. That incidentally is why power, which the proletariat thought to seize by making the revolution, must always elude their grasp and fall into the hands of a small body of intelligent leaders. The people are incapable of governing themselves. The proletariat are slaves and slaves need masters."

"You would hardly describe yourself any longer as a good democrat, I take it," said Charley with a twinkle in his blue eyes.

Simon impatiently dismissed the ironical remark.

"Democracy is moonshine. It's an unrealizable ideal which the propagandist dangles before the masses as you dangle a carrot before a donkey. Those great watchwords of the nineteenth century, liberty, equality, fraternity, are pure hokum. Liberty? The mass of men don't need liberty and don't know what to do with it when they've got it. Their duty and their pleasure is to serve; thus they attain the security which is their deepest want. It's been decided long ago that the only liberty worth anything is the liberty to do right, and right is decided by might. Right is an idea occasioned by public opinion and prescribed by law, but public opinion is created by those who have the power to enforce their point of view, and the only sanction of law is the might behind it. Fraternity? What do you mean by fraternity?"

Charley considered the question for a moment.

"Well, I don't know. I suppose it's a feeling that we're all members of one great family and we're here on earth for so short a time, it's better to make the best of one another."

"Anything else?"

"Well, only that life is a difficult job, and it probably makes it easier for everybody if we're kind and decent to one another. Men have plenty of faults, but there's a lot of good in them. The more you know people the nicer you find they are. That rather suggests that if you give them a chance they'll meet you half way."

"Tosh, my dear boy, tosh. You're a sentimental fool. In the first place it's not true that people improve as you know them better: they don't. That's why one should only have acquaintances and never make friends. An acquaintance shows you only the best of himself, he's considerate and polite, he conceals his defects behind a mask of social convention; but grow so intimate with him that he throws the mask aside, get to know him so well that he doesn't trouble any longer to pretend; then you'll discover a being of such meanness, of such a trivial nature, of such weakness, of such corruption, that you'd be aghast if you didn't realize that that was his nature and it was just as stupid to condemn him as to condemn the wolf because he ravens or the cobra because he strikes. For the essence of man is egoism. Egoism is at once his strength and his weakness. Oh, I've got to know men pretty well during the two years I've spent in the newspaper world. Vain, petty, unscrupulous, avaricious, double-faced and abject, they'll betray one another, not even for their own advantage, but from sheer malice. There's no trick they won't descend to in order to queer a rival's pitch; there's no humiliation they won't accept to obtain a title or an order; and not only politicians; lawyers, doctors, merchants, artists, men of letters. And their craving for publicity; they'll cringe and flatter a two-penny-halfpenny journalist to get a good press. Rich men will hesitate at no shabby dodge to make a few pounds that they have no use for. Honesty, political honesty, commercial honesty—the only thing that counts with them is what they can get away with; the only thing that restrains them is fear. For they're craven.

And the protestations they make, the high-flown hum-bug that falls from their lips, the shameless lies they tell themselves. Oh, believe me, you can't do the work I've been doing since I left Cambridge and preserve many illusions about human nature. Men are vile. Cowards and hypocrites. I loathe them."

Charley looked down. He was a little shy about saying what he wanted to. It sounded rather silly.

"Haven't you any pity for them?"

"Pity? Pity is womanish. Pity is what the beggar entreats of you because he hasn't the guts, the industry and the brains to make a decent living. Pity is the flattery the failure craves so that he may preserve his self-esteem. Pity is the cheap blackmail that the prosperous pay to the down-and-out so that they may enjoy their own prosperity with a better conscience."

Simon drew his dressing-gown angrily round his thin body. Charley recognized it as an old one of his which he had been going to throw away when Simon asked if he could have it; he had laughed and said he would give him a new one, but Simon, saying it was quite good enough for him, had insisted on having it. Charley wondered uncomfortably if he resented the trifling gift. Simon went on:

"Equality? Equality is the greatest nonsense that's ever muddled the intelligence of the human race. As if men were equal or could be equal! They talk of equality of opportunity. Why should men have that when they can't take advantage of it? Men are born unequal; different in character, in vitality, in brain; and no equality of opportunity can offset that. The vast majority are densely stupid. Credulous, shallow, feck-less, why should they be given equality of opportunity with those who have character, intelligence, industry

260

and force? And it's that natural inequality of man that knocks the bottom out of democracy. What a stupid farce it is to govern a country by the counting of millions of empty heads! In the first place they don't know what's good for them and in the second, they haven't the capacity to get the good they want. What does democracy come down to? The persuasive power of slogans invented by wily, self-seeking politicians. A democracy is ruled by words, and the orator seldom has brains, and if he has, he hasn't time to use them, since all his energy has to be given to cajoling the fools on whose votes he depends. Democracy has had a hundred years' trial: theoretically it was always absurd, and now we know that practically it's a wash-out."

"Notwithstanding which you propose, if you can, to get into parliament. You're a very dishonest fellow, my poor Simon."

"In an old-fashioned country like England, which cherishes its established institutions, it would be impossible to gain sufficient power to carry out one's plans except from within those institutions. I don't suppose anyone could gain support in the country and gather round himself an adequate band of followers to effect a coup d'état unless he were a prominent member of one of the great parties in the House of Commons. And since an upheaval can only be effected by means of the people it would have to be the Labour party. Even when the conditions are ripe for revolution the possessing classes still retain enough of their privileges to make it worth their while to make the best of a bad job."

"What conditions have you in mind? Defeat in war and economic distress?"

"Exactly. Even then the possessing classes only

suffer relatively. They put down their cars or close their country houses, thus adding to unemployment, but not greatly inconveniencing themselves. But the people starve. Then they will listen to you when you tell them they have nothing to lose but their chains, and when you dangle before them the bait of other people's property the greed, the envy, which they've had to repress because they had no means of gratifying them, are let loose. With liberty and equality as your watchwords you can lead them to the attack. The history of the last five-and-twenty years shows that they're bound to win. The possessing classes are enervated by their possessions, they're humanitarian and sentimental, they have neither the will nor the courage to defend themselves; their counsels are divided, and when their only chance is in immediate and ruthless action they waste their time in recrimination. But the mob, which is the instrument of the revolutionary leaders, is a thing not of reason but of instinct, it is amenable to hypnotic suggestion and you can rouse it to frenzy by catchwords; it is an entity, and so is indifferent to the death in its ranks of such as fall; it knows neither pity nor mercy. It rejoices in destruction because in destruction it becomes conscious of its own power."

"I suppose you wouldn't deny that that entails the killing of thousands of inoffensive people and the destruction of institutions that have taken hundreds of years to build up."

"There's bound to be destruction in a revolution and there's bound to be killing. Engels said years ago that the possessing classes must be expected to resist suppression by every means in their power. It's a fight to the death. Democracy has attached an absurd importance to human life. Morally man is worthless and it's no loss to suppress him. Biologically he's of no consequence; there's no more reason why it should shock you to kill a man than to swat a fly."

"I begin to see why you were interested in Robert Berger."

"I was interested in him because he killed, not for any sordid motive, not for money, nor jealousy, but to prove himself and affirm his power."

"Of course it remains to be proved that communism is practicable."

"Communism? Who talked of communism? Everyone knows now that communism is a wash-out. It was the dream of impractical idealists who knew nothing of the realities of life. Communism is the lure you offer to the working classes to rouse them to revolt just as the cry of liberty and equality is the slogan with which you fire them to dare. Throughout the history of the world there have always been exploiters and exploited. There always will be. And it's right that it should be so because the great mass of men are made by nature to be slaves; they are unfit to control themselves, and for their own good need masters."

"That's rather a startling assertion."

"It's not mine, old boy," Simon answered ironically. "It's Plato's, but the history of the world since he made it has amply demonstrated its truth. What has been the result of the revolutions we've seen in our own lifetime? The people haven't lost their masters, they've only changed them, and nowhere has authority been wielded with a more iron hand than under communism."

"Then the people are duped?"

"Of course. Why not? They're fools, and they deserve to be. What does it matter? Their gain is substantial. They're not asked to think for themselves any more; they're told what to do, and so long as they're obedient they have the security they've always hankered after. The dictators of our own day have made mistakes and we can learn by their errors. They've forgotten Machiavelli's dictum that you can enslave the people politically if you leave their private lives free. I should give the people the illusion of liberty by allowing them as much personal freedom as is compatible with the safety of the state. I would socialize industry as widely as the idiosyncrasy of the human animal permits and so give men the illusion of equality. And since they would all be brothers under one yoke they would even have the illusion of fraternity. Remember that a dictator can do all sorts of things for the benefit of the people that democracy is prevented from doing because it has to consider vested interests, jealousies and personal ambitions, and so he has an unparalleled opportunity to alleviate the lot of the masses. I went to a great communist meeting here the other day and on banner after banner I read the words Peace, Work and Well-Being. Could any claims be more natural? And yet there man is after a hundred years of democracy still making them. A dictator can satisfy them by a stroke of the pen."

"But by your own admission the people only change their master; they're still exploited; what makes you think that they'll put up with it?"

"Because they'll damned well have to. Under present conditions a dictator with planes to drop bombs and armoured cars to fire machine guns can quell any revolt. The possessing classes could do the same, and no revolution would succeed, but the event has shown that they haven't the nerve; they kill a hundred men, a thousand even, but then they get scared, they want to compromise, they offer to make concessions, but it's too late then for concession or compromise and they're swept away. But the people will accept their master because they know that he is better and wiser than they are."

"Why should he be better and wiser?"

"Because he's stronger. Because he has the power, what he says is right *is* right and what he says is good *is* good."

"It's as simple as A B C but even less convincing," said Charley with some flippancy.

Simon gave him an angry scowl.

"You'd find it convincing enough if not only your bread and butter but your life depended on it."

"And who, pray, is to choose the master?"

"Nobody. He's the ineluctable product of circumstances."

"That's a bit of a mouthful, isn't it?"

"He rises to the top because he has the instinct to lead. He has the will to power. He has audacity and enthusiasm, ability, industry and energy. He fears nothing because to him danger is the salt of life."

"No one could say that you hadn't a good conceit of yourself, Simon," smiled Charley.

"Why do you say that?"

"Well, I suppose you imagine yourself to possess the qualities you've just enumerated."

"What makes you suppose it? I know myself as well as any man can know himself. I know my capacities, but I also know my limitations. A dictator must have a mystic appeal so that he excites his followers to a religious frenzy. He must have a magnetism which makes it a privilege for them to lay down their lives for him. In him they must feel that they more greatly live. I have nothing in me of that. I repel rather than attract. I could make people fear me, I could never make them love me. You remember what Lincoln said: "You can fool some of the people all the time, and all the people some of the time, but you can't fool all the people all the time." But that's just what a dictator must do; he must fool all the people all the time and there's only one way he can do that, he must also fool himself. None of the dictators has a lucid, logical brain; he has drive, force, magnetism, charm, but if you examine his words closely you'll see that his intelligence is mediocre; he can act because he acts on instinct, but when he begins to think he gets muddled. I have too good a brain and too little charm to be a dictator. Besides, it's better that the dictator brought to power by the proletariat should be a member of it. The working classes will find it more easy to identify themselves with him and thus will give him more willingly their obedience and devotion. The technique of revolution has been perfected. Given the right conditions it's easy for a resolute body of men to seize power; the difficulty is to hold it. The Russian revolution in the clearest possible way, the Italian and the German revolutions in a lesser degree, have shown that there's only one means by which it can be done. Terror. The working man who becomes head of a state is exposed to temptations that only a very strong character can resist. He must be almost superhuman if his head isn't turned by adulation and if his resolution isn't enfeebled by unaccustomed luxury. The working man is naturally sentimental; he's kind-hearted and so accessible to pity; when he's got what he wants he sits back and lets things slide; he forgives his enemies and is surprised when they stick a knife in him as soon as his back is turned. He needs at his elbow someone who by his birth, education, training and character, is indifferent to the trappings of greatness and immune to the debilitating influence of success."

Simon for some time had been walking up and down the studio, but now he came to an abrupt halt before his friend. With his white unshaven face and dishevelled hair, in the dressing-gown huddled round his emaciated limbs, he presented a grotesque appearance. But in a past that is not so distant other young men as pale, as thin, as unkempt as he, in shabby suits or in a student's blouse, had walked about their sordid rooms and told of dreams seemingly as unrealizable; and yet time and opportunity had strangely made their dreams come true, and, fighting their way to power through blood, they held in their hands the life of millions.

"Have you ever heard of Dzerjinsky?"

Charley gave him a startled look. That was the name Lydia had mentioned.

"Yes, oddly enough I have."

"He was a gentleman. His family had been landowners in Poland since the seventeenth century. He was a cultivated, well-read man. Lenin and the Old Guard made the revolution, but without Dzerjinsky it would have been crushed within a year. He saw that it could only be saved by terror. He applied for the post that gave him control of the police and organized the Cheka. He made it into an instrument of repression that acted with the precision of a perfect machine. He let neither love nor hate interfere with his duty. His industry was prodigious. He would work all night examining the suspects himself, and they say he acquired so keen an insight into the hearts of men that it was impossible for them to conceal their secrets from him. He invented the system of hostages which was one of the most effective systems the revolution ever discovered to preserve order. He signed hundreds, nay, thousands of death warrants with his own hand. He lived with spartan simplicity. His strength was that he wanted nothing for himself. His only aim was to serve the revolution. And he made himself the most powerful man in Russia. It was Lenin the people acclaimed and worshipped, but it was Dzerjinsky who ruled them."

"And is that the part you wish to play if ever revolution comes to England?"

"I should be well fitted for it."

Charley gave him his boyish, good-natured smile.

"It's just possible that I'd be doing the country a service if I strangled you here and now. I could, you know."

"I daresay. But you'd be afraid of the consequences."

"I don't think I should be found out. No one saw me come in. Only Lydia knows I was going to see you and she wouldn't give me away."

"I wasn't thinking of those consequences. I was thinking of your conscience. You're not tough-fibred enough for that, Charley, old boy. You're soft."

"I daresay you're right."

Charley did not speak for a while.

"You say Dzerjinsky wanted nothing for himself," he said then, "but you want power."

"Only as a means."

"What to do?"

Simon stared at him fixedly and there was a light in his eyes that seemed to Charley almost crazy.

"To fulfil myself. To satisfy my creative instinct. To exercise the capacities that nature has endowed me with."

Charley found nothing to say. He looked at his watch and got up.

"I must go now."

"I don't want to see you again, Charley."

"Well, you won't. I'm off to-morrow."

"I mean, ever."

Charley was taken aback. He looked into Simon's eyes. They were dark and grim.

"Oh? Why?"

"I'm through with you."

"For good?"

"For good and all."

"Don't you think that's rather a pity? I haven't been a bad friend to you, Simon."

Simon was silent for a space no longer than it takes for an over-ripe fruit to fall from the tree to the ground.

"You're the only friend I've ever had."

There was a break in his voice and his distress was so plain that Charley, moved, with both hands outstretched, stepped forward impulsively.

"Oh, Simon, why d'you make yourself so unhappy?"

A flame of rage leapt into Simon's tortured eyes and clenching his fist he hit Charley as hard as he could on the chin. The blow was so unexpected that he staggered and then, his feet slipping on the uncarpeted floor, fell headlong; he was on his feet in a flash and, furious with anger, sprang forward to give Simon the hiding he had often, when driven beyond endurance, given him before. Simon stood quite still, his hands behind his back, as though ready and willing to take the chastisement that was coming to him without an effort to defend himself,

269

and on his face was an expression of so much suffering, of such consternation, that Charley's wrath was melted. He stopped. His chin was hurting him, but he gave a good-natured, chuckling laugh.

"You are an ass, Simon," he said. "You might have hurt me."

"For God's sake, get out. Go back to that bloody whore. I'm fed to the teeth with you. Go, go!"

"All right, old man, I'm going. But I want to give you a little presy that I brought you for your birthday on the seventh."

He took out of his pocket one of those watches, covered in leather, which you open by pulling out the two sides, and which are wound by opening.

"There's a ring on it so you can hang it on your key-chain."

He put it down on the table. Simon would not look at it. Charley, his eyes twinkling with amusement, gave him a glance. He waited for him to say something, but he did not speak. Charley went to the door, opened it and walked out.

It was night, but the Boulevard Montparnasse was brightly lit. With the New Year imminent there was a holiday feeling in the air. The street was crowded and the cafés were chock-a-block. Everybody was taking it easy. But Charley was depressed. He had a feeling of mortification, as one might have if one had gone to a party, expecting to enjoy oneself, and because one had been stupid and tactless, had come away conscious that one had left behind a bad impression. It was a comfort to get back to the sordid bedroom at the hotel. Lydia was sitting by the log fire sewing, and the air was thick with the many cigarettes she had smoked. The scene had a pleasant domesticity. It reminded one of an interior of Vuillard's, with its intimate, cosy charm, but painted by Utrillo so that it had at the same time a touching squalor. Lydia greeted him with her quiet, friendly smile.

"How was your friend Simon?"

"Mad as a hatter."

Lighting his pipe, he sat down on the floor in front of the fire, with his back against the seat of her chair. Her nearness gave him a sense of comfort. He was glad that she did not speak. He was troubled by all the horrible things Simon had said to him. He could not get out of his head the picture of that thin creature, his pale face scrubby with a two days' beard, underfed and overworked, walking up and down in his old dressing-gown and with a cold-blooded, ruthless malignance delivering himself of his fantastic ideas. But breaking in upon this, as it were, was the recollection of the little boy with the big dark eyes who seemed to yearn for affection and yet repelled it, the little boy with whom he went to the circus during the Christmas holidays and who got so wildly excited at the unaccustomed treat, with whom he bicycled or went for long walks in the country, who was at times so gay and amusing, with whom it was jolly to talk and laugh and rag and play the fool. It seemed incredible that that little boy should have turned into that young man, and so heart-rending that he could have wept.

"I wonder what'll happen to Simon in the end?" he muttered.

Hardly knowing that he had spoken aloud, he almost thought Lydia had read his thoughts when she answered:

"I don't know the English. If he were Russian I'd say he'll either become a dangerous agitator or he'll commit suicide."

271

Charley chuckled.

"Oh well, we English have a wonderful capacity for making our wild oats into a nourishing diet. It's equally on the cards that he'll end up as the editor of *The Times*."

He got up and seated himself in the armchair which was the only fairly comfortable seat in the room. He looked reflectively at Lydia busily plying her needle. There was something he wanted to say to her, but the thought of it made him nervous, and yet he was leaving next day and this might well be his last opportunity. The suspicion that Simon had sown in his candid heart rankled. If she had been making a fool of him, he would sooner know; then when they parted he could shrug his shoulders and with a good conscience forget her. He decided to settle the matter there and then, but being shy of making her right out the offer he had in mind, he approached it in a round-about way.

"Have I ever told you about my Great-Aunt Martha?" he started lightly.

"No."

"She was my great-grandfather's eldest child. She was a grim-featured spinster with more wrinkles on her sallow face than I've ever seen on a human being. She was very small and thin, with tight lips, and she never looked anything but acidly disapproving. She used to terrify me when I was a kid. She had an enormous admiration for Queen Alexandra and to the end of her days wore her hair, only it was a wig, as the Queen wore hers. She always dressed in black, with very full long skirts and a pinched-in waist, and the collar of her bodice came up to her ears. She wore a heavy gold chain round her neck, with a large gold cross dangling from it, and gold bangles on her wrists. She was appallingly genteel.

She continued to live in the grand house old Sibert Mason built for himself when he began to get on in the world and she never changed a thing. To go there was like stepping back into the eighteen-seventies. She died only a few years ago at a great age and left me five hundred pounds."

"That was nice."

"I should have rather liked to blue it, but my father persuaded me to save it. He said I should be damned thankful to have a little nest-egg like that when I came to marry and wanted to furnish a flat. But I don't see any prospect of my marrying for years yet and I don't really want the money. Would you like me to give you two hundred of it?"

Lydia, going on with her work, had listened amiably, though without more than polite interest, to a story that could mean nothing very much to her; but now, jabbing her needle in the material she was sewing, she looked up.

"What on earth for?"

"I thought it might be useful to you."

"I don't understand. What have I done that you should wish to give me two hundred pounds?"

Charley hesitated. She was gazing at him with those blue, large, but rather flat eyes of hers, and there was in them an extreme attention as though she were trying to see into the depths of his soul. He turned his head away.

"You could do a good deal to help Robert."

A faint smile broke on her lips. She understood.

"Has your friend Simon been telling you that I was at the Sérail to earn enough money to enable Robert to escape?"

"Why should you think that?"

She gave a little scornful laugh.

273

"You're very naïve, my poor friend. It's what they all suppose. Do you think I would trouble to undeceive them and do you think they would understand if I told them the truth? I don't want your money; I have no use for it." Her voice grew tender. "It's sweet of you to offer it. You're a dear creature, but such a kid. Do you know that what you're suggesting is a crime which might easily land you in prison?"

"Oh well."

"You didn't believe what I told you the other day?"

"I'm beginning to think it's very hard to know what to believe in this world. After all, I was nothing to you, there was no reason for you to tell me the truth if you didn't want to. And those men this morning and the address they gave you to send money to. You can't be surprised if I put two and two together."

"I'm glad if I can send Robert money so that he can buy himself cigarettes and a little food. But what I told you was true. I don't want him to escape. He sinned and he must suffer."

"I can't bear the thought of your going back to that horrible place. I know you a little now; it's awful to think of you of all people leading that life."

"But I told you; I must atone; I must do for him what he hasn't the strength to do for himself."

"But it's crazy. It's so morbid. It's senseless. I might understand, though even then I'd think it out-rageously wrong-headed, if you believed in a cruel god who exacted vengeance and who was prepared to take your suffering, well, in part-payment for the wrong Robert had done, but you told me you don't believe in God."

"You can't argue with feeling. Of course it's unreasonable, but reason has nothing to do with it.

274

I don't believe in the god of the Christians who gave his son in order to save mankind. That's a myth. But why should it have arisen if it didn't express some deep-seated intuition in men? I don't know what I believe, because it's instinctive, and how can you describe an instinct with words? I have an instinct that the power that rules us, human beings, animals and things, is a dark and cruel power and that everything has to be paid for, a power that demands an eye for an eye and a tooth for a tooth, and that though we may writhe and squirm we have to submit, for the power is ourselves."

Charley made a vague gesture of discouragement. He felt as if he were trying to talk with someone whose language he could not understand.

"How long are you going on at the Sérail?"

"I don't know. Until I have done my share. Until the time comes when I feel in my bones that Robert is liberated not from his prison, but from his sin. At one time I used to address envelopes. There are hundreds and hundreds of them and you think you'll never get them all done, you scribble and scribble interminably, and for a long time there seem to be as many to do as there ever were, and then suddenly, when you least expect it, you find you've done the last one. It's such a curious sensation."

"And then, will you go out to join Robert?"

"If he wants me."

"Of course he'll want you," said Charley.

She gave him a look of infinite sadness.

"I don't know."

"How can you doubt it? He loves you. After all, think what your love must mean to him."

"You heard what those men said to-day. He's gay, he's got a soft billet, he's making the best of things.

275

He was bound to. That's what he's like. He loved me, yes, I know, but I know also that he's incapable of loving for very long. I couldn't have held him indefinitely even if nothing had happened. I knew that always. And when the time comes for me to go, what hope have I that anything will be left of the love he once bore me?''

"But how, if you think that, can you still do what you're doing?"

"It's stupid, isn't it? He's cruel and selfish, unscrupulous and wicked. I don't care. I don't respect him, I don't trust him, but I love him; I love him with my body, with my thoughts, with my feelings, with everything that's me." She changed her tone to one of light raillery. "And now that I've told you that, you must see that I'm a very disreputable woman who is quite unworthy of your interest or sympathy."

Charley considered for a moment.

"Well, I don't mind telling you that I'm rather out of my depth. But for all the hell he's enduring I'm not sure if I wouldn't rather be in his shoes than yours."

"Why?"

"Well, to tell you the truth, because I can't imagine anything more heart-rending than to love with all your soul someone that you know is worthless."

Lydia gave him a thoughtful, rather surprised look, but did not answer.

X

CHARLEY'S train left at midday. Somewhat to his surprise Lydia told him that she would like to come and see him off. They breakfasted late and packed their bags. Before going downstairs to pay his bill Charley counted his money. He had plenty left.

"Will you do me a favour?" he asked.

"What is it?"

"Will you let me give you something to keep in case of emergency?"

"I don't want your money," she smiled. "If you like you can give me a thousand francs for Evgenia. It'll be a godsend to her."

"All right."

They drove first to the Rue du Château d'Eau, where she lived, and there she left her bag with the concierge. Then they drove to the Gare du Nord. Lydia walked along the platform with him and he bought a number of English papers. He found his seat in the Pullman. Lydia, coming in with him, looked about her.

"D'you know, this is the first time I've ever been inside a first-class carriage in my life," she said.

It gave Charley quite a turn. He had a sudden realization of a life completely devoid not only of the luxuries of the rich, but even of the comforts of the well-to-do. It caused him a sharp pang of discomfort to think of the sordid existence that had always been, and always would be, hers.

"Oh well, in England I generally go third," he said

apologetically, "but my father says that on the Continent one ought to travel like a gentleman."

"It makes a good impression on the natives."

Charley laughed and flushed.

"You have a peculiar gift for making me feel a fool."

They walked up and down the platform, trying as people do on such occasions to think of something to say, but able to think of nothing that seemed worth saying. Charley wondered if it passed through her mind that in all probability they would never see one another again in all their lives. It was odd to think that for five days they had been almost inseparable and in an hour it would be as though they had never met. But the train was about to start. He put out his hand to say good-bye to her. She crossed her arms over her breast in a way she had which had always seemed to him strangely moving; she had had her arms so crossed when she wept in her sleep; and raised her face to his. To his amazement he saw that she was crying. He put his arms round her and for the first time kissed her on the mouth. She disengaged herself and, turning away from him, quickly hurried down the platform. Charley got into his compartment. He was singularly troubled. But a substantial luncheon, with half a bottle of indifferent Chablis, did something to restore his equanimity; and then he lit his pipe and began to read *The Times*. It soothed him. There was something solid in the feel of the substantial fabric on which it was printed that seemed to him grandly English. He looked at the picture papers. He was of a resilient temper. By the time they reached Calais he was in tearing spirits. Once on board he had a small Scotch and pacing the deck watched with satisfaction the waves that Britannia traditionally rules. It was grand to see the white cliffs of Dover. He gave a sigh of relief when he stepped on the stubborn English soil. He felt as though he had been away for ages. It was a treat to hear the voices of the English porters, and he laughed at the threatening uncouthness of the English customs officials who treated you as though you were a confirmed criminal. In another two hours he would be home again. That's what his father always said:

"There's only one thing I like better than getting out of England, and that's getting back to it."

Already the events of his stay in Paris seemed a trifle dim. It was like a nightmare which left you shaken when with a start you awoke from it, but as the day wore on faded in your recollection, so that after a while you remembered nothing but that you had had a bad dream. He wondered if anyone would come to meet him; it would be nice to see a friendly face on the platform. When he got out of the Pullman at Victoria almost the first person he saw was his mother. She threw her arms round his neck and kissed him as though he had been gone for months.

"I told your father that as he'd seen you off I was going to meet you. Patsy wanted to come too, but I wouldn't let her. I wanted to have you all to myself for a few minutes."

Oh, how good it was to be enveloped in that safe affection!

"You are an old fool, mummy. It's idiotic of you to risk catching your death of cold on a draughty platform on a bitter night like this."

They walked, arm in arm and happy, to the car. They drove to Porchester Close. Leslie Mason heard the front door open and came out into the hall, and then

Patsy tore down the stairs and flung herself into Charley's arms.

"Come into my study and have a tiddly. The whiskey's there. You must be perished with the cold."

Charley fished out of his great-coat pocket the two bottles of scent he had brought for his mother and Patsy. Lydia had chosen them.

"I smuggled 'em," he said triumphantly.

"Now those two women will stink like a brothel," said Leslie Mason, beaming.

"I've brought you a tie from Charvet, daddy."

"Is it loud?"

"Very."

"Good."

They were all so pleased with one another that they burst out laughing. Leslie Mason poured out the whiskey and insisted that his wife should have some to prevent her from catching cold.

"Have you had any adventures, Charley?" asked Patsy.

"None."

"Liar."

"Well, you must tell us all about everything later," said Mrs. Mason. "Now you'd better go and have a nice hot bath and dress for dinner."

"It's all ready for you," said Patsy. "I've put in half a bottle of bath salts."

They treated him as though he had just come back from the North Pole after a journey of incredible hardship. It warmed the cockles of his heart.

"Is it good to be home again?" asked his mother, her eyes tender with love.

"Grand."

But when Leslie, partly dressed, went into his wife's

room to have a chat with her while she did her face, she turned to him with a somewhat anxious look.

"He's looking awfully pale, Leslie," she said.

"A bit washed out. I noticed that myself."

"His face is so drawn. It struck me the moment he got out of the Pullman, but I couldn't see very well till we got here. And he's as white as a ghost."

"He'll be all right in a day or two. I expect he's been racketing about a bit. By the look of him I suspect he's helped quite a number of pretty ladies to provide for their respectable old age."

Mrs. Mason was sitting at her dressing-table, in a Chinese jacket trimmed with white fur, carefully doing her eye-brows, but now, the pencil in her hand, she suddenly turned round.

"What *do* you mean, Leslie? You don't mean to say you think he's been having a lot of horrid foreign women."

"Come off it, Venetia. What d'you suppose he went to Paris for?"

"To see the pictures and Simon, and well, go to the Français. He's only a boy."

"Don't be so silly, Venetia. He's twenty-three. You don't suppose he's a virgin, do you?"

"I do think men are disgusting."

Her voice broke, and Leslie, seeing she was really upset, put his hand kindly on her shoulder.

"Darling, you wouldn't like your only son to be a eunuch, would you now?"

Mrs. Mason didn't quite know whether she wanted to laugh or cry.

"I don't suppose I would really," she giggled.

It was with a sense of peculiar satisfaction that Charley, half an hour later, in his second-best dinner-jacket, seated himself with his father in a velvet coat, his mother in a tea-gown of mauve silk, and Patsy maidenly in rose chiffon, at the Chippendale table. The Georgian silver, the shaded candles, the lace doyleys which Mrs. Mason had bought in Florence, the cut glass—it was all pretty, but, above all, it was familiar. The pictures on the walls, each with its own strip-lighting, were meritorious; and the two maids, in their neat brown uniforms, added a nice touch. You had a feeling of security, and the world outside was comfortably distant. The good, plain food was designed to satisfy a healthy appetite without being fattening. In the hearth an electric fire very satisfactorily imitated burning logs. Leslie Mason looked at the menu.

"I see we've killed the fatted calf for the prodigal son," he said, with an arch look at his wife.

"Did you have any good food in Paris, Charley?" asked Mrs. Mason.

"All right. I didn't go to any of the smart restaurants, you know. We used to have our meals at little places in the Quarter."

"Oh. Who's we?"

Charley hesitated an instant and flushed.

"I dined with Simon, you know."

This was a fact. His answer neatly concealed the truth without actually telling a lie. Mrs. Mason was aware that her husband was giving her a meaning look, but she paid no attention to it; she continued to gaze on her son with tenderly affectionate eyes, and he was much too ingenuous to suspect that they were groping deep into his soul to discover whatever secrets he might be hiding there.

"And did you see any pictures?" she asked kindly.

"I went to the Louvre. I was rather taken with the Chardins."

"Were you?" said Leslie Mason. "I can't say he's ever appealed to me very much. I always thought him on the dull side." His eyes twinkled with the jest that had occurred to him. "Between you and me and the gatepost I prefer Charvet to Chardin. At least he is modern."

"Your father's impossible," Mrs. Mason smiled indulgently. "Chardin was a very conscientious artist, one of the minor masters of the eighteenth century, but of course he wasn't Great."

In point of fact, however, they were much more anxious to tell him about their doings than to listen to his. The party at Cousin Wilfred's had been a riot, and they had come back so exhausted that they'd all gone to bed immediately after dinner on the night of their return. That showed you how they'd enjoyed themselves.

"Patsy had a proposal of marriage," said Leslie Mason.

"Thrilling, wasn't it?" cried Patsy. "Unfortunately the poor boy was only sixteen, so I told him that, bad woman as I was, I hadn't sunk so low as to snatch a baby from his cradle, and I gave him a chaste kiss on the brow and told him I would be a sister to him."

Patsy rattled on. Charley, smiling, listened to her, and Mrs. Mason took the opportunity to look at him closely. He was really very good-looking and his pallor suited him. It gave her an odd little feeling in her heart to think how much those women in Paris must have liked him; she supposed he'd gone to one of those horrible houses; what a success he must have had, so young and fresh and charming, after the fat, bald beastly old men they were used to! She wondered what sort of girl he had been attracted by, she so hoped she was young and pretty, they said men were attracted by the same type as their mother belonged to. She was sure he'd be an enchanting lover; she couldn't help feeling proud of him; after all, he was her son and she'd carried him in her womb. The dear; and he looked so white and tired. Mrs. Mason had strange thoughts, thoughts that she wouldn't have had anybody know for anything in the world; she was sad, and a little envious, yes, envious of the girls he had slept with, but at the same time proud, oh, so proud, because he was strong and handsome and virile.

Leslie interrupted Patsy's nonsense and her own thoughts.

"Shall we tell him the great secret, Venetia?"

"Of course."

"But mind, Charley, keep it under your hat. Cousin Wilfred's worked it. There's an ex-Indian governor that the party want to find a safe seat for, so Wilfred's giving up his and in recognition he's to get a peerage. What d'you think of that?"

"It's grand."

"Of course he pretends it means nothing to him, but he's as pleased as Punch really. And you know, it's nice for all of us. I mean, having a peer in the family adds to one's prestige. Well, it gives one a sort of position. And when you think how we started . . ."

"That'll do, Leslie," said Mrs. Mason, with a glance at the servants. "We needn't go into that." And when they left the room immediately afterwards, she added: "Your father's got a mania for telling everyone about his origins. I really think the time has now arrived when we can let bygones be bygones. It's not so bad when we're with people of our own class, they think it's rather chic to have a grandfather who was a gardener and a grandmother who was a cook, but there's no need to tell the servants. It only makes them think you're no better than they are."

"I'm not ashamed of it. After all the greatest families in England started just as humbly as we did. And we've worked the oracle in less than a century."

Mrs. Mason and Patsy got up from the table and Charley was left with his father to drink a glass of port. Leslie Mason told him of the discussions they had had about the title Cousin Wilfred should assume. It wasn't so easy as you might think to find a name which didn't belong to somebody else, which had some kind of connection with you, and which sounded well.

"I suppose we'd better join the ladies," he said, when he had exhausted the subject. "I expect your mother will want a rubber before we go to bed."

But as they were at the door and about to go out, he put his hand on his son's shoulder.

"You look a bit washed out, old boy. I expect you've been going the pace a bit in Paris. Well, you're young and that's to be expected." He suddenly felt a trifle embarrassed. "Anyhow, that's no business of mine, and I think there are things a father and son needn't go into. But accidents will happen in the best regulated families, and well, what I want to say is, if you find you've got anything the matter with you, don't hesitate but go and see a doctor right away. Old Sinnery brought you into the world and so you needn't be shy of him. He's discretion itself and he'll put you right in no time; the bill will be paid and no questions asked. That's all I wanted to tell you; now let's go and join your poor mother."

Charley had blushed scarlet when he understood what his father was talking about. He felt he ought to say something, but could think of nothing to say.

When they came into the drawing-room Patsy was playing a waltz of Chopin's and after she had finished his mother asked Charley to play something.

"I suppose you haven't played since you left?"

"One afternoon I played a little on the hotel piano, but it was a very poor one."

He sat down and played again that piece of Scriabin's that Lydia thought he played so badly, and as he began he had a sudden recollection of that stuffy, smoky cellar to which she had taken him, of those roughs he had made such friends with, and of the Russian woman, gaunt and gipsy-skinned, with her enormous eyes, who had sung those wild, barbaric songs with such a tragic abandon. Through the notes he struck he seemed to hear her raucous, harsh and yet deeply moving voice. Leslie Mason had a sensitive ear.

"You play that thing differently from the way you used," he said when Charley got up from the piano.

"I don't think so. Do I?"

"Yes, the feeling's quite different. You get a sort of tremor in it that's rather effective."

"I like the old way better, Charley. You made it sound rather morbid," said Mrs. Mason.

They sat down to bridge.

"This is like old times," said Leslie. "We've missed our family bridge since you've been away."

Leslie Mason had a theory that the way a man played bridge was an indication of his character, and since he looked upon himself as a dashing, open-handed, free-and-easy fellow, he consistently overcalled his hand and recklessly doubled. He looked upon a finesse as un-English. Mrs. Mason on the other hand played strictly according to the rules of Culbertson and laboriously counted up the pips before she ventured on a call. She never took a risk. Patsy was the only member of the family who by some freak of nature had a card sense. She was a bold, clever player and seemed to know by intuition how the cards were placed. She made no secret of her disdain for the respective methods of play of her parents. She was domineering at the card table. The game proceeded in just the same way as on how many evenings it had done. Leslie, after over-calling, was doubled by his daughter, redoubled, and with triumph went down fourteen hundred; Mrs. Mason with her hand full of picture cards refused to listen to her partner's insistent demand for a slam; Charley was careless.

"Why didn't you return me a diamond, you fool?" cried Patsy.

"Why should I return you a diamond?"

"Didn't you see me play a nine and then a six?"

"No, I didn't."

"Gosh, that I should be condemned to play all my life with people who don't know the ace of spades from a cow's tail."

"It only made the difference of a trick."

"A trick? A trick? A trick can make all the difference in the world."

None of them paid any attention to Patsy's indignation. They only laughed and she, giving them up as a bad job, laughed with them. Leslie carefully added up the scores and entered them in a book. They only played for a penny a hundred, but they pretended to play for a pound, because it looked better and was more thrilling. Sometimes Leslie would have marked up against him in the book sums like fifteen hundred pounds and would say with seeming seriousness that if things went on like that he'd have to put down the car and go to his office by bus.

The clock struck twelve and they bade one another good-night. Charley went to his warm and comfortable room and began to undress, but suddenly he felt very tired and sank into an armchair. He thought he would have one more pipe before he went to bed. The evening that had just gone by was like innumerable others that he had passed, and none had ever seemed to him more cosy and more intimate; it was all charmingly familiar, in every particular it was exactly as he would have wished it to be; nothing could be, as it were, more stable and substantial; and yet, he could not for the life of him tell why, he had all the time been fretted by an insinuating notion that it was nothing but make-believe. It was like a pleasant parlour-game that grown-ups played to amuse children. And that night-mare from which he thought he had happily awakened —at this hour Lydia, her eyelids stained and her nipples painted, in her blue Turkish trousers and her blue turban, would be dancing at the Sérail or, naked, lying mortified and cruelly exulting in her mortification, in the arms of a man she abhorred; at this hour Simon, his work at the office finished, would be walking about the emptying streets of the Left Bank, turning over in his morbid and tortured mind his monstrous schemes; at this hour Alexey and Evgenia, whom Charley had never seen but whom through Lydia he seemed to know so well that he was sure he would have recognized them if he met them in the street; Alexey, drunk, would be inveighing with maudlin tears against the depravity of his son, and Evgenia, sewing, sewing for dear life, would

288

cry softly because life was so bitter; at this hour the two released convicts, with those staring eyes of theirs that seemed to be set in a gaze of horror at what they had seen, would be sitting, each with his glass of beer, in the smoky, dim cellar and there hidden amid the crowd feel themselves for a moment safe from the ever-present fear that someone watched them; and at this hour Robert Berger, over there, far away on the coast of South America, in the pink-and-white stripes of the prison garb, with the ugly straw hat on his shaven head, walking from the hospital on some errand, would cast his eyes across the wide expanse of sea and, weighing the chances of escape, think for a moment of Lydia with tolerant affection—and that nightmare from which he thought he had happily awakened had a fearful reality which rendered all else illusory. It was absurd, it was irrational, but that, all that seemed to have a force, a dark significance, which made the life he shared with those three, his father, his mother, his sister, who were so near his heart, and the larger, decent yet humdrum life of the environment in which some blind chance had comfortably ensconced him, of no more moment than a shadow play. Patsy had asked him if he had had adventures in Paris and he had truthfully answered no. It was a fact that he had done nothing; his father thought he had had a devil of a time and was afraid he had contracted a venereal disease, and he hadn't even had a woman; only one thing had happened to him, it was rather curious when you came to think of it, and he didn't just then quite know what to do about it: the bottom had fallen out of his world.

*This book was designed
by William B. Taylor
for Heron Books, London*

Printed in Switzerland